Chasing Home

PIPER RAYNE

About Chasing Home

It was straight out of a rom-com—until two pink lines changed everything.

Zander Shaw is country music's hottest star. So, when he singled me out of a packed arena and had me pulled backstage, I should've known I wasn't his forever. One signed NDA later, I was sneaking onto his tour bus, wrapped up in his world, and him. But it ended before it really started when he ghosted me.

Then he shows up on my family's ranch to film his new music video, a surprise to us both. Now I'm his appointed tour guide around the ranch, stuck sharing all my favorite places with the man who carelessly discarded me.

The more time we spend together, the harder it is to guard my heart because his flirty half-smile makes me forget my anger. But Zander's made it clear, he's not looking to ride out into the sunset with anyone.

Which would be fine... if I wasn't carrying his baby.

CHASING HOME

<u>**The Noughtons Family**</u>
Parents
Bruce and Daisy (deceased) Noughton
Children
Ben Noughton – Gillian Adams
(*The One I Left Behind*)
Jude Noughton – Sadie Wilkins
(*The One I Stood Beside*)
Emmett Noughton – Briar Adams
(*The One I Didn't See Coming*)

<u>**The Owens Family**</u>
Parents
Brad and Darla Owens
Children
Lottie Owens – Brooks Watson
(*Chasing Forever*)
Bennett Owens – Delaney Richards
(*Chasing Love*)
Romy Owens – Zander Shaw
(*Chasing Home*)

<u>**The Ellis Family**</u>
Parents
Wade and Bette Ellis
Children
Poppy Ellis
Jensen Ellis
Scarlett Ellis

To see more of the Plain Daisy Ranch
family tree visit our website:
https://piperrayne.com/noughton-family-tree

Chapter One

ROMY

I inhale a sharp breath and tear open the plastic package. I've held onto this test too long, pretending what I know in my heart to be true isn't my actual reality. But my breasts ache, I'm devouring every snack in sight, and my period is two weeks late. The test feels like a formality at this point.

Still, I go through the motions. I pee on the stick. I snap the cap back on. I set it on the counter. When I reach for my phone to start a timer, my thumb stalls over the screen. A video of Zander Shaw teasing his hot new single to the world fills the feed. No doubt it's a fake-ass love song written by someone with an actual heart.

He's striding off his tour bus, surrounded by camera flashes and screaming fans, walking into a sold-out arena. His shirt is wrinkled as if he just picked it up from the corner of the room, and his dark hair is disheveled—probably from someone's fingers. My chest tightens, because once—okay, three times—I was that someone.

Does he have to be so damn gorgeous? I squeeze my eyes shut, and I'm right back there, on that narrow bed in the back of his bus relaxing after he'd just taken me against the wall, his

1

fingers grazing down the valley of my breasts, whispering things that made me believe I wasn't just another notch on his belt.

God, what an idiot. I can't believe I ever fell for his bull-shit. I blame the hopeless romantic in me. Correction. The *former* hopeless romantic.

I swipe the video up before my heart caves in again.

A knock rattles the bathroom door. "Romy, are you in there?" my cousin Scarlett asks.

"Yeah, I'll be out in a minute."

Why Scarlett's at The Knotted Barn today is beyond me. We don't have a wedding booked for this weekend. Business has been slowing ever since Walker Matthews announced and then spent a gazillion dollars on his knock-off venue on Wild Bull Ranch.

Scarlett knocks again.

"I heard you the first time. Give me a second, okay?" I attempt to keep the irritation from my voice, then glance at my phone.

How many minutes since I peed on the stick?

Damn Zander. Even when he's not here, he's pulling my focus. And if this test is positive, he won't just haunt me. I'll be tied to him for life.

No. Not happening.

I cling to denial. There's a chance I'm not pregnant, right? I haven't had any pickle-and-peanut-butter cravings. And there's been not one ounce of morning sickness. That means something, right? I'm fine. Totally fine. Not growing a little one inside me, that's for sure.

"I have a surprise for you." Scarlett's voice is lighter than usual, bubbling with excitement.

"And I said I'd be a minute." This time I don't manage to keep my irritation hidden.

She growls in frustration, a more familiar Scarlett sound, then her heels click away down the hall.

The mental timer in my head buzzes. I face the counter, shut my eyes, palms clammy. This is it. If there are two lines, my life will never be the same.

"Romy!" Emmett pounds on the door.

"Is this a family reunion I don't know about?"

"Jeez... calm down. Are you hangry?"

I snap my gaze back to the test, and my stomach flips. Because there they are. Those two pink lines.

No fucking way.

My lungs seize, my heart hammers, and sweat prickles my hairline. I grab the second test, desperate for a different answer, and sit again, rocking forward, willing my bladder to cooperate.

This can't be real. And yet it is.

I already know that even though this wasn't planned, I'll be having this baby. My options flash through my mind, but the only one that feels right to me, no matter how messed up this situation might be, is becoming a mother.

How the hell am I supposed to tell Zander Shaw he's going to be a father? He never wants to see me again. He had his security guy DeSoto make that abundantly clear already.

"Romy..." my older sister, Lottie, singsongs through the door.

Seriously? Can I not have two damn minutes to myself?

"In a minute!" I shout, pressing down, rocking, trying to squeeze out enough pee for the second stick.

The knob rattles. "Why is the door locked? Are you alone in there? Or are you with your mystery boyfriend?" She laughs.

"Go find somewhere to bang Brooks!"

My sister and her new husband are always eye-fucking

each other, even at family dinners. That kind of thing used to make me swoon, but now it makes me feel sick.

The door jiggling stops. "You're scaring me. What's going on?"

I hear her whisper to someone else.

"Sweetie, are you okay?"

My eyes shut with frustration when I hear my mother's voice. "Yes, Mom!"

I snap the cap on the second test, jam both sticks back in the box, and shove it into the farthest corner under the sink. Then I face the mirror. My reflection looks... off. My cheeks are flushed, my hairline damp. I practice a neutral expression. Maybe I can get away with saying I have food poisoning or something.

It's just my family. There're so many of us, and with whatever is going on out there, there should be so much chaos that no one will catch onto the fact that something is up with me.

I open the door.

Lottie and Mom are plastered against the opposite wall, staring at me as if I just got released from jail.

"Why are you all here?" I ask.

Mom arches a brow and looks right and left. "I think I own the place, no?"

"What's going on? You look sick. Are you sick?" Lottie frowns. "It's probably from the girls. Bet they brought something home from school. I tried to tell Mom—"

"I'm fine," I interrupt Lottie, my voice sharper than I mean it to be. "What's going on?"

We head toward the barn's main room, the old beams strung with lights, the vineyard visible through the French doors that lead to the balcony.

Scarlett spots me and claps her hands. "Oh yay!"

Most of the family's here, minus a few who must still be working.

"Spit it out!" I snap.

Mom shoots me her disapproving look, but I don't care. My nerves are frayed to threads.

Scarlett raises a finger, then swings open the double barn doors like I do when a gorgeous bride is on the other side, about to walk down the aisle to her groom.

Light spills in from outside, making me squint a bit.

Lottie hooks her arm through mine, her grin way too wide.

And then, DeSoto steps inside and does a double-take, his eyes asking the same question mine are—*what the hell are you doing here?*

But my stomach drops fully when the man behind DeSoto appears.

Zander walks in as though we should all fall to our knees over sharing the same space as him. It's his practiced rock star look. Pompous cocky asshole.

Sorry, little one.

My hand drifts to my stomach before I snatch it back.

"Mr. Shaw... Zander..." Scarlett stammers. "This is my cousin, Romy. She runs The Knotted Barn and is a huge fan of yours."

For the first time ever, Zander Shaw's camera-ready smile slips.

Chapter Two

ROMY

I stick out my hand toward Zander, forcing myself to keep it there and not recoil. "Nice to meet you."

"That's it?" Scarlett murmurs, gaze darting to meet Lottie's.

Zander's chin raises slightly, as if he's questioning why I'm pretending I don't know him. Then his large hand slides into mine. His calloused fingertips graze along my palm, and an uninvited memory of those fingers sliding between my legs forces itself front and center. I lock my jaw, willing it back down.

"Scarlett says you're a really big fan. I love meeting fans."

It takes everything inside me not to smack that smug smile off his face.

He doesn't strip his gaze off me. It's as though he's daring me to acknowledge our prior relationship, which clearly wasn't a relationship to him. He opens his mouth to say something else, but Scarlett interrupts.

"He's going to film his new video here! Can you believe it?" Scarlett is so excited she looks as if she could pop a blood vessel. I'm not sure I would mind if she did, just to have an excuse to stop staring at him.

"Oh?" I press my lips together and nod.

"Yeah, can you believe it?" She grins at me, then lowers her voice. "I thought you'd be more excited."

I hate the disappointment in her eyes, but I'm doing my best here.

Lottie grips my arm so tightly, I wonder if she knows something.

"We all did," Emmett says from the back of the room. "I gotta go get Colter. Welcome to Plain Daisy Ranch." Emmett walks past us, smacking Zander on the shoulder.

DeSoto steps forward, but Zander gives his head a shake, and DeSoto stands down. That's the way it goes. It takes me back to the first night when DeSoto put his hand on my elbow and ushered me past the security detail at Zander's request. It's the same hand that barred me from entry, eyes apologetic, when he told me I was no longer on the list.

I pull my hand out of Zander's, and his lingers in the air a beat before he shoves it in his pocket. All easygoing and casual. Annoyingly in control of his emotions.

"Why here?" I ask him.

My mom nudges me in the side with her elbow. "Romy," she whispers.

"Why not?" Zander shrugs.

"Can't you make a set like this on some soundstage or something?" My bitterness seeps out before I can rein it in. If I'm not careful, my whole family will piece together the fact that Zander Shaw was my mystery man.

"I want this to feel authentic."

"Hmm." My lips press together.

"Well, let me show you around the rest of the ranch. We've reserved The Getaway Lodge for you and your entourage." Scarlett gives me a questioning glare as she holds out her arm to escort Zander away, but he doesn't turn around.

I raise my eyebrows, afraid to open my mouth because my family are like detectives who will compare notes and swap knowledge until they figure out my secret. And this one I need to keep so I can wrap my head around it before I have to deal with everyone else's opinions. Besides, I need to make sure I tell Lottie before anyone else. She deserves to be the first to know.

"Are you coming?" Zander asks.

"You should go, Romy," my mom encourages.

"Yeah, we have room in the UTV for you." Scarlett waits, looking between us.

"Nah, I'm good. I have work to do here."

Zander's smile falters. It's a crack in his rock star façade that makes my chest ache. Reminds me of the man I thought he was.

Get a grip. He's probably just upset his super fan isn't starstruck in his presence in front of her family.

"Okkkaayy," Scarlett says, her gaze searching out Lottie once again. "This was my birthday present to you, so I guess I'll have to go shopping now. Hope you wanted some wool socks."

A few of my family members laugh at Scarlett's rare show of humor.

Dread washes over me—guilt, more precisely—because no one in this room knows my history with this man. They don't know how much I thought it was some sign that Zander and I were meant to be the night he had DeSoto pluck me out of the crowd to go backstage. I inserted myself into the plot of one of the romance books I read, thinking that I was the special one he'd want to keep around.

They turn to leave, and my mom gives me a disappointed look over her shoulder.

"Sorry. I'll go," I say before my brain can catch up and ask me what the fuck I'm doing.

Zander circles back around. He holds out his hand for me, and my mom coos as if it's romantic. I ignore his outstretched hand and unwind myself from Lottie, walking around them toward the door.

"Me too." Lottie's playing protective sister although she has no idea what she's protecting me from. But she obviously must sense that something is up.

DeSoto steps in front of her.

Oh, this isn't going to be good.

"We don't have room," he says in that stern voice he likes to use to intimidate people.

I was never on the other end of it, but I heard it plenty. When he denied me entry, there was a sadness in his eyes and a gentleness in his tone. Hell, he offered to get me a ride back to the airport or wherever I needed to go.

Now it makes me wonder how many times Zander had put him in that position.

"Sorry, big guy, but this here." Lottie circles her finger in the air. "This is my family's ranch. So, I can go wherever I want, and this whole bodyguard act isn't necessary. I doubt anyone knows Zander is even in town, and if they did, there's only one person you would've had to protect him from, but she doesn't seem as interested as she once was. So why don't you take the afternoon off and go feed our chickens or something?" Lottie breezes past him out the door, leaving DeSoto with his mouth hanging open.

Her husband, Brooks, saunters over. "Yeah... she's gonna do what she wants when she wants. Get used to it, and if you have a problem... well... you can talk to me, but it won't do you any good. I'm on her side every damn time." He follows her out.

"I'm good, DeSoto. Why don't you go settle in at the

lodge?" Zander gives him a meaningful look and waits for Scarlett to lead him out.

DeSoto glances at me before he follows.

No chance in hell he's going to just head off to go chill at the lodge.

The sun hits my eyes, almost blinding me, and the chill of fall lingers in the air.

Sure enough, DeSoto is in his own UTV with my mom as the driver.

God help him. I shoot him a sympathetic smile because she's going to talk his ear off, and based on my experience, he's not a talkative guy.

By the time I reach the UTV, only one seat is available. The one right next to Zander. Lottie is in the third row with Brooks. I guess I was wrong about her sisterly intuition.

Scarlett and Poppy are in the front seat, leaving me no choice but to sit next to Zander.

His jean-clad thigh brushes against mine even with me pressing my thighs together to give him as much room as I can.

Scarlett presses the gas, and we all fly back in our seats.

It's going to be a bumpy ride for more than one reason.

Chapter Three

ZANDER

S he hates me.

Deservedly so, but it doesn't make the confirmation that I'm a complete asshole any easier.

Romy... how many times have I said that name? Probably a shit-ton if I add up all my dreams and every time I fist myself with her name on my lips.

Her blonde hair is pulled up into a ponytail, and her cheeks are flushed. Once upon a time, I coaxed that blush from her with just a smile in her direction. Now her cheeks are red from anger, and I'm the one who flipped the switch.

How the hell did I get here?

Did my manager, Beau, not do any investigation as to whose ranch this is and put two and two together? He's supposed to be in charge of details and shit. All I ever knew was when Romy would arrive and when she had to leave. Although each time I begged her to stay just one more night. That's when I realized I was in too deep with her. That last night, when I was glaring at her small suitcase by the door as though it had personally offended me, I knew that every second with her was putting me on the verge of destruction.

Either I was always just distracted by Romy, or I didn't hear her ever tell me about this place. All I knew was that she had a big family and ran a venue that was a restored barn. Honestly, when she was with me, I'm not sure I was ever fully listening because she was doing something to me that no one else had. My attention was on the cute dimple in her left cheek, the bow of her rosy top lip, and the way her body weaved with mine as the miles stretched out on the tour bus.

Fuck. I need to get a hold of myself.

We drive to a big hill covered in daisies after we've already ridden past the cattle ranch and the cornfield that looks as if it's being mapped out for a corn maze now that the season is over.

"This is Daisy Hill," Scarlett calls over her shoulder before stopping the UTV.

Romy's mom gets out of the driver's seat. "Let's go pay our respects," she says, looking over at me and then her daughter. "You two don't have to join us."

Everyone else climbs out of the UTV.

"Mom..." Romy sounds annoyed that they all think she wants to be alone with me. They couldn't be more wrong.

DeSoto glances at me from the other UTV to see if I'm going to go, but Romy hasn't slid out of her side yet.

"Are you going?" I ask.

She glances at me and climbs out, but instead of going up the hill like the rest of her family, she walks in the opposite direction.

DeSoto's head volleys between her and back to me, waiting to see what I want to do.

I should stay right where I am. I definitely shouldn't follow her.

"Damn it," I mumble and jog after her. DeSoto moves to join me, but I put out my hand. "I'm fine. Stay with them."

"Okay," he says, ever the faithful employee.

It takes me only a few moments to catch up, but she doesn't slow her pace. Thankfully, I have longer legs.

"Hey," I say like an idiot when I finally catch up to her. My hand reaches out to grasp her elbow, but I retract it before I touch her.

"It's a really big ranch." She walks steadily, not slowing her pace or looking in my direction. "So big that two people can coexist on it and not ever have to see each other."

She continues walking, crossing her arms. Her closed-off body language is like a set of iron gates with chains across them. And she's right to keep them in place where I'm concerned.

But she doesn't see me. Not the true me. She sees Zander Shaw, the man who sings songs about love and heartbreak I've never experienced because to do that, I'd have to allow someone to get close enough to break me.

"So, it's fine. And this will be really good for the ranch. You can film your video here, and my family will benefit from it. Which is good. Didn't you always say any type of publicity is good?"

Is she throwing that in my face from that night I lost my shit because a guy grabbed her arm on the way to the tour bus?

"We'll make it work. You being here and all. Scarlett is great, and she'll make sure you've got everything you need. Jensen, my other cousin, is a great chef, so you'll eat well at The Getaway Lodge. Might want to tell him about your shell-fish allergy, though."

"You remember that?" I didn't even know where she lived, and she remembered my stupid story about when I went into anaphylactic shock from shrimp.

She stops finally. Thank God, because my heart is racing, and I'm winded. I thought I was in shape until this mile-long trek along uneven ground in my cowboy boots.

"It's my job to remember things like that. I don't want someone dying at one of the events I plan. Don't think you're special or something." She flips back around, and I swear she's stomping her feet as she walks away.

"I would never," I say, more truth in those three words than she'll ever know. "Romy." I finally get the nerve to grasp her elbow to force her to stop.

She does, but she doesn't turn toward me. Instead, she turns toward the lake briefly before she groans and faces me with an expression that reveals how much I hurt her.

It's me. I'm the problem, not you.

"Enjoy your stay, and please just..." She stops right as we reach a sign that says, *This way to The Getaway Lodge.* "They're my family... my everything, Zander. I know that they're all on board with this decision to bring you and your big show here, but please respect them."

"Of course." What kind of monster does she take me for?

The one you proved to be.

She points at a path. "Head that way." She walks straight past it.

I watch her, wishing I could follow. Damn, she's even more beautiful than in my memories.

I can't do this. I'm not going to upend her life again. Not to mention, being able to control myself and stay away from her feels impossible since every fiber in me is begging me to follow her right now.

I turn to the sign and walk up the path to find Beau so I can tell him we need to find somewhere else to shoot this video.

The sound of an engine comes from behind me just as the lodge comes into view.

"There you are," Scarlett says, pulling up in the UTV.

Beau steps out onto the porch, phone to his ear. He glances at us, then does a double-take, his eyebrows furrowed.

You brought me right into her orbit again, asshole.

He quickly hangs up and pockets his phone, jogging down the front steps of the lodge.

"How was the tour?" he asks, looking at me.

"We need to talk," I say under my breath.

"Okay, big guy." He pats me on the shoulder.

I grab his elbow. "Now."

He stops and must see the seriousness on my face because he nods and looks around.

"Is everything okay?" Scarlett asks. "Beau, if you'd like a tour, I'm happy to take you out."

Beau shoots her that smile of his that appeases people. Immediately puts them at ease when I'm acting like a shithead. "Nah, I'll make my way around. I just have some important business to discuss with Zander, so..."

"Settle in," Scarlett says.

Lottie climbs out of the UTV, and she and her husband say something to her mom and walk away on the gravel path. I'm half tempted to follow, thinking they're going to Romy. Every muscle in me twitches to chase Romy down and explain.

"All right, let's go. I'll head over for copies in about an hour, Scarlett. Thanks for everything." Beau puts his hand out toward her, and they shake hands.

"Is everything okay though?" she asks again. "Romy really is a big fan, not sure what's put her in a bad mood, but I apologize if she was rude. I'll talk with her."

"It's fine," I say. "Don't worry about talking to her."

Her eyes widen then narrow. "Okay then. See you all later." She climbs back into the UTV and drives off.

I spin and face my manager as soon as she's out of earshot. "What the fuck do I pay you for?"

Beau's head tilts, and he glances at DeSoto for answers.

"She's here," DeSoto says. "It's her family ranch." I'm happy DeSoto can answer him.

"Who?" We both glare at Beau, and his head rocks back. "Oh, shit. No way."

"Get me out of this. Now." I stomp up the stairs of the lodge, my boots stopping at a picture of her and her family right there in the center of the wall.

Her smile and that damn dimple are like a sucker punch.

I need out of here, so I head to my room to get my suitcase and get the hell away from Plain Daisy Ranch.

ROMY

Tears slip down my cheeks the minute I break apart from Zander.

Seeing him in the flesh, moments after taking the test that will change my life, has somehow shattered all the anger I've been clinging to. The weight of the secret growing inside me has crumpled all the walls I built.

My hand falls to my flat stomach, finally able to settle on this new reality with no witnesses. We're going to have a child, and I have no idea how to tell him or what his reaction will be when I do. The man didn't even have the decency to tell me to my face that he was done with me. He let his lackies do it. Surely, he won't be pleased to find out that I'm having his baby.

Finally reaching my house, I pray Poppy and Scarlett are still with the tour group.

I'm sure everyone has a million questions about how the country singer I've been the biggest fan of—hell, I could have been the president of his fan club—didn't garner the reaction they thought it would from me. Scarlett looked so upset that I didn't jump him. Had I been the earlier version of myself, I would have screamed, run to him, thrown my arms around him like a crazy fan. Hell, maybe I even would have cried happy tears. Not now that I know the real Zander Shaw.

I walk into the house where I live with my cousins Poppy and Scarlett. Lottie moved in with Brooks after they built a house on her piece of land on the property. Bennett and Delaney are in the process of building theirs next to Lottie's. I always wondered how long my lot would stay vacant, and it seems a hell of a lot longer than I'd hoped. But if my brother, Bennett, could raise my niece, Wren, in a house with two other men, I can raise this baby in a house with my cousins.

I sit on the couch, wipe the tears from my face, and try to process the fork in the road my lifepath just took in the last hour.

That lasts for about a second because I hear Brooks and Lottie outside, arguing about the back deck being built at their place. We all know Brooks will give in, and Lottie will get her way. It's just foreplay for them.

I slide to the edge of the couch to escape to my room, but I don't move fast enough because the screen door opens. Lottie stops when she sees me. Immediately, she turns around to Brooks, puts her hand on his chest, and whispers something to him.

He nods, kisses her briefly, and circles back around.

"You don't have—"

"You're my sister. Now what's going on?" She sits on the couch next to me. "You've been crying."

As if her words are an explosion against the dam, my tears break free again, falling so fast they topple over one another in a race down my cheeks. I hiccup and shudder for breath, snot running down my nose.

She slides the box of Kleenex off the table and gives me a few of them. "Talk to me, what is it?"

Guilt is like a stone lodged in my throat. How do I say it to the sister who can't carry her own children, who once cried in my arms over it? How do I say I got pregnant by accident, and by a man who used me?

"I'm so sorry," I wail, my head falling into my hands.

"For what? The way you treated Zander Shaw?" She huffs. "No one cares. I can't say I wasn't surprised. I mean, I thought when you disappeared the night of his concert… like… did you hook up with that DeSoto guy or someone from his road crew? I know if you'd met Zander Shaw, you'd have told us all a thousand times by now. Either that, or you did meet him and were thoroughly unimpressed."

I peek up through the web of my fingers. "What?"

Her shoulders fall. "You came home at six in the morning, and it was DeSoto who came and got you to take you backstage, right? It looked like him. Maybe all those security guys look alike."

I nod, silently telling her to go on.

"I figured someone from backstage saw you and requested you. I guess I'm wrong?"

I need to get her off this track since I signed an NDA, and I'm not sure of anything until I talk to Zander myself. But I don't want her to be surprised or blindsided by my pregnancy either. I want her to hear it from me.

I suck in a breath and straighten my back, facing her. "I'm pregnant," I say, dodging any question of who I hooked up with that night.

She'd never believe me if I said Zander Shaw himself spotted me in the crowd, asked DeSoto to bring me backstage, and that it snowballed into a handful of nights that burned themselves into my bones. Nights I thought meant something to him. Turns out I was just a naïve groupie hearing what I wanted to hear, seeing what I wanted to see.

"Pregnant?" Lottie's eyes widen.

I nod, swallowing past the lump in my throat.

"When? Who?" Her gaze dips to my stomach.

"It's early. I just took the test right before Scarlett came to get me. That's why I was in the bathroom."

Her mouth opens in an "oh" expression, and she slides closer, wrapping her arm around my shoulders. "Oh, Romy. And then we put you on parade out there. Of course you were curt, you're probably freaking out."

I nod, and she draws me into an embrace. I fall into her arms, and she holds me tightly. Cue the ugly cry.

"It's going to be fine. We're going to get through this. So, this is the mystery man's baby?"

I nod against her chest, hoping she doesn't ask for specifics. My confession is on the tip of my tongue, wanting to let everyone know what I've been hiding these past months, but I want her to be the first to know.

"You're not mad?" I draw back and wipe the tears from my face. "Upset?"

Her head rears back, and her forehead wrinkles. "No." Then her shoulders fall as she must realize what I'm referring to. "No, Romy. I came to terms with my situation a long time ago, and Brooks and I have talked. Sure, my path will look a lot different than yours, but it's my path. I'm at peace with that. Do you know what you're going to do?"

I nod weakly. "Become a mother, I suppose."

A small smile tips the edges of her lips. "I'm happy to have another niece or nephew to love but seeing you so worked up upsets me. This should be a happy thing."

I scoff.

"Sure, the situation isn't ideal, and I have no idea who this mystery man is or what he's going to do when he finds out. Will he be a part of our new bundle of joy's life, I don't know. But Romy... a baby? What's not to love about it?" She squeezes my shoulder.

My chest twists. If she only knew the mystery man is in another building on the ranch right now. That he's someone whose songs she's danced to. Someone whose touch I still ache for. But she's right that this baby deserves love no matter what.

My hand goes to my stomach again. "I'm not sure he'll want to be a part of this."

"His fucking loss. Tell me who he is and where he lives, and I'll pay him a little visit."

She'd go over and pull him out of the lodge by his ear probably. And I love that she'll always protect me, but I have to deal with this with Zander on my own.

"Can we keep this between us? For right now?"

Her head tilts with compassion, but she's not one to leave things be. I'm more of a patient, feel things out person while Lottie is all quick reactions and think on it later.

"Whatever you want. And if you need me to go with you to tell the loser, I'll drive you. Or come with you to the doctor's appointment. I'm your partner in this until you fire me." She puts her arm around my shoulders again.

I lean my head on her shoulder. "I'll be okay? Like, I can do this?"

She laughs. "Yes, you can do this. And you have an entire ranch of your annoying, overbearing family to help you."

Her head falls to mine, and we sit on the couch for what feels like forever. She doesn't rush me to get up but comforts me instead. My heart aches with the unfairness that Lottie will have to fight for her chance at motherhood, while I stumbled into it by accident. If she and Brooks choose that path, she'll make a great mom. A mamma bear, more than likely. A grizzly bear.

No matter what, she'll be an auntie bear, and I'm grateful to have her in my corner because I'm pretty sure I'll be raising this one on my own. And maybe that's why I'm hesitating to tell him—because if Zander tries to make this go away, to sign a check and erase me and his baby from his life, he'll break my heart all over again.

Chapter Five

❧

ZANDER

Beau follows me to my room at the lodge. No doubt DeSoto is a few steps behind.

"We signed a contract. I can't just get you out of it," Beau says, impatient as he should be. This is going to cause him a shit-ton more work.

"Then get me a better lawyer. I'll pay, do whatever you need to, but I can't be on this ranch. It's not fair—"

"To whom?" Beau asks as we walk up the stairs toward my room.

Lucky me, I got the honeymoon suite with a Jacuzzi tub and a walk-in shower big enough for five. Because there's nothing like sleeping solo in a suite built for two people in love as a reminder of what the rest of your life will look like.

I scan my keycard, and the door unlocks.

The door shuts behind Beau, and he leans his back on it as if he's DeSoto and afraid I'm going to make a run for it, and he'll have to tackle me to the ground. I pick up my suitcase from the corner of the room and throw it on the luggage holder to pack my bag.

"Have you thought this could be a sign?" he asks.

25

I glance at him. Beau is my best friend. A fellow foster kid who got his shit together a lot sooner than I did. Although he hasn't ventured onto a path of love or family, he's had healthy relationships in his past. He never cheats, goes on actual dates, and tries—tries to find his one.

How did we both come from such fucked up childhoods, yet he can be so centered? I'll never understand. Maybe it was always meant to be this way.

Beau looks like a teenager's heartthrob with his golden-blond hair, blue eyes, pressed slacks, and shoes that cost more than some people's mortgage payments. Even on a ranch, he's dressed as if he's on his way to a board meeting.

Whereas I'm the darker half of our duo with dark hair, dark eyes, and a beard that I keep because I feel like it hides a part of me from people. If Beau is the angel on someone's shoulder, I'm the devil feeding them bad ideas.

"Give me a break." I unzip the suitcase and splay it open.

He drops onto the couch, forearms resting on his thighs. "Zan, you can't just run away from this. We signed a contract. We guaranteed them money."

"I don't give a shit. I don't want to film the video here. It didn't feel right the minute we drove onto the property."

Lies, all of it, and Beau probably knows it. He just won't call me out on my shit. *Yet.* The truth? The second I pulled onto this ranch, looked up the hill at the rehabbed barn, I swear something cracked in my chest. As if I'd been here before. There was something familiar about it, but I had no idea it was because it's where the one woman who scares me the most was raised. That changes everything.

Beau stands. "Fine. I'll go to Scarlett and see what I can do. But you need to know, you can't keep living this way. One day, you need to deal with your demons—"

"Do you like your Ferrari?" I toss my T-shirts in the suitcase. "How about your mansion?" My pants go in next. "All the expendable cash... the vacations?"

He crosses his arms and glares at me.

"That can all go away. We both know what it's like to be piss poor, and I sure as hell don't ever want to be there again. Do you?"

"Of course not, but—"

"I don't need a lecture right now, Beau. What I need is to get the fuck off this property. You're my manager, so make it fucking happen."

I'm not even sure why I'm this pissed, but it's as if every speck of dirt on this ranch is choking me. All I want to do is seek Romy out, kiss her, touch her, make it all okay now that I know she's nearby. Which is exactly why I need to get the hell out of here. Because I'll only end up hurting her again.

He holds up his hands. "Fine. You'll have to pay them at the very least. They've closed the entire ranch for us." His eyes flash with concern. He's always thinking of other people before himself. He's like my conscience.

Some of the heat in my temper dissipates. "I'm sorry to have you do it. Pay them whatever you think is fair. I obviously—"

"I know. I'll handle it." He claps a hand on my shoulder, meeting my gaze. "I'm not gonna bother giving you advice, but did you ever think this might be just the place for you to find some peace? To get away from it all? We've got security at every entrance. Everything you need is here. Maybe... maybe you need this... for you." He smacks his hand on my chest.

"I don't need peace. I need to get this video going. It's my directorial debut, and this song has the potential to reach new heights, even for me. After the single, I need to record an album to go along with it."

"This might be a good place to find some inspiration." His eyebrows waggle like a smart-ass.

"Or kill it. I can't risk that. There's another ranch we can use somewhere. Find it."

"There's one down the road. It'd save on expenses. Trucks wouldn't have to go far. We already have everything set up to come to the area, and this way, no airline changes or rerouting." He pulls out his phone, finally on board with me.

There. Even he gets it. I need space from Romy if I'm gonna make this album work. If I stay, every lyric I write will bleed with heartbreak.

"Wild Bull Ranch," he says, flashing a picture on his screen. "I'll call them when I'm done with Scarlett. But we've got to get out of this before we can sign with them."

"Please, Beau. Just make it happen."

He nods but chews the inside of his cheek—his tell when he thinks I'm being a dipshit but does what I want anyway because, technically, I sign his paychecks.

"Consider it done," he says, then pauses. "You gonna be okay here until I get back?"

"I'm not a toddler," I grumble, tossing my phone charger in the suitcase.

"You throw tantrums like one."

I shake my head and give him my back as I walk into the bathroom to collect my stuff. "Funny."

"I like to think so. I'll take it as a compliment."

I shove my toiletry bag into the suitcase. "I guess one of us has to be."

How many times has Beau's humor kept me from spiraling? It's his defense mechanism—thank God. Especially since mine is shutting down so hard I self-isolate.

I glance at him.

He chuckles, stepping back and raising both hands. "I'm going..."

"Hey," I call, and he turns back to me. "Thanks." I hope he sees I mean it.

"Yeah, yeah. Always doing your dirty work." He nods before opening the door to the hallway. "Hey, DeSoto, you make sure no chickens come pecking at our guy, will ya?"

The door shuts before I catch DeSoto's reply, but I'm sure it was just as sarcastic.

I sit on the edge of the bed and drag my hands down my face.

I'm making the right decision. Nothing good will come from me staying here. Not for me and sure as hell not for Romy.

Chapter Six

ROMY

My family has taken this whole Zander Shaw surprise way too far.

They scheduled a board meeting that everyone else was already in on to talk about the logistics and special requests from Zander's team while they film on the ranch. Normally, nothing new gets approved without a majority vote, but this time, they signed the contract behind my back, assuming I'd be thrilled. And I *would* have been thrilled. Zander Shaw filming here? Before everything went down, I'd have popped a bottle of champagne and probably made myself his damn welcoming committee.

That was before he kicked me to the curb and those two pink lines showed up.

A foot nudges me under the table, and I snap back to reality, straightening in my chair as a dozen sets of eyes turn toward me.

Thanks, big sis.

"Sorry, what?"

"What's going on with you?" Mom asks, her brow furrowing. "You've been off all day."

"Nothing. Just… got a wedding on my mind."

The fake one Zander's about to film. The one that will never be my life.

Scarlett leans back in her chair. "I was saying how The Knotted Barn was the most interesting location to Zander when I sent them the pics and videos. He sees it as the focal point—the heart of the video. He wants to keep circling back to it with flashes of the rest of the ranch."

"Okay." My voice is flat and emotionless.

Mom zeroes in on me. "Are you going to be able to dial back that attitude with him?"

"Did he deny you backstage access or something?" Emmett throws in, grinning because he has no idea how close he is to the truth. No doubt he's heard the rumors from someone in the family about the first time I was backstage and got delivered home at six in the morning.

"No," I say, forcing a shrug. "I just… don't think he's all that anymore. I'm allowed to change my mind."

Emmett's brows lift, but I don't give him the satisfaction of a reaction.

"I'll put on a nice face." I grin, big and fake, stretching it wide as if they can't tell.

Sighs echo around the table. It would be so easy to spit out the news and let the silence descend. I should warn them that their shiny opportunity might implode the second I tell Zander he's going to be a father. That he'll run. That this entire video shoot will be over before it begins.

"How long did they say they'd be here?" I ask.

Scarlett pauses, flicking a glance at Lottie. She suspects I've told her why I'm like this. She's right, but Lottie would never breathe a word to her. Lottie just shifts slightly, as though she wants to carry some of this for me.

"For the entire gap we have in the schedule. We're lucky

we had no events booked and could accommodate them when they approached us." Scarlett passes papers around the table. "This is the current plan. I'm still working with Beau, Zander's manager, to finalize the rest. His team's coming in tomorrow, so we'll have a full crew meeting for intros."

Jude groans. "I don't have time for this. The maze is a mess, and the cattle schedule is stacked."

Ben raises a hand. "I'm in the middle of football season at the high school. Do I really need to be here for all this?"

"We *all* agreed to do what it would take to make this work," Scarlett says pointedly. "Well—everyone but Romy."

"I didn't think he'd care about the cattle ranch. Now he wants to play cowboy too?" Jude shoves his paper away with a grumble.

He's always so grumpy—except with his wife, Sadie, and baby girl.

"I'll do it with him," Emmett volunteers. "Probably better if Jude doesn't interact with Zander. Dealing with Romy will be bad enough."

I snap my gaze toward Emmett, scowling.

He laughs. "Just saying, you're usually a sweetheart, but you looked ready to throat-punch the guy."

"I get it," Lottie cuts in gently. "She's just protective. The Knotted Barn is hers, and who knows what kind of circus they're planning to bring into it."

I offer her a silent thank you.

"She's taking the brunt of this, and she didn't get a chance to agree to it," Poppy adds. "The least the rest of us can do is handle our small parts."

Emmett puts up his hands in defense. "All right, girl army, calm down. It was just an observation."

"Anything else?" Uncle Bruce stands from his chair as though we're already done. He's never been one for distractions during these meetings. He likes them clear-cut and to the point.

"No, that's it. You have your itineraries. Just everyone be available tomorrow night. Jensen is going to cook an old west cookout for us all to get to know one another."

My cousin Jensen has done that for a few of the dude ranches we've put on that Emmett and Briar have organized, but never for this many people. My family is pulling out all the stops.

"Thanks, Jensen," Emmett says. "I hope you're making that brisket."

"Not for your sorry ass," he says, standing to leave as well.

As the room clears, chairs scrape and boots shuffle, and a new weight settles on me. The pressure to pretend. The dread of what's coming. What will the next meeting look like? I'll probably have all eyes on me, thinking I ruined it for them.

"Romy, can you stay for a sec?" Scarlett asks.

Lottie pauses, silently asking if I need her. I shake my head.

As they leave, I hear Ben joke, "So what does the big ol' sheriff think about all this ruckus in his town?"

Scarlett sinks into the chair beside me. "I'm really sorry, Romy. I shouldn't have sprung this on you. I was just so excited when I got the call. Out of all the ranches, they picked ours. And you were always such a big fan... I thought I was doing something special, but it was wrong of me to keep you out of the loop and make a big spectacle of it."

"I appreciate that, but it's okay. I was just taken by surprise." Little does she know the surprise I'm referring to is the one I had before walking out to find Zander in the venue. One day I'll be able to explain myself. "I'll be fine. Honestly."

She looks out the windows that face our iron archway at the gate of our ranch. It's been in our family for years. First our great-grandparents, then our grandpa's, then Uncle Bruce until my mom and Aunt Bette decided to build businesses on their parts of the land. Now, we're all fortunate to live together and work together. Sure, sometimes we don't all get along, but I love being close to my family and would never want to be anywhere else.

"This is going to be really good for us," she says, her eyes not leaving the dirt road into our farm. There seems to be more she's not saying. "Four generations."

"No worries on my front and thank you for the apology. I just..."

A knock lands on the conference room door.

We turn to see Beau. I should've known he was on the ranch. He's never very far from Zander.

His usually easygoing persona is absent. He seems tense. Beau might be the most attractive male I've ever seen, although I like mine a little edgier—like his best friend, unfortunately.

For a moment, I wonder if he'll be an uncle to my child. If Zander decides he wants a relationship with his son or daughter, will Beau be the one who gets them juice boxes and sneaks snacks to him or her? Will he make them laugh, and they'll come back from visiting their dad telling stories of Uncle Beau?

"Sorry to interrupt," he says, flashing a smile I want to punch off his face. I don't want his sympathy.

"I was just leaving," I say. I hug Scarlett tightly, wishing I could whisper I'm sorry for all the work she put into this only for me to blow it up.

Beau steps in front of me, blocking the door. "What? No hello?" He opens his arms.

"I'm sorry?" I pretend to not know what he's getting at, but his eyebrows scrunch.

Sure, Beau was the guy who arranged for me to come and go. We stood on the side of the stage together, and I thought we were building a friendship. Back when I was delusional about what was transpiring with Zander.

He pulls me into a hug, and I wonder what Scarlett is thinking. This isn't good for my secret. "I love the guy, but he can be an asshole."

I pat his back, hoping he'll let go, but he hugs me tighter.

"C'mon. You're making me feel creepy," he says.

I give him a real squeeze and blink away the sob clawing its way up my throat.

"You were too good for him anyway," he whispers.

"What am I missing?" Scarlett asks behind me.

I stiffen. Beau looks at me, then her. Realization dawning in his blue eyes.

"Well, shit," he mutters. "Seems I'm the asshole."

I circle back around to Scarlett. "I'll explain later."

Scarlett's face goes pale, but she nods.

"I'm sorry," Beau tells me. "I assumed—"

"Not all women brag about having him." I give him a caustic smile.

His expression softens, eyes dimming. "I should've known."

"Welcome to Plain Daisy Ranch," I say, a hollow laugh escaping me.

He smiles. I'm assuming he's as surprised as the rest of us. He'd never put Zander in this spot. "It's amazing."

"I'm sure I'll see you around." I squeeze past him.

I go to the bathroom, and on the way back, I have the thought that I need to get that pregnancy test out of The Knotted Barn's bathroom cabinet.

"You can't do that," Scarlett snaps from the conference room.

The door's cracked open, so I can hear her, and when I hear the edge of panic in her voice, I stop to peek inside. Beau's leaned back in a chair, hands raised while Scarlett stands across from him, clearly furious.

"I'm sorry," he says. "He wants out. He's willing to pay."

"Pay? You think that fixes this? This ranch was counting on him. On this." Her usually calm voice is breaking.

Beau sighs. "We'll make it good. I promise."

"And where will you even go?" There's a desperation I've never heard from Scarlett before.

"I'm talking to another ranch. The one that was our second choice," Beau says.

"Who?" she asks. I'm surprised fire isn't flowing out of her mouth.

"Wild Bull Ranch. I'm not a big fan of the guy we were dealing with, but—"

"You committed to us. We closed our ranch for you. This has been in the works. You cannot do this to us. I'm calling our lawyer." Scarlett drops into a chair, her fingers pressing against her temples.

"Hey, I tried to change his mind, but he's the boss. You don't want to involve lawyers and pay those bills. No one wins in cases like this. We can pay for the expense of closing the ranch, make it worth it to you."

Her arms fall to the table. "Listen, we're having our worst year ever. Tourism is down because of the economy. Walker Matthews from Wild Bull Ranch is draining us dry by constantly competing with our businesses. This was our chance to put our ranch on the map. We *need* this."

I close my eyes.

Beau grunts, and the back of the chair pops up. They're about to square off over this.

The knot in my throat sinks to my stomach from Scarlett's confession. We're down this year, and she was banking on this video. Not only will Zander be paying for his time here, but afterward we'll be able to advertise the fact that the video was filmed here. Maybe even increase our event pricing as a result.

I can't imagine not having this ranch. I've seen the downfall of other ranches over the years. One bad year turns to two then three, and soon enough there's a *For Sale* sign up on the fence post. That can't happen to my family. Too many of us are counting on this, which leaves only one way to fix it.

Zander always gets his way, so there's only *one* way to make him stay.

Chapter Seven

ZANDER

My suitcase is already packed.

DeSoto's been hovering outside my door as though I'm still on tour, guarding a hotel hallway instead of a family ranch in the middle of nowhere. I told him to knock it off. The only people trying to breach security out here might be the set of little girls I saw running around earlier.

I scroll through my phone to keep my head busy. Not that I'm hot on reading blatant lies written about me. Beau and the team did a good job spinning my absence as a post-tour break, but you can't hide a caravan of trucks and an army of new faces in a small town. Everyone will know where I am soon enough.

My phone pings with a text from Zara.

> What is there to do out in Nebraska?

My thumbs hover my screen when a knock lands on the door.

"Beau, you get it handled or what?" I mutter, tossing my phone onto the bed and yanking open the door.

It's not Beau.

"Romy?"

Her eyes are steady, and her chin is lifted. She tilts her head toward the room. "Mind if I come in?"

I step back. "Uh... yeah, sure."

She walks past me, eyes scanning the room. "Not surprised they gave you the honeymoon suite." She scoffs as if I'm undeserving.

"It's the biggest room." I shrug.

She shakes her head but doesn't comment. Instead, she crosses the space to the farthest corner, deliberately keeping her distance from me. There's resolve in her face and a tightness in her shoulders.

"Listen," she says, her voice firmer than I've heard prior, "I know this is uncomfortable. But I'm not here to stalk you. I haven't told my family what happened between us, so you don't have to worry about them hating you on my behalf."

I clench my jaw.

"I overheard Beau telling Scarlett you want out."

"I do." I force myself to hold her gaze.

She nods once. "Then let me make this easy for you. You don't have to worry about me. I get it—it was a fling. Less than a fling. I was just another rabid screaming female in the crowd you picked out to pass the time with."

My chest tightens. I want to stop her. Tell her she wasn't like the others. That she's still under my skin. But if I do that, I'll give her hope that this can be something it can never be. Hope that I might be a different person than she thinks. That would make me even more of a bastard.

"Just..." She swallows hard, her voice catching. "I know you don't owe me anything, but please... stay. Film the video here."

Her words slice deeper than I expect. I study her. She's

flushed, but not the way she used to be when I kissed her. This looks more like exhaustion.

"Help me understand," I say, arms crossing, feet planted wide.

Her eyes narrow. "You don't have to understand."

"Then I'm leaving."

Her jaw drops open, disbelief sparking in her eyes.

You're being a dick. Stop it.

"God, isn't my asking enough?" Her voice rises, sharp edges breaking through. "Do you think I'd humiliate myself like this if I wasn't desperate?"

Her fierce gaze locks with mine. And just like that, I'm dragged back to the memory of her beneath me as I slid into her. How I wanted to slow down, savor her, memorize every second because I knew even then she was too good for me.

"So, in just a few hours, you've changed your mind?" I ask, my words sharper than I intend. "What happened to *it's a big ranch. We don't have to cross paths?*"

Her annoyance spikes. "Fine. Whatever. Leave. I'm not surprised." She storms toward the door, putting as much space between us as possible.

Let her go. Let her go. Get off this ranch.

But my hand betrays me, reaching out, fingers curling around her wrist.

She freezes. But she doesn't turn or pull away.

"Fine," I say, my voice low. "If it matters that much to you... I'll stay."

She exhales as though the air's been punched from her lungs. I force myself not to trace the pulse on the inside of her wrist with my thumb. We just stand there, breathing the same air.

"Thank you," she whispers.

I let go, and after a beat, she walks to the door.

"Romy," I say.

Her hand stills on the knob, but she doesn't look back. "You should be careful," she warns. "This might be a small town, but there are plenty of women who'd kill to get into this room. Maybe DeSoto should stick to the hallway instead of raiding the complimentary peanut butter cookies downstairs."

I smirk. "They're good cookies."

Her shoulders loosen slightly. "Nothing compared to the pistachio ones."

Our exchange garners the barest shift in her posture before she slips out.

I don't try to stop her. Whatever drove her to me had to be monumental because I'm the last man she'd ever want to ask for help.

I walk to the window just to torture myself, desperate for one more glimpse.

She's crossing the lot, climbing into a UTV. That blue dress of hers catches the fading light, hem fluttering around those long, tan legs I used to dream about being wrapped around me.

Still do, asshole.

Another UTV pulls up with Scarlett and Beau. He walks over to Romy, holding papers. He's smiling, but she breaks the distance, her hand touching his arm, and his smile falls. He nods. They talk for one or two seconds before she climbs into the UTV and drives off.

Then Beau glances up at me. He sees me watching then shakes his head, laughing to himself.

Great. Now he's gonna give me hell.

I wait for the knock, but he doesn't bother. The door clicks open.

"Last I checked, this isn't your room," I grumble.

"Figured you wouldn't let me in." He tosses the papers onto the bed and finishes off the cookie he must have taken when he passed by reception. "These are some of the best cookies I've ever had."

"I guess the pistachio ones are the best."

"Really? Says who?"

"So?" I change the subject, not wanting to talk about Romy and how when she confessed her favorite cookie, I wanted to go down to the kitchen and beg the chef to teach me how to make them just to impress her.

"Here's the deal. I granted your wish. Again. Which makes this a helluva lot more than three, so you're out of genie requests. Then I hear you changed your damn mind?"

I grab my guitar, sitting on the edge of the mattress and settling it on my lap.

"Zan?"

"Yeah," I mutter. "We're staying."

Beau glares at me when I glance up at him. "You're a fucker, you know that? Scarlett Ellis isn't all sunshine and fucking roses. She threatened my balls. Promised to slit my throat. Might've cursed my unborn children. She's probably gone back to that office of hers to put a hex on me."

I arch a brow.

"Okay, maybe not," he admits. "But it wouldn't shock me if that's next. So now I have to tell her we're back on?"

"Yep." I strum a chord casually.

"I quit."

"You say that every day."

"And if you weren't such a sorry ass, I'd mean it."

"No, you wouldn't."

He shakes his head, muttering as he grabs the papers again. "I should."

"Probably."

He stops in the doorway. "You're buying me a new shirt. This one's soaked in sweat."

I chuckle.

"Stop laughing, asshole."

The door shuts, and I'm sure he's flipping me off behind it, but I'm thankful when the silence returns.

I scribble a line into my notebook, words coming fast and furious since Romy left.

Maybe Beau's right. Maybe this ranch is exactly what I need. For inspiration or peace or mental torture, I don't know.

It could be a good thing or a bad thing, but if I'm stuck here, I might as well benefit from it.

Chapter Eight

ROMY

The sun slips behind the hills, but the plethora of string lights trailing from one tree or pole to the next cast a warm glow.

The huge buffet that Jensen must have planned for weeks is over, though a few of the desserts are still out for people to enjoy as they mill about. The fire is low enough that it's not throwing too much smoke, just warmth into the crisp evening air. Someone fiddles with a Bluetooth speaker, then curses when it loses connection.

Everyone groans. I look at my phone to see how much longer I might be required to stay. Maybe I can slide out early.

After numerous people try to fix the speaker, Beau walks over with Zander's guitar.

My stomach sinks.

He sets it in front of Zander with a grin, but Zander scowls and shakes his head.

"One song," Beau nudges, loud enough for everyone nearby to hear. "They deserve a little concert after all the hard work that went into tonight."

The hard lines on Zander's face soften. "Which was amazing. Thank you for the spread and your gracious hospitality," Zander says, voice dry, but his mouth curves in a half smile.

Flutters erupt in my stomach. It's the same half smile that won me over every damn time we were together.

"Get on with it then." Beau nudges the case closer with his foot.

The people closest cheer in agreement, egging Zander on. I roll my eyes so hard they nearly stick. Zander's gaze finds mine over the flames of the fire, and thankfully I have the excuse of the heat from the flames for why my cheeks are so red.

Zander smiles and opens the case. The guitar gleams in the firelight, the warm wood reflecting the flickers of the flames. He slings the strap of the guitar over his shoulder and positions the guitar in his lap. The movements are flawless, showing how his guitar is just an extension of him. He adjusts the strap, strums a few test chords, letting out a breath.

And then—

He sings.

I wonder if anyone will notice if I bolt.

His voice isn't the one filling a stadium when he's on tour or the polished studio version that plays on the streaming services. It's lower, rougher, and more intimate. The notes drop into the night sky and float away, quieting the murmurs of the bystanders.

I tell myself to not watch. I tell myself to drown him out with my thoughts or go help Delaney chase down the last marshmallow sticks for the girls. And I definitely tell myself to get up off the log across from him and disappear into the backdrop of darkness so I'm invisible to curious eyes.

But I don't move.

My gaze finds him as if it's being pulled by magnets. Zander sits forward, head tipped slightly down, lashes lowering as his thumb drags steadily over the strings. There's tension in his jaw, a faint furrow in his brow. I always loved when he did an acoustic rendition at his concerts, and everyone would raise their phones and shine their flashlights. It always felt more personal, as if he was letting me in a little. How naïve was I?

The fire crackles, and people link arms, swaying together. I sit stiffly, arms wrapped around my knees, trying not to let the heat pooling in my chest spread.

Of course he had to pick *this* song.

The one he used to strum quietly in the bus, when the crew was gone and it was just us. I was foolish enough to think our stolen nights together meant something to him. Back then, I pretended not to hang on every word.

Halfway through the second verse, his eyes lift, finding mine.

Technically, it's just a glance, but it lingers a little longer than it should, pinning me in place. My pulse trips at hearing him sing the loving lyrics I once dreamed could be about me.

I make the mistake of not forcing myself to look away. And when he looks back over at me a minute later, it's as if we're in a game of chicken, and I have to win. But once he has me, he doesn't let go. He holds my gaze as his voice dips softer.

I clench my jaw. My face stays blank, but inside, I'm as tumultuous as a thunderstorm.

"Hard to believe that something so intimate comes out of him, right?"

I jolt at Beau's voice.

He slides in next to me on the log, close enough that I smell the faint cologne that probably costs more than I make in a week. His blond hair gleams in the firelight, and as usual, his smile is warm.

I give him a side-eye. "He's all right."

He laughs and shakes his head. "Yeah, not impressive at all. He should keep his day job for sure." He gestures lazily toward Zander, still singing, still lost in the lyrics. "But you have to admire the way he can make everyone stop breathing and hang on his every word for three minutes."

"Jealous?" I say, keeping my tone light.

Beau chuckles, cups his drink in his palms. "People don't always appreciate how heavy it is, carrying the weight of that kind of attention."

"Right," I mutter, eyes fixed stubbornly on the crackle of flames instead of Zander now. "Must be exhausting being so adored."

In my periphery, I see Beau tilt his head, studying me. "Believe it or not, he doesn't love it. Twists your view on who is authentic."

I snap my gaze to him. "You don't need to be cryptic, Beau. Just say what you came over here to say."

"I just want you to know that though most people think he has everything, that's not true. He has fame. He has money. Hell, he has good looks. I mean, he's not nearly as good-looking as me, but..." He smirks faintly. "But there's more to life than all that."

My chest tightens. "Are you expecting me to feel sorry for him?"

I think about the baby growing inside me and what will happen to that baby when I have to explain that his or her daddy didn't show up for his scheduled visit.

"Maybe," he says easily. "I wasn't in those rooms with you. I don't know the conversations you had, but you got him to stay here and that says something. At least to me. You know, his best friend for almost his entire life."

The words hit me square in the heart. "Why are you telling me this? Clearly, he wanted things between us to be over. And I don't appreciate—"

"I'm just pointing out the facts." He sighs and takes a quick glance at Zander. "Sometimes he gets in his own way."

I stiffen, not entirely sure what he's getting at but not

willing to put any hope into what Beau's implying. Zander was very clear about where we stood when he barred me from entry without any explanation.

Beau grins, apparently satisfied that he got under my skin, then goes quiet, letting the song fill the space between us.

Zander's voice dips to the last line, softer, almost breaking. For a heartbeat, the world stills. Then the last chord rings out, and everyone reacts to the mastery they just witnessed.

People cheer, whistle, and clap as though he just gave them a concert's worth of music and not one song. Zander tips his head, mouth curving in gratitude, but his gaze goes straight back to me, then to Beau, and back to me.

"Don't worry, I didn't tell him," Beau says.

"What are you talking about?"

"He didn't stick around because he feels bad for your family. He's here because you asked him to be. I want to make sure you know that."

I stare at him for a moment, then back at Zander, who is still looking at us.

"I have a feeling he was only singing to one person just now."

I stand abruptly, brushing dirt off the butt of my jeans. "Good night, Beau."

Before he can respond, I slip into the darkness, needing to put distance between us, but the lyrics still flow through my mind, as does the hum of the melody of a song I've listened to so many times.

But no matter how far I walk from the campfire, I can still feel his eyes on me.

Chapter Nine

ZANDER

I've been in my fair share of commercial kitchens since my music took off. Chef's tables in every city, seven-course meals with small flowers put on with tweezers when I'd have killed for a burger and fries.

Romy says her family doesn't know about us, and I believe her. But that doesn't mean I'm not on edge. Because if they *do* find out, they'll probably boot me off the ranch in a stampede. And I wouldn't blame them.

Beau said her cousin Jensen wanted to go over the food with me. I'm not picky though, and I'm sure someone already passed along that I'm deathly allergic to shellfish.

When I walk into the back kitchen of The Getaway Lodge, the smell of garlic and butter hits me. It's like stepping into heaven. Heads lift from workstations, and I get a few polite nods along with a few curious stares. It's better than the outright gawking that sometimes happens.

I met Jensen during the cookout, but it was a brief encounter since he was running around in all different directions, making sure everything was the way he wanted.

He was dressed casually last night like the rest of us. Today, he wears a chef coat that isn't the typical black or white, but the kind of plaid you'd find on a flannel shirt. It makes him look more like a cowboy. His shoulders are more relaxed than the other night, and he's got a pen tucked behind one ear and a piece of paper in front of him.

His eyes lift, and he straightens. "Zander, thanks for coming." He closes the distance with an outstretched hand. Romy's family is so welcoming and kind. Something I don't deserve.

I shake his hand. "The kitchen smells amazing."

He folds his arms, glancing around as if he can't believe it's his. "Took a long time to build out. Now I just stand here asking myself, 'What next?'"

I nod. "It's like finishing an album. All that work, all those hours, and the minute it's out, I'm sitting there wondering what to do next."

He grins. "Except you make another one. I'm not sure I could do this again."

"It's just strumming strings," I say with a smirk.

He chuckles and pats my shoulder. "Right. Easy peasy. Come on, let's get your info down." He leads me over to the counter, slips the pen out from behind his ear, and poises it over the paper. "So, favorites?"

"Anything but shellfish."

Jensen gives me a look. "Beau mentioned that. How severe are we talking? Like... EpiPen or just some hives?"

"Stab me in the thigh allergic," I deadpan.

"Got it." He jots down no shellfish and circles it at least five times. "I'll bold and highlight once I type this up for all my employees."

I tap the counter. "Appreciate it. If I die, there'll be a mob after you."

He laughs and leans his hip against the counter. "Guess then I'd never be a Food Network star."

"Career over. You'd be stuck here for life."

We both laugh, then the kitchen door swings open. I glance over my shoulder and see Romy walk in. Her hair is in a high ponytail, and she's dressed in faded jeans and a T-shirt that hugs her waist. She has a clipboard clutched in one hand.

She freezes when our eyes lock. It's only for a second, but I catch the flicker of something before she snaps back into remembering she hates me.

"Oh," she says. "It's you."

I flash her my most charming smile. "Don't sound so excited."

She brushes past me without a second glance. "Jensen, when you've got a sec, I need to talk to you about Ben and Gillian's wedding."

"Sure, give me, like, ten," he says.

"I'll save you some time," I say to him, still watching her. "I'm not picky. Nothing fancy and make sure the plates are big enough to fill me."

"And no shellfish," Romy adds.

My grin deepens. I tilt my head.

She catches herself and rolls her eyes. "I'd like the ranch *not* to trend for killing a country music star. Call me crazy."

"Wow." I press a hand over my heart. "Your concern warms me."

"We've got the allergy noted," Jensen says, pointing at his notes.

One of his employees politely interrupts us. Jensen excuses himself and heads off to another station, leaving Romy and me alone.

She glares at my smirk. "What?"

I shrug, leaning against the stainless-steel counter. "Nothing."

"Stop looking at me like that." She hugs the clipboard to her body and looks down at it.

"Like what?"

"Like you're assuming I'm worried about you or something."

"You *have* mentioned the allergy more than once." I chuckle deep in my throat.

She doesn't look up. "We don't want to be sued if you drop dead."

I narrow my eyes. "So, your concern for my well-being is just a legal precaution?"

"Pretty much," she says, finally meeting my gaze.

We stand in silence for a beat.

This. This is exactly why I can't be around this woman—because of what I can't stop myself from revealing to her.

I lean in and whisper, "You looked really good in firelight, by the way."

She doesn't miss a beat. "You'd look really good *in* the fire."

I chuckle, but she's already shifting back into business mode.

"Tell Jensen to text me when he's ready," she says, turning to go.

"Wait—"

She hesitates just enough to let me know she's listening.

"I don't want it to be like this between us."

She lets out a quiet breath. Her shoulders drop, and I see the soft edges she's been trying to hide take shape. The part of her that used to open up to me, that trusted me isn't so far under the surface.

"What? You want to be friends?" she asks.

I shrug. "I guess so, yeah."

What I want is more, but I can't have it. Don't deserve it. Wouldn't know what to do with it even if I had it.

"You don't sound so sure."

"I just don't want to spend my time on the ranch dodging each other."

Her smile is tight, and I hate that what I did was morph her from someone who was open and had all this love to share to someone who is guarded and untrusting. "Fine. Stop flirting, and we can be cordial."

"Cordial?" I repeat, as if it's a foreign word.

"What do you want, Zander?" Her voice rises a little. "You just—" She cuts herself off, swallows. "It doesn't matter. You're doing me a favor by being here, so if you want to be friends, we'll be friends."

I want to explain. I *do*. But what am I supposed to say? That I asked DeSoto to keep her away because I was scared? Because she made the ground shift out from under me? Because she made me question a lifetime of choices and everything I ever thought I wanted?

I was scared and couldn't make sense of all the conflicting feelings inside me. Wasn't sure that she'd want me or my life for the long term. Sure, I was exciting and mysterious, but when she got to know the guy underneath the stardom, she'd find out I wasn't good enough for her. She'd see the parts of me that aren't made for stadium tours and song lyrics and realize I don't have anything real to offer.

"Good, want to do lunch?" I force a smile.

She shakes her head. "I was thinking more like... wave from a distance kind of friends."

Jensen walks back over and joins us. "Okay, what are your top five favorites?"

"I'll be back," Romy says, disappearing before either of us can say anything.

He looks at me. "Everything okay?"

I lie through my teeth. "Yeah. All good." Then I rattle off my answers, "Burgers, chicken sandwiches..."

He jots it all down then asks about breakfast, snacks, and drinks.

My answers are quick and easy, but my head's still at the door she walked through, wondering how the hell I'm going to make it through this while pretending all I want from Romy Owens is *friendship*.

Chapter Ten

ROMY

I stand in my office in front of the corkboard of ideas for my cousin Ben and his fiancée Gillian's wedding. Even though they've decided not to have the reception at The Knotted Barn, they've asked me to help with the planning.

They're hosting the reception in the backyard of Uncle Bruce's house. The same yard where we always have the Fourth of July parties. I think it's a special place for them.

I unpin the piece of fabric I got for the tablecloths and hold it against a swatch I ordered online. To anyone else, the corkboard probably looks chaotic, but I've never been able to build one digitally. I need to touch and feel and compare, to see the pieces side by side.

"You never told me you were so talented," a voice says behind me, sinking into my skin before I even turn around. "Although I'm not surprised."

My spine stiffens. His boots cross the floor until he's standing right beside me. Close enough that his scent drifts over. Just as I remembered—sandalwood and leather.

I hate how easily he makes me forget how to breathe.

"How would you know? I feel like we barely talked." I keep my eyes glued to the board.

"That's what happens when you're so good at doing other things together." Zander's tone carries enough heat that my pulse jumps. He nods at the board. "This is for a wedding?"

I press down hard on the flutter in my stomach, on the memory of how badly I used to want his hands, his lips, his body pressed to mine. Our chemistry was like a wildfire. We never stopped long enough to talk, just pieced each other together in shared fragments. Regardless, I felt as though I knew him. It felt like the start of something.

"Ben and Gillian. He's the football coach."

Zander smirks, amused. "That's all, huh? Just a high school football coach?" His chuckle rumbles low, since he knows Ben's a retired professional football player, a small-town legend, and Gillian is the high school sweetheart he left behind. I overheard them talking around the fire the other night.

"Now he is."

"One day I'll be just a music teacher, I suppose." His soft voice dips.

The sadness in his tone makes my chest squeeze. I suppose his worst nightmare would be to be stuck somewhere small like Willowbrook for the rest of his life. "You teaching kids how to play the guitar—it's hard to imagine."

A flash of him with our own child on his lap, teaching him or her how to play, flashes in my mind, and I force it back.

"Thanks for the compliment." He steps closer to the board, shoulder brushing mine, and my anxiety spikes.

I hate showing these boards to anyone before the bride and groom see them. For him to see my work at this raw stage makes me want to throw my body in front of it and shield it.

"I like the way you have the lights falling down off the

branches instead of being strung across. Feels more romantic. Not as commercial."

His words land too warmly, pressing into the part of me that likes it when people appreciate my vision. I shove away the feeling. "Strung lights are still romantic."

A silent chuckle makes his back rise and fall. "Take the compliment, Romy."

I want to fight him, to push back, to prove I don't need his approval. But what's the point? Every night I remind myself that eventually I have to tell him he's the father of the baby growing inside me. That I don't want him back, not really, but I want him to show up, to co-parent, to love our little one. It isn't the baby's fault we were careless.

"Thank you," I say quietly.

He circles around, thumbs hooked in his pockets, wearing that arrogant grin I want to smack off his face. "Whoa. That seemed too easy."

I shrug, pretending to dig through papers on my desk. "We did agree to be cordial."

"We agreed to be friends actually," he clarifies.

I glance over my shoulder, catching the way he's smiling at me. "Right."

"After seeing this," he gestures to the board, "I'm hoping you might help me dress the set for the wedding in the video. I get that it won't be easy to work together, but it's not like I know a lot about this netting stuff." He fingers a scrap of tulle.

"Netting?"

"See? I don't even know what it's called."

"Tulle."

"You're the expert. That's why I'm asking you to help."

I huff out a breath, staring at Ben and Gillian's board. I love finding beauty in scraps and sketches, building something magical out of a blank canvas. But never in my life did I imagine doing it for an audience as big as this music video will have.

"I'm sure you could hire a professional to do it." I arch an eyebrow at him and make my way over to take a seat at my desk.

"That's what I'm attempting to do right now."

I frown. "I mean some Hollywood type."

"I want you. You're the one who's put together who knows how many weddings in the venue, not some Hollywood type."

I want you.

I try not to let the words settle into my bones, but it proves difficult. If only he meant them the way I'd once hoped he would.

"I'd give you the credit. And I'll pay you obviously."

My chest tightens. That's how he keeps people at arm's length. He makes it transactional and professional. "I don't need either. You're already doing enough for the ranch."

He comes around my desk, looming tall, taking up space until I can't think straight. "I want to. It's the fair thing to do."

"Or it's just to ease your guilty conscience." My hand goes to the second drawer out of habit, and I freeze. The pregnancy test is still there. I couldn't bring it home, didn't know where to hide it, but for sentimental reasons, I couldn't throw it away. This baby might not have been planned, but he or she is still very loved, and I want to remember when I first found out I was going to be a mom.

"I'd really like your help on this," he says softly. "This is clearly your thing. It's not mine—"

I scoff. "What? Romance and love?" I interrupt with that bitter tone I keep trying not to let out.

Our gazes lock.

"It would seem so."

A heavy weight charges the air. I should say no again. I should shut this down before I get pulled back under. Being around him, talking about romance, about forever, is the last thing I need when I'm carrying this secret.

But maybe if I help him quickly, he'll leave quickly. And once he's ready to leave and all the lights and cameras roll off the ranch, I'll tell him about the baby.

"Strictly professional?" I ask.

He nods slowly, finally stepping back. "Of course."

"Okay."

He nods. "Do you mind walking me around the venue? Do you have some videos or pictures from previous weddings?"

"Yeah. But we're not copying anything I've already done. We'll make it unique. First though, we have some things to go over, so let's walk the venue." I move toward the hall, desperate for distance.

"Lead the way."

I don't know what the hell I've just agreed to. Alone time with Zander Shaw is dangerous, but I need to keep reminding myself that he isn't who I thought he was.

Chapter Eleven

ZANDER

I step into The Knotted Barn and scan the space. Romy's nowhere in sight.

I've deliberately kept out the crew. This video is the first I'm co-directing. I want it to be entirely my vision, but even that's a risk. Since I'm going to be in front of the camera, I've brought on Jack, who I've worked with before, to help as the other co-director. Still, if it fails, it's on me... He might be helping me execute, but I'm in charge of the direction we're going, and it'll be my vision everyone sees on-screen.

A loud crash rings out from somewhere in the back.

"Son of a bitch." Romy's voice carries through the quiet.

I follow the noise, my heart thudding with concern. There's an open door I haven't noticed before.

"Romy?" I call, stepping in.

"Yeah... shit... in here."

The room is packed tight with wedding décor. There're arches, chairs, and floral pieces scattered around.

"Be careful!" she calls from somewhere behind a stack of archways. They're all stained different colors and etched with unique designs. "I do not need you spraining an ankle or getting some gash on your forehead."

I find her sitting on a table, sucking on her finger, glaring at a jagged nail sticking out of one of the arches.

"You okay?"

"It's nothing. Just a cut. Someone didn't take out a nail, and it cut me." She yanks her finger away from her mouth, inspecting the blood that's still pooling.

"Let me see." I hold out my hand.

"I'm fine," she says quickly, standing before I reach her. "I just need a Band-Aid."

She moves past me, still nursing her finger, winding through the room as though she's mastered the chaotic labyrinth. I follow close on her heels.

She stops abruptly outside the bathroom door and points at the frosted glass with *Women's* stamped in bold black letters on it.

I shrug. "No one's here."

"You don't know that."

"I do."

She pushes the door open with her shoulder. "I don't need help."

I don't move. "Look, I know you don't think very highly of me, and that's fair. But I'm not going to let you bleed out without at least checking the cut. You might need stitches or a hospital visit."

She rolls her eyes. "You're being dramatic." But she doesn't argue when I catch the closing door with my boot.

"Dramatic?" I lift a brow. "If you'd just let me help you, I wouldn't have to start listing all my reasons."

"It's just a cut." She pulls her finger from her mouth again, and blood drips in a slow, lazy trail down to her palm.

"Yeah, looks like you have it totally under control." I slide my hands to her waist and easily lift her onto the counter.

"Zander," she warns, her voice tight with resistance.

I pick up her hand. The cut's deep. Not stitches-deep, but it's not a nick either. "First-aid kit?"

"In my office," she mumbles, still concentrating on the cut.

"I'll be right back. Sit still. Be a good patient."

"Do I get a sticker if I don't cry?"

"You can have a lollipop if you're really good," I say, chuckling as I head out.

But the second I leave the room, I hear her jump off the counter.

"Actually—I'll get it!"

"Relax. Where is it?" I keep walking down the hall, already knowing she won't tell me.

Sure enough, I feel her presence behind me before I see her. Her fingers clutch the back of my T-shirt, and she yanks me out of the way. "I said I can get it."

"Romy," I warn, sidestepping her as she lunges for the drawer in her desk.

She pulls out the kit with victorious flair, holding it up as if she just captured the flag and is declaring victory. "Got it!"

"Congrats. You're bleeding again." I nod toward her hand.

She looks down and frowns. "Shit."

I take the kit gently, brushing past her on the way back to the bathroom. She follows me in and hops back up on the counter, wiggling her ass, suddenly being the most cooperative patient ever.

I turn on the faucet and guide her finger under the cool stream of water, rinsing the blood away. Then I pat her finger dry and gently press gauze on the cut. "Keep pressure on that."

"Yes, doctor," she says lightly.

"You into roleplay?" I glance at her from beneath my lashes.

"You sure know your way around a first-aid kit," she says, staring at my items all lined up in order of how to help her, completely ignoring my flirtatious comment.

She's right to ignore it. I don't know why I say half the shit that comes out of my mouth when she's around. I just can't seem to help myself.

"Foster kid." My voice drops. Giving her a bit of my past that I usually let people discover on their own feels strange. Although it's not a secret and since she was a big fan of mine, she probably already knows.

Her smile falters. "And that makes you an expert at patching people up?"

I grab the antibiotic cream. "More like... I struggled to keep my emotions in check, and I had to fix myself up after a lot of fights." I peek up at her. "On the rare occasions I didn't win." I wink, but she doesn't smile or laugh at my joke.

"You had to bandage yourself?"

I shrug. "Most of the time."

She's quiet. And when I glance up, her mouth is pinched, her eyes softening with the one emotion I hate—pity.

She grew up on this big ranch with her pick of family members to turn to whenever she needed support. She'll find my childhood sad and depressing. It was, but I don't want people's pity. I've made a helluva life for myself by anyone's standards.

"Don't pity me, Romy."

She inhales when I touch her again, wrapping the Band-Aid carefully over the wound. "Pity a superstar? Give me a break."

I smooth the edges of the bandage, then make the mistake of looking up.

She's smiling. An honest and unguarded one.

It's her first real one since I stepped on this ranch.

The words rush out before I can stop them. "I'm sorry." My voice is quieter than it should be.

She meets my gaze, and I swear, for a second, all the bullshit between us slips away.

But then she blinks, pushes off the counter, and cleans up the wrappers and gauze. "Yeah, we're not doing this." She tosses away the trash. "Thanks for your help."

I cover her hands with mine. "Romy... just let me say it. I was an asshole. I handled everything in the wrong way, and you didn't deserve it."

Her head tilts, and her brown eyes sear me down to my soul. Every ounce of my energy is being used to hold me back from lowering my head enough to press my lips to hers. To feel their warmth, her want and her desire for me.

But I know the truth. She'd be kissing Zander Shaw, the famous singer. And I'd be kissing the woman I can't stop thinking about, the one who might actually be able to break down everything I've built to keep people out.

"Thank you," she says softly. She turns, closes the first-aid kit, and walks over to the door. "I should get back to work."

Her hand hovers over the handle, and I brace for her to bolt. For the door to swing shut and lock me out again.

But instead, she glances over her shoulder. "Did you want to go through the storage room? See if there's an arch you like? Seems senseless to build a new one."

I blink and wait a beat until I realize she's not pushing me away. Then I smile. "I'd love to. But you better be careful. My medical expertise ends at cuts and bruises. No promises on broken bones."

She laughs. Actually laughs.

And I just stand there, stunned like a fucking idiot. Because that laugh is dangerous.

I don't know what's worse, her hating me... or her friendship. Because when this ends, one of us is going to walk away hurting. And I'm worried it won't be her.

Chapter Twelve

ROMY

My boots crunch up the gravel path toward The Knotted Barn. Lottie runs up beside me, breathless like she sprinted the whole way from her house.

"You're a hard woman to find," she says, panting.

"You haven't been looking very hard. I haven't left the ranch in, like, two weeks."

She's dressed in her Harvest Depot long-sleeve shirt and jeans, probably on her way into work. "Well, you know how busy the store is during the fall season. It's the one part of the ranch that's open, and everyone and their sister wants to visit to try to get a glimpse of Zander."

I stop in my tracks, stomach tightening. "People in town have figured it out?"

She nods, her face pinched. "Yep, word is out. Brooks said people keep asking him questions about it. He's kind of annoyed, but I think he's just a little hurt Zander's crew doesn't need him. You know how he feels about his role in this community." She looks genuinely upset for him, and of course she does. He's her husband. "Anyway, how are you?" Her gaze flicks down to my stomach as though it's glowing neon.

"Fine." My throat is tight, and the word sounds like a lie even to me.

"Did you tell mystery man?" she whispers.

"No."

"Because you don't want to do it over the phone?" She falls in step beside me as we climb the hill toward the barn.

"No, I just haven't yet." The words scrape out of me.

"What about seeing a doctor?" she presses.

The crack in my patience isn't her fault. It's the weight of spending these past few days with Zander. The way I've almost blurted out the news several times. Then I play out the conversation in my head. *You're going to be a father... how do you feel about that? Gotta go? Yeah, I get it, you're not ready for me or a kid. See ya.*

"Nope."

"Romy." She tugs on my arm, halting us at the back door.

"What?"

"You can't just ignore it." Her matching brown eyes dig into mine.

"I'm not... I'm just trying to survive, you know?" My voice cracks, and I hate the weakness there. Why can't I just tell him and be done with it?

She nods, and that sympathetic look nearly undoes me. "I know, but you need to take the necessary steps. Do you want me to call? I'll do it. I might be able to pass as you."

I blow out a breath and shake my head.

"I can call, really. Let's call Briar and get a number for her OBGYN." Her eyes are pleading.

I take her hands, grounding both of us. "I'm fine. I'm good. I appreciate the help. I do. And after I can get this Zander... Shaw's thing up and running, I'll make the plans. It's still really early."

She exhales a frustrated sigh, and I feel the weight of her

worry. I'm sure it's hard since she's the only one in our family who knows. It's never fun bearing a secret alone.

"Hey." Zander's voice cuts in, pulling my spine up taut.

He clocks us, looking over with a confused sort of expression, and suddenly I'm hyperaware of the flush on my face and the way my sister's hands are clasped in mine.

"Where's your big bad bodyguard?" Lottie asks.

"He's on his rounds of the security detail." He looks inquisitive, and I hope he doesn't suspect anything.

"Leaving you all alone on the ranch, huh?" Lottie says.

Zander slides his thumbs into his jean pockets, rocking back as if he's posing without even trying. "It appears so. Is there a mean side of Romy I should be worried about?"

Lottie looks at me, then at him. "Um... no. We all have our roles in this family. *I'm* the mean one, Bennett is the straight-laced one, and Romy is the romantic and eternal optimist."

Zander's gaze snaps to mine with curiosity. "Is that so?"

Lottie follows his look, smirks, then adds, "She used to be, but there's this guy—"

I cut her off before she detonates my dignity completely to the least romantic man I've ever met. "We gotta go, and you better get to the store."

"Saylor's there holding down the fort. What are you two up to today?" She lingers, nosy as ever, and Zander's eyelids lift.

"Actually, I was hoping Romy would play hooky today," he says.

"Hooky?" Lottie's smile deepens as she swings her gaze between us. "That's fun. What are your plans? A plane ride to Paris for dinner at the Eiffel Tower? Or I bet you're going to take her to an opera in San Francisco."

"This isn't a romcom," I whisper, mortified. "And it's not like that." How could she think it would be, knowing my situation?

"Do you like big things like that?" Zander asks softly.

I shake my head quickly.

"It's called wooing. I get that you probably don't have to do too much. I'm sure a whole slew of women beg and plead for you to take them on your tour bus. But one of these days, Zander Shaw, you're going to find a woman who flips your world around, and you'll be whisking her away to Paris." Lottie hugs me tightly, then shoots him a wink. "Gotta go. You know how crabby Brooks gets when his coffee isn't ready on time." She smacks Zander lightly on the arm. "See ya."

"I don't understand. Isn't she married to Brooks?" Zander asks, watching her walk off.

"It's their thing." I fumble for my key.

"Their thing?" He holds the door open for me once I've unlocked it.

"You know how couples have things..." In my office doorway, I hesitate, torn between wanting space and wanting him. I feel as if an arrow is hovering over the drawer with the test in it. "Seriously?"

Something shifts across his face. Could it be embarrassment?

"Right, you're not into those types of relationships." My bitterness is loud and clear.

He braces his hands against the top of the doorframe, shirt tugging up, revealing skin and a line of dark hair that disappears into the waistband of his jeans.

My body reacts before my brain can scold it. Why is he so damn sexy?

"So, their thing is her making him coffee in the morning? Wouldn't it be better to have her bring coffee to him in bed or, I don't know, wearing lingerie or, hell, naked?"

A full-body shiver rocks me. "Okay, first, I don't want to think of Brooks in a bed and definitely not my sister bringing him coffee naked."

He chuckles. "That's a tad immature, no? They obviously have sex."

I arch an eyebrow. "Do you have siblings?"

He shakes his head.

Right. Foster kid, you idiot.

"Okay, think about Beau or better yet, DeSoto. Imagine him naked, beating off."

His brows rise, but he nods in mock understanding.

"See what I mean?"

"Yeah." He grimaces. "Now I have to think of how to banish that image from my head."

His smile—his real smile—breaks out. The one that used to belong only to me. Or so I thought. Maybe a lot of women think that smile is theirs. My chest aches at the memory of the nights when that grin was mine and mine alone.

I clear my throat, desperate to redirect this line of conversation. "Anyway, you said something about playing hooky?"

Still leaning forward on the doorframe, biceps straining, he says, "I don't want the whole video shot in the barn. I wanted to have flashbacks to where they fell in love. So, I thought maybe you could show me around the ranch, and we can brainstorm?" His voice dips, sounding shy in a way that disarms my anger completely.

"You already got the tour."

His smile falters. "Yeah, but I could barely concentrate then."

"Why?" I cross my arms, bracing myself.

"Because I wasn't expecting you."

Heat floods my cheeks, betraying me and my unresolved feelings for him.

"So, what do you say? Jensen said he'd pack us a lunch basket, and we could take the horses up to this spot a lot of you guys like. Some place by a creek?"

"Do you ride?"

Please say no. Please, God, say no.

"Yeah. I assume you do?"

I nod. "I can call down to Nash and ask him if we can take the horses."

Which he will say no to because I will not be making that call.

"Jensen mentioned it's his best friend who manages the horses."

I latch onto that, trying to derail the conversation about the horses. "A picnic lunch sounds a little too romantic. Not very friend-like."

"It could be friend-like, and besides, I didn't say picnic lunch. I just said he's packing a basket. We have to eat, right?"

I think of my growing baby and sigh. "I suppose."

His arms drop, and he steps into the room. "Listen, I know I don't deserve your kindness, but you're the one I feel the most comfortable with, and that's not an easy thing for me to come by. I know I could ask your brother or one of your cousins. Emmett seems really helpful, but I want you."

I want you.

Ugh. How many times have I dreamed of hearing those words from him? Just in a different context.

"I also think you have a great eye for some romantic possibilities."

And there's the real reason. Well, at least if he's thinking about it that way, he just needs me there for business reasons. Which will make it all clear-cut in the end. We're in this together until he leaves, then our future is up in the air.

"Okay."

His eyes widen. "Really?"

I nod. "Really. I'll grab the keys to the UTV, and I'll pick you up at The Getaway Lodge."

"Can I drive? We can head to the lodge together and pick up the basket and then head out."

For a man who never has to plan anything himself, he's got this day mapped out.

"Sure. Let's go."

I grab the keys, lock my office, and follow him out.

Another day with Zander Shaw sounds like a slow form of torture. Just another day of holding my heart together while it quietly breaks into pieces.

Chapter Thirteen

ZANDER

Luck has been a foreign word my entire life. I'm sure some people think I got where I am because of luck, but they didn't walk in my shoes. But Romy agreeing to go out with me after everything I've done to her? Maybe my luck is changing.

That blush on her cheeks... I can't stop admiring it, wanting to be the reason for her flush again.

Fuck. What am I doing? What's the end game? What's my plan? Hell if I know. All I know is that now that she's back in my life, I feel like a fucking fool for kicking her out of it in the first place. Even if it was the right thing to do.

Regardless, I'll take what I can get today. I saw her wince when I suggested a horseback ride and the picnic, and I didn't realize until after the words were out of my mouth how romantic they sounded. I don't deserve her even entertaining a day with me, let alone a picnic.

She closes up her office and locks the door. I find it funny how she and her family swear up and down that my security detail and DeSoto are ridiculous, that Plain Daisy Ranch is safe, but she locks that door up tighter than a drum every time she leaves.

She steps into the hallway, and I motion for her to go first because though I wasn't raised behind a white picket fence, I'm not a total douchebag. Or maybe I am because all I can think is that the view is a nice reward for being gentlemanly. I remember gripping those plump ass cheeks as she rode me on the bench of my tour bus.

We walk out the back door, and she keeps going.

"Aren't you going to lock the door?" I ask, searching for a reason why she'd lock her office but not the venue itself.

She shrugs. "My mom will probably come by, and besides, this is Plain Daisy Ranch."

"But you lock your office." My eyebrows raise.

She shoots me a smile that feels a little flirtatious. My dick takes notices. "Well, I can't let everybody know all my secrets."

She pauses as though she's going to say something more but turns away from me and walks toward the UTV.

"You sure you can drive this?" she asks, dangling the keys in front of me. "When's the last time you even drove yourself around anywhere?"

I chuckle, hold my hand out, and our fingers brush. Electricity shoots up my arm. It's a bad sign. A really bad sign. I can't entertain something with Romy again. My lifestyle doesn't afford us anything more than what we already shared. My lifestyle and *me*.

We climb into the UTV. I place the key in the ignition and turn to her. "Just so you know, I do have a license, and sometimes I even drive instead of DeSoto... all by myself, if you can believe it. There's a lot more to me than just the singer and the star."

She holds my gaze. Something tells me to turn around, break our connection.

Romy floors me when she says softly, "I know."

And damn, I feel more seen in this moment than I ever have. The time I spent with Romy was limited—three dates. Extended dates, but still only three. And somehow, even in that short time, I always felt like she saw a different version of me. One I don't show anyone else. Not even Beau.

Unbeknownst to me, maybe I let her in a little at a time. A sliver here and a sliver there. Not through vomiting out my trauma to her, but her listening and observing. And I think that's what kills me the most now. I pushed her away because I didn't want anyone to know the real me. Letting someone in means giving them the power to destroy you, and I mastered the lesson of keeping everyone at arm's length a long time ago.

I straighten, clear my throat, start the engine, and we drive toward The Getaway Lodge. Jensen's already inside. We both duck in, grab the basket, and get out before anyone really notices—although Darla gave us a second glance from the dining room where the crew is eating.

As we drive, I decide to bring up the horseback riding again to gauge how she feels about it. "Point me in the direction of the stables."

She hems and haws. "I actually have another spot I want to show you, but we need the UTV cause it's a little farther away. Is that okay?"

She shifts in her seat, and her gaze shifts away from me. I've been around enough people in my life to know when someone's lying. Years of foster care drilled that into me. The fake smiles, the empty promises. The "we love you, we want you here forever" right before they send you packing for one reason or another.

Romy's hiding something. But for today, I'll give her a pass. God knows I've kept enough shit from her.

She directs me around the ranch in a more sweeping tour than the introductory one on the day I arrived. This place is fucking massive. We pass the lake, and she points out the dock and says it'd be a good spot to show the couple splashing around in the water. We pass the horse stables, but don't actually go in. She introduces me to their ranch mascot Bessie, a Guernsey cow they all tell their problems to. She is super sweet as we stand by the fence line. Then Romy shows me the flower shop, the greenhouse, the bee area, the vineyard her uncle tends to, and a lot of the land where the cows graze.

As we drive past Daisy Hill, she directs me up another path. "I don't know if Scarlett mentioned this, but please don't film anything on Daisy Hill."

"I figured when your mom mentioned paying your respects. Is it a family cemetery?"

"Yeah, my Aunt Daisy, who the ranch is named after, died young. She's buried there, as well as all my grand and great-grandparents. I get that it would probably be great for the video—"

I place my hand on her thigh. "It's off-limits. I got it."

Her body relaxes under my touch, and as much as I don't want to pull my hand away, I do. "Thanks."

"I get it." And I do. She's so rooted in family. While I've mostly been on my own my entire life, I can spot it easily. Probably because it's something I grew up wanting.

We head toward a creek and an open field.

"Is this the spot everyone wanted us to use?" I ask.

She smiles. "Yeah, but there's a better one. At least I think so. I like to keep it to myself, but I'll share it with you. Only because I think it's the best spot on the ranch."

"I'm honored." I cover my heart with my hand.

It's a nice change of pace, having the freedom to drive around the ranch with her next to me and not having to worry about people's assumptions.

After a while, Romy directs me to drive up a hill and park the UTV. We step out and—

"Holy shit," I breathe. "You're telling me nobody else knows about this spot?"

She shrugs. "Not that I know of. I'm sure some of my family do. But no one's ever said anything. I found it by accident one day when I needed some space."

My head swims with questions about when she needed the space and time to think. Was it after I pushed her out of my life? No. It had to have been way before that.

Jensen packed a blanket with the basket. We spread it out, and I put the basket down to stop the slight breeze from turning up the corner, and we both sit down. She slips her shoes off and extends her legs, leaning back on her arms.

There might not be a creek here, but it's a full view of the ranch with the sun shining across their land.

"I can't believe you're sharing this with me," I admit, feeling unworthy.

She shrugs, which seems to be her thing when she doesn't want to give me any more information.

I'm undeserving of sharing her sacred spot. The one she goes to in order to think. God, did she come here after DeSoto told her she wasn't welcome backstage that night? I treated her as though she was disposable. And now she's giving me the gift of this view and a piece of her to share with the world through my video.

"It's amazing here. I can't believe this is where you grew up."

She pulls her knees to her chest and rests her chin on them, staring out at the view. "I know. I'm lucky. I had an amazing childhood."

Romy glances at me. I catch a flicker of pity in her eyes. My spine straightens, and I feel my defenses snap into place, but I swallow it down. Maybe it's okay if she feels bad for me. Maybe that's just who she is. The truth is, I liked that she was always searching for more from me than what it was like to be

Zander Shaw, country music star. How many women didn't ever ask me anything, didn't care about me? They just wanted to tell people they got on my tour bus and made it into my bed —even if they hadn't.

She goes quiet, then murmurs, "I'm sorry you didn't have this."

I laugh. It's a nervous and automatic response, not genuine laughter in the least. My past isn't something I like talking about, but that doesn't mean it doesn't haunt me daily. "You aren't any of the people who didn't want me."

"I know, but I think everyone should have a place where they feel safe."

"Everyone is dealt a different hand. Mine was shit, but I can't complain. I bet on myself, and it paid off." I doubt Romy agrees with me because I have a lot, but other than Beau and maybe DeSoto, I don't really have the kinds of things in my life that she's referring to.

We stay on the hill, the only sound the long grass below swishing in the breeze. Eventually I open the picnic basket to keep my mind from wondering what it would have been like to grow up somewhere like here, rather than the way I did.

Jensen did good. Chicken salad sandwiches, apples, even little pumpkin bars.

"He really is an amazing chef," I say. "I've enjoyed everything he's prepared."

Romy smiles. "Yeah, sometimes I think it's strange. He should be famous and long gone from here, but that's not Jensen's style." She crosses her legs and turns to the basket, peering inside.

"Do you think it's a family obligation for him? To stay here? Like maybe that's why he hasn't left?" I hand her a chicken salad sandwich.

Part of being raised the way I was made it easy to cut ties and live life on the road. I was out of the system as soon as I was eighteen and never looked back. I had Beau of course, and we just kept pushing to make my music career happen. Sometimes I feel like we should stop and look back at everything we've done, appreciate it a little more. Take the foot off the gas, but... those what-ifs are hard to push aside.

Romy thinks on my question for a while. "I'm not sure that's it. I think we all just want to be here. I know some people would call us crazy because they want to get as far as they can from their family. And some of us have left. Bennett moved away for college, lived in California for a while, but he came back. Ben left to play football but returned after his retirement. I don't know... I just can't imagine not living here... having my kid grow up somewhere else..." Her voice fades.

Again, she looks away. There's probably something personal she doesn't want me to know. The realization that I can't be the person who hears her hopes and dreams hits me square in the chest, like a knife between the ribs.

"What were you going to say?" I ask, pressing in the hopes that she'll share.

"Nothing. It's just—" She turns to face me, and I watch her chest rise and fall as if she's gaining the courage to share something with me.

This is it. She's going to tell me off. Tell me how badly I hurt her and how undeserving I am to talk to her about anything other than this video. How I don't deserve to know the phenomenal woman who hides under the layer of hurt I painted her with.

"Zander. There's something I think—"

But she stops again. I'm desperate to get something from her, even if it's her wrath. If she lets it out, we can move on maybe.

Then I hear the click of a camera shutter.

I whip around to find a photographer ducking behind a tree.

"Fuck," I say. "We gotta go." I shoot up off the blanket, quickly pack up what's left of the food, and lead her back to the UTV.

Who did I think I was out here? Some average Joe who can just roam around? Of course, the paps are going to find a way onto the property and search me out. But it's not only me. Now I've put Romy in this shit situation.

Obviously, word's gotten out that Zander Shaw is at Plain Daisy Ranch.

I drive fast and get us back on the path in enough time that I'm hoping he didn't get too many decent shots. By the time we get back to a more public part of the ranch, where a photographer wouldn't dare push their luck, I'm fuming.

The UTV rattles idle outside The Knotted Barn as I turn to her. I will not allow them to ruin our conversation.

"What were you going to say?" I ask, keeping one hand on the steering wheel, the other braced on my thigh.

She shakes her head, ponytail slipping over her shoulder. "Nothing. Don't worry about it. I just... I hate that we got interrupted."

The cool breeze whips through the open cab. "Me too. It's the price you pay for this life, I guess. They're just trying to make a living."

"Yeah, but they're preventing you from having a life in order to chase theirs." Her voice is edged with frustration. The UTV rocks slightly as she shifts in her seat. "They could do something else to earn money."

I glance past her toward the barn. "I'm not going to fault someone for trying to feed their family. I put myself in the spotlight. I made that choice. Knew the deal. I have to deal with the consequences."

She takes me in, gaze sharp. For a second, it's as if she can see past every wall I've ever stacked up.

"That doesn't mean it's right or fair to you." Her hand curls tightly around the grab bar. "So you should sacrifice your life because you make music?"

"All I said is, it's the price you pay." My voice is steady. I fought the paps and the shitty, dishonest reporters for a long time. And I lost every time, so now I try not to put myself in that situation.

Her eyes soften. "You pay a lot to be who you are, Zander. Will you ever stop paying for it?"

The engine ticks after I kill it. There's not much to say. She doesn't understand the day to day, but I really want to know what she was going to tell me earlier. It felt important.

Before I can press her, she climbs out.

I stay behind the wheel, watching her walk away, and just like that, the perfect day I had with her... is over.

Chapter Fourteen

ROMY

Today's the day. Today's definitely the day I'm gonna tell him. I have no choice. Yesterday made me realize how much he lost out on, being a foster child and not having a family to call his own. This little one growing inside me *is* his family. I want Zander to have the opportunity to have everything that comes along with that, should he choose to.

If only all the feelings I developed for him had gone away, it would make this whole situation feel different.

I walk into The Knotted Barn and am surprised to find he's already there. My mom too. An entire crew is circled around Zander, who is on top of a ladder explaining how he wants the lights.

I guess I'm the last one to the party. I grab a muffin from the tray and go into my office to figure out how to get him alone now that he's finally allowed the crew to come in. A touch of sadness that our time alone here is over hits me, but I brush it aside.

My key is in my office door lock when my mom comes down the hall. "Why is your office door always locked now?"

"Well, it's my office, so…"

"It's like when you used to lock your bedroom door as a teenager. Nothing good goes on behind a locked door. Plus, you've been acting strange lately." She gives me the once-over with narrowed eyes. Her mom look used to work on me, but not anymore.

I walk into my office and put away my purse. "No, I haven't. I'm fine." I round my desk to go back out to the main part of the building.

"They've been here since right after breakfast. Zander asked me if I could let him in. He didn't want to bother you, and they wanted to start doing some of the lighting."

"Okay. Thanks, Mom."

Why she's being so informative, I'm not sure. It's not as if I would take offense that she let them in.

She heads to the storage room. I forgot she has a key for that too. I'd feel much calmer if she was at The Getaway Lodge, being social with everyone eating breakfast. I'm already strung tight knowing the conversation I have to have today.

In the venue area, Zander is still on the ladder, and they're talking about the lighting and some other things. I watch him from the archway and realize this announcement I'm about to make will change everything. It'll change the world as he knows it, and the weight of that settles on my shoulders like hundred-pound bricks.

Then again, maybe that's not the case. Maybe he'll want nothing to do with our child. But even if he walks away, continuing to chase stardom and leaving this baby behind, he'll still know a piece of him is out there. He could come back into our lives at any time, without warning. And with his resources, is that something I should be wary of? Will I always be worried about him returning?

I could push for papers, force something official, but god,

I don't want to think about that. I'm not asking for forever with Zander. I know he doesn't want that, not with me anyway. But still... he deserves to know. I saw what finding out he had a child he didn't know about did to my brother, and I can't do that to Zander. Whatever happens needs to be his decision.

He climbs down the ladder, catches me watching from across the room, and smiles that damn half smile that makes my heart flop. It makes me shiver, makes me think that he was lying when he pushed me away. That there *is* something between us, and I wasn't a fool to believe I was becoming important to him. But if he can't admit it, I sure as hell am not going to push it. We have enough to figure out without bringing *us* into it.

Zander crosses the room, and whoever else was with him —somebody from the crew—takes over his spot on the ladder. He stops right in front of me.

Okay, hormones, calm the fuck down.

"Hey," he says. "Did you sleep in this morning?"

"Yes... no." I didn't sleep in. I've barely slept since I found out I'm pregnant. It's probably why there are dark circles and bags under my eyes every morning. "No, I just had some things to catch up on."

It's a lie he seems to believe. Because why wouldn't he? He has no idea the torment that's been in my head since that positive pregnancy test.

"All right," he says. "I was wondering if we could go down to The Perfect Petal and pick out some flowers. Do you think they'd have any availability to talk to us today? Maybe even walk through the greenhouse, get some suggestions?"

I nod absentmindedly. "Sure. Yeah, we can do that. Of course. They'll make time for us. Did you have an idea of what you were thinking?"

"I don't know anything about flowers, so you should definitely be the leader on this one."

"Okay. All right, we'll make—I'll call Poppy and see."

"Sounds good. Thanks."

I go back to my office to call Poppy to figure out if she or Delaney have time for us today. They'll definitely have better ideas than me if he wants something unique and special.

His footsteps fall behind me as I make my way down the hall. My mom comes out of the storage area and eyes Zander behind me.

"Oh my god, you two. I love the arch you picked out the other day," she says. "I can't wait. I loved it when it was used in that one wedding." She snaps her fingers. "Remember, Romy, that one where the bride was pregnant?"

My stomach lurches. "Um... vaguely."

"Sure, you do." She puts her hand on my arm and squeezes, then turns her attention to Zander. "The groom was drunk the entire time and threw up all over the balcony. Uncle Wade was going to..." She eyes Zander and stops talking. "Well, anyway, seemed like such a waste for such a great piece. They didn't make it two months. Sad."

"Doesn't sound like the best premonition for the project," he says.

My mom cringes. "But it's just a music video. Not like real life, you know?"

"Okay, Mom," I say. "I need to go make a phone call."

"Oh, to who?"

Thankfully I dodge her before we get the lecture about signs and fate and kismet. She's where I learned to believe in fairytales. What a disappointment that turned out to be.

"Don't worry about it," I say, annoyed now from that story about another couple that got pregnant before their wedding and then divorced. She just squashed that pea-sized amount of hope I had that maybe there could be a chance

Zander and I could raise this baby together. I need to exorcise that delusional, romantic side of myself.

"Just give me a second. I need to grab a pen," Mom says.

I wave for her to go into my office, not that she cares to have my permission.

"I don't know what your song's about, Zander, because you're not sharing much information about it." She gives him a look that says she would like to know. So nosy. "But I think the arch is so whimsical and romantic and will fit a music video perfectly."

"Thank you, Darla," Zander says, and my mom's face lights up.

"I used to love watching music videos," she says mindlessly, scribbling something on a piece of paper.

"You know, back in her day. The eighties," I joke.

I'm waiting by the door for her to leave, and she doesn't even realize it. I try to convey my apology to Zander that I have no idea what she's doing.

Mom sticks out her tongue at me, and she and I laugh. My humor dies the minute her hand lands on the drawer with the test in it.

My spine straightens. "Why are you going in there?"

"You're making me think there's something in this office you're hiding. What's your dirty little secret, Romy?" She laughs, but I don't.

"Nothing. Nothing. Just—Mom, god—just what do you need? I'll get it for you." I stand in the doorway, blocking Zander from coming in.

"I'm perfectly capable of finding tape. I know your office pretty well because, oh yeah, once upon a time it was my office." She points at herself. I have her distracted now, but I'm not sure for how much longer.

My heart races. She cannot see that test before I have time to tell Zander. No, no, no, no.

"It's not in there."

She shifts to look into the drawer, and my stomach drops. My instincts take over, and I slam my office door shut, planting myself in front of it, leaving Zander and me in the hallway with my hand clamped around the knob.

Zander's confused gaze flicks to mine, searching. It's now or never. God, I can't believe this is how it's going to come out —that he's going to find out he's a father with my mom banging on the other side of a door. I should have told him sooner. He should've been the first to know, not the third if my mom just saw that test.

"Romy!" My mom pounds so hard the wood shakes. "What the hell are you doing? What is wrong with you? Open this door right now." She's using her mom voice. The one that used to make us all freeze as kids.

"Mom, just—just give me a second!" My voice cracks. My throat is closing, and my heart's about to pop out of my chest.

Zander doesn't move. He doesn't even blink, just watches me. Doesn't this chaos make him wonder what I could be hiding? Does he already know? Suddenly I'm spiraling—am I showing? Do I look different? Did I touch my stomach too much? Has he already guessed?

But he doesn't say a word.

Another pound rattles the door. "Romy, let me out of here right now! I don't—you know how I am in closed-off spaces."

"Then you shouldn't have gone into my office in the first place!" I snap, panic sharpening my words. "I told you I would've just gotten whatever you needed."

When I turn back, Zander is still looking at me, and I feel dizzy. I can't take the silence and pressure anymore. The words rip out of me before I can stop them.

"I'm pregnant." My voice cracks. "I'm sorry I haven't told

you yet, but my mom is about to find something in that drawer, and yeah... I'm pregnant."

For a beat, there's nothing. No reaction at all. He stands there stone-faced.

Then his face drains of color. His mouth parts as though he can't find enough air.

Nope. He had no idea.

Chapter Fifteen

ZANDER

Did she just say... *pregnant?*

Chapter Sixteen

ROMY

"Okay... okay... let me explain. I can explain. Please." I let out a breath since I feel as though I'm about to hyperventilate. "I know, I know. I can see on your face that you're a little surprised."

"A little?"

My mom keeps turning the doorknob, and I keep holding it tightly. She bangs on the other side. "Romy! Romy, let me out. This is not funny."

I look at Zander. "I have to let her out."

It's obvious to me that my little stunt with the door has distracted my mom from looking in the drawer, otherwise, she'd be less concerned with getting out. She'd either speak softly to me and ask me to open the door because she wants to comfort me, or she wouldn't be trying to get out at all because she'd be sitting there stunned.

He stares at my hand on the knob and doesn't say anything. I have no idea what he's thinking. I want to know what's going on in his head. He's probably thinking the baby isn't his. The words *paternity test* must be flashing in his mind like a neon sign. He's thinking about his money and that I'm

97

going to want to take him for everything he has. He's thinking this one woman that he spent very little time with is now a part of his life forever.

My mom yanks on the door even harder, and I have to use every muscle I have to hold the door shut until he can grasp what I've just told him and put on some kind of fake act, as if I didn't just shatter his world with two words.

Right before I release the doorknob, I say, "I'm really sorry."

I let go. My mom swings the door open, heaving for breath, totally pissed and giving me the meanest look I have ever seen her give any of us. Even when Bennett crashed the truck at sixteen for a second time.

Zander turns and walks away.

"What is going on? Why would you lock me in there?" I don't answer, my eyes on Zander's back as he pushes out the back door, and she says, "Romy, I want answers."

I raise my hand. "Just give me five minutes, Mom. Just five minutes."

I follow Zander without waiting for her to reply.

"You've got five minutes, and then I want some answers!" She sucks in a breath. "Jesus, I can't believe you did that."

"I swear I'll be right back," I say as I push out the door.

Zander is already halfway to the edge of the vineyard, heading down the hill.

Maybe I should give him some time to process things, but once I get close enough, I can't stop myself from spitting it all out. "Let me explain. I know I should have told you. I get that. I know—"

"Damn right you should have."

He whips around, and I'm taken by surprise. I stumble back and trip on a small rock behind me. He grabs my arms and holds me steady. Then he just stares into my eyes. His pain flickers through, and my heart sinks for holding onto this information.

"Zander, I found out the day you showed up here. Like, minutes before. I was just trying to make sense of this whole situation before bringing you into it." Wetness pricks at my eyes. My nose stings. My throat is closing up. I can't hold these tears in any longer. I just want to crumble. I just want to— "I don't expect anything from you if that's what you're worried about."

Zero emotion lines his face.

"Just tell me what you're thinking right now," I plead. One tear falls, then another before I cover my face with my hands from embarrassment.

"Fuck, don't cry." He pulls me into him, wrapping his arms around me.

I'm surprised but comforted at the same time. My fingers grip the back of his shirt as I breathe in his scent. And damn it if that doesn't somehow make me feel worse and better with every breath.

I hold onto him while I mumble, "I'm sorry. I'm sorry."

He draws back but keeps his hands linked behind my back. "Why do you keep apologizing?"

"I don't know. Because... I feel like I just ruined your life."

He smirks, gives me that half smile. *Who is this man?*

"Last I checked, you didn't make this baby by yourself. Didn't they teach you in school that it takes two to make a baby?"

His response floors me. It's the total opposite of what I thought I'd get. "But you—you walked away after I told you. I thought you were mad."

"I left because your mom was coming out of that room, and I didn't want her to see my reaction. Clearly, you're keeping this a secret from everybody, including me. I didn't want your mom to ask a bunch of questions."

He lets his hands drop from behind my back and walks toward the vineyard again. I follow, unsure if he even wants me to.

"It was that one time, right? After that show, in the tour bus?"

I nod. It's the only time we didn't use a condom, so it has to be. He pulled out, but clearly that didn't work.

"You know, all my life, I've always heard it only takes once. Only one fucking time. Damn it all to hell, they were right."

I nod—because yeah, it did only take one time. He must've been on a high after his show, and he took us into that bus, locked the door, and told Beau to keep everybody out. I don't know if it was the song he sang at the end or seeing everybody adoring him. I have no idea what made him pull me away, but he took me, and we didn't even think about protecting ourselves. We still thought, what are the chances? One in a million, right? I remember saying how I'd heard we'd have a better chance at winning the lottery, and we laughed.

And now we're here.

"I guess all those health teachers were right, huh?" My breathing has started to settle, and I inhale slowly.

Zander chuckles. His laugh actually sounds really nice compared to the other sounds I thought he'd be making now. I thought I'd hear cursing and shouting, maybe sobbing and lamenting his life choices.

"God, you're taking this so much better than I thought you would."

He still has that smile as he says, "Believe me, my head's playing war with me right now. But anger isn't going to help. I'm sure you don't want this any more than I do."

His words sting, but they don't surprise me. My hand falls to my stomach, and he clocks the movement instantly, transfixed on it. I don't want to read anything into the panic in his eyes, how real it seems to be becoming to him. I've had a couple of weeks to digest this news, and he's had all of five minutes.

His eyes still don't shift from my stomach.

I guess it's time I lay it all out on the line. He has to know exactly what my plans are moving forward. "There's something else you have to know, Zander."

Alarm shifts his features. "Is there something wrong? Have you already been to the doctor? Is it the baby?" He reaches out but retracts his hand before it can make contact with my stomach. "How far along are you? I mean, I can guess how far along you are, but I don't know how they calculate those things. Something's wrong, isn't it? Something that's—"

I shake my head. "No... well, not that I know of. I've just decided... I'm keeping the baby. I want to keep the baby."

He nods and blows out a breath. "Okay."

For some reason, that's more of a comfort to me than anything else. I'm still in shock over how he's handling the news, and I have no idea where we go from here.

"Do you want to take some time to think about what you want to do?" I broach the subject about finding our way forward.

By now we're right at the edge of the vineyard, where the grapes are plump enough to harvest. Uncle Wade always does one harvest in September and the other in early October, so these must be for that one.

"I—I don't know. There's... a lot of logistics, I guess. I should probably talk to Beau, figure out the next steps, but right now, I can't even think about any of that. Honestly, I'm still in shock. The thought of me as—" He breaks off, dragging a hand down his face. "God. Me? A dad? Who would even want that? I'm such a screw-up. I have commitment issues, keep people away. I don't know how the hell a real family functions because I've never been a part of one." His voice falters. "How the hell am I supposed to be somebody's father?"

He lays all his vulnerabilities at my feet. I'm unsure if he's expecting me to answer him or not. Should I tell him that I think he'll be an amazing dad and that he should give himself the chance? That I saw a glimpse of who he truly is and could be, and that man will be a wonderful father? But then does it sound like I'm pressuring him to be involved? So, I stay silent and let him have his moment—the same moment I did, though I was able to have it without witnesses.

I look at him, then look up at The Knotted Barn, seeing my mom standing on the balcony watching us. Her mamma bear tendencies have never gone away, even as my siblings and I grew into adulthood. She wants to know what the hell is going on with me, although I'm assuming she has an inkling if she went back and opened that drawer. I guarantee she did after I ran off.

"I think I'm going to go back up. I'm going to let you digest this information, and then if you want to talk—whenever you want to talk—we can."

He turns and walks right up to me. I stand frozen, worried about what he's going to say, but he wraps his arms around me and squeezes me tightly. All he says is, "Thank you."

I don't know what the thank you means. I don't know if it means thank you for telling me or thank you for giving me time to process. But I nod, and he gives me one last squeeze. Then he walks away, down one of the rows, farther back into the vineyard.

I watch him for a moment, a little relieved that the truth is out, that I no longer have to hold this secret inside me. I'm going to have to go up there and tell my mom, and she's either going to give me her sarcastic wit or judgment—maybe a little of both. She won't like that I kept this from her. The guilt will be real. She would've wanted to see me through this moment, but it was important for me to make sure Zander knew before my whole family. It was only fair.

I walk up the hill and see my mom leave the balcony. Moments later, she's out the back door, and as I reach the top of the hill, she holds out her arms.

She's seen the test.

All the tears that have been welling up spring free, and I can't hold them in any longer as I walk into her arms.

Her hands run up and down my back as she whispers, "It's gonna be okay. It will all be okay."

I hope she's right.

Chapter Seventeen

ZANDER

I don't know which way is up right now.

As I walk around the vineyard, guilt coats me like a fine mist for leaving Romy behind. I feel bad that she's seeing my back once again. And on top of it, at the worst time. But I need to wrap my head around this news before I do or say something stupid.

That's my track record, right? I push people as far away as I can. I've been through my hours of therapy. Sat in that chair while the therapist told me over and over how I can't keep living my life without any meaningful connections. He gave me exercises and taught me what to do and how not to be such an angry person, how not to expect the worst from everybody. I know it's conceivable that not everybody will abandon me or use me. But still—a baby. A kid. A kid who will rely on me.

I have so many fucking people who already rely on me— from my road crew to Beau and DeSoto, my entire security detail, music producers, songwriters, my band, concert promotors, to every food vendor in the packed arenas. Many of them support their families because of me and my success. All those people look to me to make a difference in their lives, to make sure they can put food on their table and clothes on their kids. But that's different. I've learned to live with the pressure to keep producing hit after hit and keep everyone's bank account flush.

But a baby needs comfort, love, and nurturing. How am I ever… I'm not meant to be a father.

No one would ever say, *You know, Zander Shaw, he'd be father of the year.* Nobody would ever look at me and be like, *That's who you should choose to have your baby with—good job, Romy.* I mean, sure, there are women who have wanted my baby over the years, but they just wanted the checks to roll in. They wanted the lifestyle and notoriety they thought would come with their kid being Zander Shaw's. Their motivation had nothing to do with me being a father to a child.

Goddamn it. I can't believe I'm gonna be a father. She's so sure. And god, I would never ask if it's mine. I'm sure it's mine. Romy isn't the kind of woman to try to pull one over— of that, I'm sure. I mean, I probably *should* ask the question, but how offensive is that? To ask, *Are you sure it's mine?* How ridiculous would that be? She already hates me. She'd hate me even more if I did that.

I stomp away from the vineyard, which—who the fuck has a vineyard in Nebraska? I can't believe they make their own wine. I guess that's something I should entertain incorporating into the video. I should ask Romy because it seems like a pretty romantic area for the video—but that's for another time. I need to push business out of my mind and start worrying more about how I'm going to provide love and care to a baby.

So, I go back to The Getaway Lodge, and I don't go to my room. This is why Beau gets paid the big bucks. He's gonna talk me down. He's gonna tell me it'll be okay. He's gonna tell me how we navigate this.

I'm so overwhelmed I don't even realize I've knocked on

his door until it swings open, and Beau stands there, still dressed in his damn slacks and button-down. *Talk about a wound that needs healing.*

Beau grew up with nothing, maybe even worse off than me. I remember the holes in the bottoms of his sneakers, the worn-out jeans, and shitty T-shirts when I first met him. Now he always makes sure the first impression anybody gets of him is how well-dressed he is. How expensively dressed he is, to be more precise. He wants people to know he's no longer that down-and-out kid with nothing to his name.

"What's up, man?" His gaze runs up and down my body.

I'm sure I look like shit. The guy knows me probably better than I even know myself at this point.

I push in past him. "She's pregnant."

He stands in the doorway for a second before he shuts the door and flicks the lock. He's ultra-paranoid about anyone having access to us. "What are you talking about?"

"You worried someone is going to bust in here and see my sorry disheveled ass?"

He follows my line of sight to the lock on the door. "Always better to be safe. So, talk to me like I'm four... *Who* is pregnant?"

"Romy."

His mouth falls open, and he shoves his hands into his pockets. His laptop sits open on the desk because the man works more than he does anything. One day, I hope he actually finds someone to share his life with, but that's for another time.

"Yeah, you heard me. I'm gonna be a fucking father."

My anger isn't about being a father. If anything, when the words first came out of Romy's mouth, I couldn't process what she was saying. Then I just thought, *Hell yeah, I'm gonna be a dad.* I'll give that kid a great life. One I never had, that's for sure. But then reality snapped into place. My lifestyle is tailor-made to tear apart that particular dream. My career has given me status, security, and money, but it ruins everything else I'd ever want.

"Shit, man. I mean, why the fuck didn't you use a condom?"

I shouldn't be surprised that Beau's first reaction is judgment. He's always warning me against situations like this. *Think with your head, never your dick.* I always agreed with him, always been right there alongside him.

But that time with Romy... I don't know what to say except that I damn well lost all control. I was singing the encore, a ballad to close out my concert. I glanced to the side stage, and she was swaying back and forth, standing next to Beau. I just thought, I could spend the rest of my life with her. That's just the thought that popped into my head. And something about that didn't scare me like I would have thought. It exhilarated me. I couldn't end the concert and get off that stage fast enough. I grabbed her hand, lead her to the tour bus, and told Beau to keep everybody out.

I wanted her naked. My lips were on hers, my hands everywhere. It started as fucking, but my pace slowed, and I looked into her brown eyes as I slid in and out of her. Then the next thing I knew, I was coming, and I didn't even realize it because of the intensity of the situation, but I'd forgotten to put on a condom. I assumed Romy would be on the pill or have one of those things put in her arm. I thought for sure she'd be protected. But she told me no. And then I thought to myself, what are the chances when I pulled out at the last minute? You know, the chances of me actually... it would be, like, one in a million.

But apparently, as Romy said, those health teachers were right because now I'm going to be a dad.

"It just got out of hand."

Beau's face screws up. "You can't let it get fucking out of

hand! Goddamn it. Do you know what this is gonna cost you?"

I press my palm to my forehead, run my hand over my hair, and tug on the back of my neck. "It's not gonna cost money. It's gonna cost *me*." Gonna cost my child for having me as a father, I think but don't say. "But fuck, man—I'm gonna be a dad."

Beau must hear the weight in my voice, the unsteadiness, the fear. He sits next to me on the edge of the couch, resting his forearms on his thighs. "Zan."

I hear it in his tone, the question that most people would ask in my situation.

"I'm telling you, it's fucking mine."

"But—"

"No. It's mine. Romy isn't like that. I'm sure she hasn't... she would never tell me if she wasn't sure. If there was an inkling it was someone else's, she wouldn't."

"Yeah, you knew her for—what? Did you see her three times? She came—"

"It doesn't matter. I just know. I know her, and this baby is mine."

He sighs and shakes his head. "I think you should at least think about a paternity test. You have things to protect. Assets, reputation, *you*. None of this works without you. Could you imagine if you go through this whole thing, and it turns out the baby was never even yours?"

I'm not going to have this conversation with him. He's just doing his job, so I can't really fault him for wanting me to get a paternity test. He probably already has a list of to-dos in his head about where we're going to go, what we're going to do, what legal paperwork we need.

"I don't know, man. I just—I gotta wrap my head around this. This is huge." I turn to look at him. He stares back at me and nods. "I mean, things are going to have to change."

And even as I say the words, I have no idea what exactly that means. I'll have to work harder. I have to make sure my kid never wants for anything—ever. He or she will never be the kid people make fun of and say they smell or the kid who goes to school in ratty clothes, half-starving.

"All right, all right," Beau says, standing, putting his hands in the air. This is stage two of Beau in the midst of any crisis. This is the we-are-gonna-get-it-handled Beau. This is the part where he wants me to let him do the worrying for me. "We got this. I'm gonna figure this out. But first things first—how did the conversation end with you two? Is she mad? Is she angry? Is she upset?"

"Aren't all three of those things the same emotion?" I arch an eyebrow.

He gives his bored look telling me to stop fucking around since we're in the middle of a crisis.

"I don't know. She seemed... okay. Upset, I suppose. She was crying. And—I don't know. I gotta talk to her more about this, but I just needed some time. I needed to figure this out for myself." I blow out a long stream of air. "A fucking father. A baby. A kid. Eighteen years this kid's gonna rely on me, and what kind of role model am I going to be?"

"You're going to be a great role model. That's what you're forgetting, Zan." He sits in a chair across from me and leans in real close to make sure I look at him. "You're the best guy I know. You're gonna be an amazing dad, and you're gonna make your child feel loved. Maybe you'll coach Little League, and I know you're going to teach them to play guitar. You're gonna talk to them, and you're gonna make them feel secure and supported. You're gonna give that child everything we didn't get, and you're gonna do right by them. This kid's gonna be amazing, and they're gonna be grateful and happy that they got you as their dad."

I wish I could believe him, but he's painting a picture of a life that doesn't exist for me.

"But what about the months spent on the road when I'm on tour? What about how I get lost in the process when I'm recording an album, and I end up disappearing for months?"

Beau shakes his head. "Yeah, man, I'm not gonna lie, that shit has to change. But it's okay. It's all right. We'll figure it out. I promise you. First thing I'll do is get you some books. We can have them loaded onto your phone, and no one has to know, okay?"

And for some reason—maybe because Beau knows everything I've been through in my life, and we've shared most of that trauma with each other—I believe him. I somehow believe that I can have both. That I can be a country music star and a father.

"Thanks, man," I say, looking at him. "I really hope so. But I gotta say—I'm scared shitless."

Beau rocks his head back and laughs. "Fuck, man, so am I."

ROMY

After my mom calmed me down and promised to keep my secret until I can actually have a conversation with Zander, I went back home and holed myself up in my room. I can't focus on work. I want to know where his head is at and what he's thinking, but I know he needs space.

Calm down, brain.

My mind is going a mile a minute with what-ifs until a knock sounds on the front door. Poppy and Scarlett are still at work, so I doubt they're expecting anyone.

I walk down the stairs and yank the door open.

It's him. Zander's standing on my porch.

"Hi." My hand grips the doorknob a little tighter.

His hands are in his pockets, and he stares right into my eyes. "I hope I'm not overstepping. I mean, it wasn't hard to figure out... someone told me where you lived."

"My mom?"

He chuckles, but it's strained. "Yeah, she's—well, I was on my way to find you, and she just happened to be in the lobby and told me where she thought you'd be."

"Oh. Well... thanks." I shake my head. "I don't know why I'm thanking you. Why am I thanking you?"

A low laugh escapes him. "I don't know."

"Do you want to come in? Or we could go for a walk?"

He peers around my shoulder, peeking inside—I think to see if anyone's here.

"I'm alone," I say quickly to put him at ease. I've already caused enough turmoil to his anxiety level today.

"Thanks. A walk, maybe?" He nods toward the porch.

"Sure. Let me just grab my sweater."

I leave him on my porch and grab my sweater off the kitchen chair. When I come back, he isn't looking into my house, trying to peer into my life out of curiosity or anything. He's turned, looking out.

"There's a path around the lake we could take." I slide my arms into my sweater and shut the door behind me.

I don't lock it, and a grin spreads across his mouth.

"So—your office. You don't usually lock it?" he asks as we walk down the steps and fall into pace alongside one other.

"No." I laugh.

"What was in the drawer, an ultrasound picture?"

"No! God, no—I haven't... I haven't done that yet." Would he be appalled or relieved if he thought I'd been to the doctor without him, that he didn't have to participate? I'm not even sure. "I've only taken the pregnancy test. And I know it's so stupid. Why keep that for sentimental reasons? Especially since it's not like we were trying or anything. Now I'm rambling and I don't even know how you feel about the pregnancy. Just so you know, when I saw the results, you know, I wasn't, like, jumping-over-the-moon ecstatic. I was scared, and I didn't... I mean—"

"My god, Romy, let me—" He takes my hand and squeezes before letting it drop. "Breathe. Just breathe. It's okay. I get it. Of course you'd want to keep it. I mean, it's a memory. I can imagine wanting to keep something tangible that you can look at that can take you back to exactly what you were thinking and feeling in that moment. I would never think that was foolish."

I draw fresh air into my lungs as we keep walking. "Thanks."

We start on the path that goes around the lake that will pass by my cousins', the Noughton brothers, houses. Each one lives in a house they built, complete with kids and forevers. This path will eventually wind around toward the Owens' part of the land, including my lot that's available for me to build on whenever I'm able.

"So... what do you want to—how do you feel?" I approach the subject, not knowing how to phrase the question. He's had, what? An hour, maybe, to digest the news. I assume he's talked to Beau.

"I'm still reeling a little bit if I'm honest." He scrubs a hand down his face.

"I understand. Me too, even after knowing for a while." I don't want him to get the wrong impression. "It's not that I don't want to—"

"I know," he says. "I mean, I'm not upset."

I shrug and shake my head. "You're welcome to your feelings. They're your feelings, and you don't have to explain them to me or worry about hurting mine."

"You've always been so easy to talk to." He lets out a long breath. "Seems kinda weird... you seem like somebody I would go to for advice about this kind of thing, but you're in it with me, facing the same thing. I mean, I'm sure you don't want my baby."

My mouth falls open, and I stare at him like I did that first time backstage when I was in shock that he had sought me out and pulled me backstage.

"No, no," he says quickly. "I mean, why would you want

to sign up for all that comes with me? I mean, god—we went up on that hill, and there was a photographer. People are going to want pictures of our baby, and others are going to pay money for those pictures. They're gonna be out for blood when they find out you're pregnant. And that's not going to make it easy whether or not you're involved with me. I mean, you won't—" He shakes his head. "I mean, you won't be with me, obviously. Obviously, we're not a couple. You know, we're going to be parents—co-parents."

I don't say anything.

"But it doesn't matter what we are—they're gonna spin it. They're going to say nasty shit. They're gonna be mean and print blatant lies about you and our baby and what I mean to you and what you mean to me. And I'm just... I'm just really sorry, Romy. I should've used a condom. I should've—I just should have protected you better."

"Oh my god, Zander, stop." I put my hand on his forearm and bring us to a halt. His corded muscles flex under my palm.

I remember this exact grip on his arm as his fingers were plunging in and out of me. I push that memory aside. Now isn't the time for my hormones to go crazy.

"Like you said, this was both of us. I was right there in that moment with you, just like you told me earlier. So please... it's okay. We're here now."

"Yeah." He looks down and shakes his head. "I guess you're right. But still, I feel like I should apologize for all the future problems you're gonna run into because of who I am."

I put my hand on my stomach and allow myself to think about the baby growing. About how large my stomach will get, and that I'm going to grow a piece of him inside me. "You know, I don't hate the idea of it that much. I know you're probably thinking I'm crazy. And it's not because I'm a romantic or because I believe in destiny or think that this is some sign for us. I don't think that. Like you said, we can be co-parents, right? We can do this. And I know you're going to be on the road, and I'm totally willing to make arrangements. I guess what I'm saying is that I don't hate the idea that I'm pregnant. And it's not because I have some fantasy that I'm going to swindle you into staying with me, or that I think you would even want a future with a wife and a kid. I get it. But I think I already love him or her. Even though I haven't heard the heartbeat or seen the ultrasound pictures, I want to protect them."

He stares at my hand on my stomach but doesn't move. Not that I'm expecting him to just put his hand over mine. I've made a complete fool of myself, rambling on.

I open my mouth to tell him to forget what I said when he breaks the distance, and his hand covers mine. His calloused fingertips run over my fingers, weaving our hands together.

"I feel the same way," he says. "I have a zillion worries rolling through my head, but... I'm scared—really, really scared. I'm so scared I'm gonna fuck this up, Romy. Jesus, how many times did I say scared?"

We both laugh, but he continues. "I hate to put that on you. You don't deserve to bear the weight of my issues. But I feel the same way. I'm not terribly upset that you're pregnant for some reason, and I want to protect our baby too."

My eyes tear up. I don't know what this means for us, or where we'll go from here. But I know one thing for sure—I have a partner in this. He's going to stay with me, and he's going to protect this little one as much as I will. And that's good enough for me.

Chapter Nineteen

ZANDER

"Absolutely not," Romy says, standing in my suite, DeSoto and Beau standing by the door. "We're not doing that."

"I understand your concern," Beau says, putting his hands up in placating gesture, because that's Beau. If he can get you to calm down, he can prove his point. Or so he thinks. "I get it, all right? It's not ideal that DeSoto has to act like your partner at the doctor, but you know DeSoto... a bit. What's the harm?"

She stares at DeSoto, and he shrugs because he too knows that this is a stupid idea.

"We can't have Zander walking into an OBGYN office with a random woman. Everybody's gonna know instantly what's going on." Beau glances at me for backup, but I don't have it in me to fight her on this.

"Well, can't he put on a baseball cap or wear sunglasses?"

God, she's so sweet and innocent. I want to throw a giant bubble over her to keep her that way and stop her from ever becoming jaded like me.

"Sadly, no," I say, trying to appease the situation.

Beau tosses his hands in the air in exasperation. "A base-ball cap and sunglasses won't hide the fact that Zander Shaw is Zander Shaw. I mean, Romy, you were a big fan at one point. Do you think a hat and sunglasses would have fooled you?"

She scoffs. "At one point I was his biggest fan."

I grunt and tilt my head at Beau with a thank you for the reminder that she doesn't think much of me anymore.

"I'll just go by myself then." She crosses her arms, looking like a defiant pre-teen.

DeSoto's lips tip up a little and damn, mine do too. It's always entertaining when someone comes back at Beau.

God, she looks gorgeous today. She's wearing a cute little skirt and shirt with cowboy boots. It makes me wish she was mine so I could pick her up and feel those legs wrapped around my waist. But she's not. I have to keep reminding myself that I'm the one who ensured that was the case. And for good reason.

"That's not an option," I say, my voice a little gruff.

Her eyes shoot to mine, and whoa, she's got a glare I didn't think she had in her.

"Well then, what do you want to do? I have to see a doctor. I have to start taking vitamins. I put it off until I told you, and now that you know—I want to confirm that every-thing is okay. After I confirm that I am indeed pregnant, I'm going to go to my parents' house for a family dinner and tell them all that you knocked me up."

"What?" I didn't even think about her telling her family. I guess because I don't have a family to tell, I never even thought about hers.

"I have to tell my parents. My mom already knows, and my sister too."

"So, two of your family members already know." Beau massages the bridge of his nose.

"Look who can do math." Romy points at him then smirks at me.

DeSoto laughs but coughs to cover it up when Beau glares at him over his shoulder. I bite my lip to stop from smiling. Now I really want to take her to bed.

"They aren't going to tell anybody I'm pregnant with Zander Shaw's baby." Her gaze drifts to mine. "I didn't mean anything by that. I shouldn't reference you like a celebrity with your first and last name, but it's kind of a habit. I should've just said Zander, I'm sorry."

I'm floored because I've never told her how I hate that people use my first and last name when they refer to me. She obviously got the gist of it just by being around me.

"Then I'll tell the rest of my family," she says nonchalantly.

DeSoto's eyebrows raise.

"What?" Beau shakes his head as if he heard her wrong. "Who?"

Romy narrows her eyes at him. "They all need to know. I'm not going to keep a secret from them."

"You can't." Beau must be desperate because he has his hands up in prayer pose now, trying to get her to understand how easily this type of news can spread. "We can't let—wait, how many people are in this family?" He turns to DeSoto. "How many people live on this ranch?"

"Why are you asking him?" Romy nods at DeSoto. "It's my family."

Beau blows out a breath and puts his hands on his hips, facing her again. "Fine, how many people are we talking about?"

She stares at the ceiling, and her lips move a little, as if she's counting in her head. "Twenty-four."

"Twenty-four?" Beau's mouth hangs open for a beat. "Twenty-four people cannot know that you are pregnant with his baby. That's a hard no, Romy. Not gonna happen." His gaze strays to me again, and I shrug, which makes his lips thin further.

"Well, it's gonna have to happen," Romy argues. "It's going to get around anyway. Believe me, my family does not keep secrets from each other. We're all very close. And I will not let them find out from someone else."

Beau's head rocks back. "I see how close you guys are. But the more people who know, the greater the chance of this getting out before we're ready for it to. If that happens, we can't spin the narrative." Romy opens her mouth to say something, but he soldiers on. "We need to keep this under wraps, Romy. It's for your protection as well the baby's. You cannot be laying this out to everybody on the ranch."

She juts out her hip, and I already know this won't go over well. "I'm telling my family. Everybody will keep it a secret. You don't have to worry."

"Did you hear that? I don't have to worry." Beau throws his hands up and rolls his eyes. "That's what everybody says. I'm not saying anyone in your family is going to sell the information to the press, but with big news like this, sometimes people inadvertently let things slip. And if they do it with the wrong person..." He shakes his head, hands on his hips. "You always think someone will keep your secret until the first sleazebag comes around with a million-dollar check and says, 'Get me a picture of the baby, and you're a millionaire.' Then everybody's ethics and values go down the drain."

"They're not going to tell anybody. If anything, they'll protect us." She begs me with her eyes.

I want to say, "Okay, I got you, baby. Yeah, we can trust your family." But the problem is, Beau is right.

She loves her family, and I'm sure they're great, but people can turn on you. Maybe she hasn't learned that harsh lesson yet, and I don't want her to ever have to learn that lesson, but it will happen sooner or later. Especially now that she's attached to me. Still, I understand, and I don't want to stress her out during her pregnancy.

"Okay, how about this?" I interrupt. "We tell the immediate family. Your mom already knows. She shouldn't be keeping it from your dad."

"Yes, couples don't keep secrets," she adds, spearing Beau with a look.

"Couples keep secrets all the time," Beau argues. "Why do you think the divorce rate is so high?"

"Romy's parents might not keep secrets." I give him a meaningful look.

"They don't," Romy confirms.

"And if Lottie knows, I'm assuming the sheriff knows—"

"Why would the sheriff know?" Beau interrupts.

"Because he's her husband. Where have you been?" Romy shoots back.

I kind of like this side of her too much.

"So, what, couples just tell each other *everything*?" Beau glances at DeSoto as if he has any clue. The man is as single as we are.

"I'm telling you, my family has to know." Romy narrows her eyes at him.

Beau shifts into negotiation mode. "Okay, how many people are we talking?"

"Well, you have my parents, then you have Lottie and Brooks."

"Brooks is the sheriff?" Beau asks.

"Yes, Brooks is the sheriff. My god, have you paid attention at all?" Romy rolls her big brown eyes at him. "And then you have Bennett and Delaney, and Wren and Leia."

"Who are Wren and Leia?" Beau asks, irritation coating every word.

"They're my nieces."

His jaw tightens. "How old are your nieces?"

"Um, they're seven." Romy glances away from him.

"Seven-year-olds definitely don't need to be in the loop. Do you think they're gonna keep a secret? They'll be like, 'My Auntie Romy is pregnant with a country singer's baby.' Actually all they have to say is, 'My Auntie Romy is pregnant,' and people are just gonna assume it's Zander's."

I try not to laugh at the girly voice Beau used to imitate the little girls.

"Why would people assume it's Zander's?" she asks.

"Yeah, why would they?" I look over at Beau, forehead wrinkled.

"Oh my god." Beau massages his temples for a beat. "This is ridiculous. Okay, we're not telling any seven-year-olds that you're pregnant. That's a done deal. I'll give you the immediate family members—Lottie, the sheriff, your brother and Delaney, your dad. But we're not telling the girls, and we're not telling anybody else at this point." He looks between Romy and me, waiting for our agreement.

"Well, when am I going to tell them? Eventually I'll be showing." She grabs a pillow off the couch and shoves it under her shirt. She bends her back and places both hands over her fake swollen belly. Something rises up inside me, some kind of feeling of possession at seeing her stomach like that. "I'm going to look like this. They aren't stupid."

Beau lets out an exasperated huff. "Fucking hell. Okay, we'll handle that when we get there. We're not there yet, right? You're still really thin." His hand runs through the air down the length of her body. "I don't know how long—I mean, when do you start showing? Eight months?"

"Eight months?" Romy says. "My god. I should take *you* to the OBGYN so you can educate yourself. And just so you know, I was a little thinner than this before."

"Well, you look great," I say to her because I can tell she

feels somewhat self-conscious about her changing body. "You look fucking fantastic."

She blushes, and I get a high over being the one to give that to her.

"Stop flirting," Beau says, his hands clenching into fists.

I scowl at him. We need to finish this conversation before things get nasty. "All right, we've got to get to the doctor, get you checked out."

Beau looks at me, and I understand. I know what he's thinking, and if he says the fucking words *paternity test*, I'm gonna murder him.

Luckily, he inhales and says, "So the best option is for me to call the doctor's office. I won't tell them who it is. I'll say we want to go in through a back door. They'll sign the NDA paperwork that says they'll owe you their firstborn if they leak any info. Or I can fly in a doctor to the ranch. Actually, that's a better idea. I'll fly in a doctor."

Romy scoffs. "You're not flying in a doctor."

"Round two," DeSoto murmurs.

I shoot him a look that says *secure your seat belt.*

"Why? The doctor I'll fly in is probably better than the doctor in town."

"Hey!" Romy raises her voice. "Don't talk about my town like that, or my town's doctors. They're fine. They're great actually. And they'll keep the secret too."

Beau shakes his head at her. "Oh, Romy, you have so much to learn about this world. You're so naïve."

She looks at him like she's going to run across the room and throttle him. "If something were to happen, I don't want my options to be to wait for your doctor to fly in or show up at the local doctor's office who I've never met and haven't established a relationship with."

"Enough," I say, putting up my hands. "Beau, call the

doctor in town. Get them to sign the paperwork. I'm going with her."

"I really don't think it's a good idea, Zander—"

"I don't care what the fuck you think, Beau. I'm going. This is the first time I get to see a picture of my baby and hear the heartbeat." I turn to Romy. "Do we hear the heartbeat first?"

"I think so. I think we hear the heartbeat before we see the picture." She smiles and that's enough for me.

Beau groans.

"I'm going. I'm going to hear the heartbeat. And I'm going to see the picture. That's what's going to happen. So just call the doctor. Romy, can you give Beau the information? He'll call. We'll go in the back door. DeSoto will be with us."

"DeSoto is not coming in. My legs are going to be spread open in stirrups. I'm not having DeSoto in the room with us."

She's fiery today. I've never seen this side of Romy, but I actually don't mind it.

"Okay, DeSoto, you'll stand outside the door."

"If he stands outside the door, that'll draw attention to you guys. Obviously, someone important is inside," Beau says.

God, the man has a mind for logistics.

"Fine. All right. DeSoto, stay in the car outside the building. I can protect myself. I don't think some pregnant woman or her husband will know I'm coming and try to accost me. I can easily go into an OBGYN office through the back door, see my baby, hold Romy's hand—"

"You're gonna hold my hand?" Romy asks, a sweetness in her voice that hasn't been there since I arrived on the ranch.

"Well, yeah." I don't know why I assumed I would. Maybe I shouldn't have, but when I picture the moment, we're holding hands.

She shrugs, but her smile. Fuck me, her smile lights up the entire room. "That's sweet."

Beau rolls his eyes.

"Anyway, that's our plan. So that's what we're gonna do. Beau, make it happen."

"Fine." He looks at Romy. "I'm telling you, immediate family only. And I'm coming to the dinner."

She narrows her eyes at him. "You're not coming to the dinner."

"Am I invited to the dinner?" I ask Romy. I should be there. She shouldn't have to do this alone.

She blinks at me in surprise. "Do you want to come to the dinner? You don't have to."

Do I really want to go to dinner? I've never met parents before. But it's not like we're dating. She's just having my baby. God, this is weird. And now her dad will know I had sex with his daughter. He's already going to hate me before I even walk in the door.

"I'm going to dinner with you," I say.

"Okay, well, you don't have to. You can think about it."

"I'm going."

"Okay, Bickersons, let's just get on with it. I'll make the phone call. You both get ready because I'm getting you in there today come hell or high water. DeSoto, get the SUV ready. Romy, you're in the back, and for extra precaution, you're gonna duck as we leave the ranch."

"Oh my god, I am not ducking."

"You're gonna duck. Because if someone finds out you're in the back seat with Zander, there'll be speculation. We'll also need to make sure nobody follows us. I'll handle the routes. Then we'll reconvene, and you'll go to the doctor."

Her shoulders sag. "Fine, I guess you're right."

Beau cups his hand around his ear. "I'm sorry, what was that. Can you repeat it for me, Romy?"

She rolls her eyes at him and chuckles. "Despite our disagreement on how we should handle things, I appreciate all your help, Beau. Thanks." All the former bitterness in Romy's tone is gone.

He looks at me and blows out a breath before he sets his gaze on her. "You're welcome, Romy."

I know he wants to say, *Why don't you get a paternity test while you're there?*

Good thing he's smart enough not to say it.

Chapter Twenty

ROMY

Beau pulled it off. Not that I'm surprised. The man moves people and things around like they're chess pieces. He's so good at what he does that I understand why he's been with Zander for so long.

Somehow, nobody follows us to the doctor's office. I picked one a couple towns over because I was worried about anybody finding out. I didn't want to go all the way to Lincoln—Briar had done that—because more people would probably recognize Zander if we were up there.

We snuck in the back door. The nurse seemed slightly annoyed but then went a little fangirlish over Zander once she figured out who the celebrity was. Beau had already called ahead and had everybody sign non-disclosure agreements and confidentiality forms. They probably each had to sign their life away in order for Zander to accompany me.

Now that we're in the room, reality hits me that I'm going to have to take off my skirt in front of Zander. Although we're not actually a couple, he's seen me naked, so does it really matter?

"I can duck out if you want privacy," he says, clearly seeing me stare at the paper sheet that's supposed to cover my hoo-ha.

"No, no, it's fine. Just... can you turn around and face the corner?"

"Like I'm in timeout?" He circles around.

"Now you know what our kid will feel like when we put him or her in timeout," I say, joking. That's another thing we will eventually have to talk about. Do we agree on punishment tactics for our child?

I hurriedly strip off my skirt and underwear and hop up on the table. The paper sheet crinkles every time I wiggle.

"Man, this is not a great view right now."

I glance over my shoulder. Zander is facing the posters showing the stages of pregnancy.

"Snap a picture for Beau. Let him know that I'm going to show a lot earlier than eight months. When does that woman's stomach finally start to show a little bit of a bump?"

Zander laughs. "I think you might pop any day."

"I probably have a little bit to wait. They say with your first baby, you don't show as fast—at least that's what I've heard. You can turn around now."

He circles, eyes finding me on the bed. "Man, there're been times I've dreamed of you in this position, but this is a little too sterile an environment even for me."

I decide to play along and keep things light. This is good that we can joke and communicate about what went down between us, right?

"That's sweet of you to say. But you never really had me in this position, did you?"

"I had you in this position." He says it with certainty.

I'm sure he's confusing me with someone else. "I don't know. I feel like half the time you were always taking me up against walls and furniture."

His eyes heat, and I feel his desire in my bones. The explosive sex between us was not easily forgettable.

"I had you lying down more than once. I'm offended you don't remember." His jaw is tight, and his voice has dipped low.

I swallow down the butterflies, telling myself it's just nerves about the exam. When the knock comes, relief floods my bloodstream since we can now push away this topic.

"Hello, I am Dr. Rojas. How are you guys today?"

She shakes both of our hands, gives Zander an extra-long look, then goes to the sink.

"So, am I supposed to pretend like I don't know who you are? I mean, I had my lawyer check over all the paperwork because I don't want to get sued, and he didn't mention anything about that." She washes her hands, dries them, then faces us.

Neither of us answer her.

Her eyebrows raise. "But seriously, am I supposed to act like I don't know that you're Zander Shaw?"

He smiles. "Not at all. I'm sorry for all the trouble. I'm sure this isn't what you were planning today, so I apologize. But these are extenuating circumstances, and we just want to make sure that this doesn't get out."

"Of course. I've spoken with your manager, Beau, on the phone. He's definitely... something. We've only told the one nurse—my head nurse, my most trusted—and she's the one who brought you in. Nobody else will know you were ever here. And you know what, to make this even better, I think from now on we'll do after-hours visits. Does that sound good?"

"That would be great." I smile at her. "Are you sure though? I'd hate to keep you after just because of us." I look at Zander for confirmation.

He nods.

"Nonsense." She waves off my concern. "As long as I can bring my husband just one time to introduce you to him. He'll sign the paperwork too." She winks, and I'm not sure if she's serious or not.

Zander chuckles. "No problem. Thanks for accommodating us. We really appreciate it."

She smiles at us. She's the cutest woman, petite with short dark hair and the kindest smile. "Okay, enough of the legal nonsense. I've had plenty of it today. No offense."

"None taken." Zander raises his hands.

"All right, let me get a little bit of information. I'll keep your chart locked in my private office cabinet, so nobody else will have access to it, and I'll give you my private number. I can't guarantee the same level of privacy at the hospital, but let's cross that bridge when we come to it. For now—Romy, when was your last period?"

I tell her. "I think I'm six weeks, maybe seven weeks, along."

"Okay, so you're not too late. And no bleeding?"

"No."

"Isn't that the issue?" Zander asks.

Dr. Rojas offers him an assuring smile. "I just want to make sure there was no bleeding after she found out she was pregnant."

Zander looks at me. "Right. Blood's not good right now."

I run my fingers down his forearm, and he winds his hand around mine, gripping it as though he needs the anchor.

"All right, so are you guys—well, you know what, that's not my business. Anyway, the urine sample you gave does indeed show that you are pregnant, Romy. Congratulations."

We smile at her.

"That was very anti-climactic, you two." She sits on the stool and slides closer. "I'll send in for bloodwork, just to make sure. And while we're here, I'd like to do an exam and then an ultrasound. Who knows—maybe we'll see something."

We nod, and Zander squeezes my hand as if he's just as excited as I am.

"Great. Do you want Zander to stay for the pelvic exam?"

I glance up at him, and he looks down at me. This is so awkward.

"Up to you," he says.

"Just stay north of the border." I motion for him to move a little more toward my head.

"Deal." He stays by my head while she wheels between my legs.

After she does the exam, she wheels back out.

"Everything looks great. Okay, I'm going to do the ultrasound. Are you ready?" She turns on the machine in the corner. "It'll be a transvaginal one, not over the stomach. Still too early for that." She stands up, takes off her gloves, and washes her hands again.

"Okay."

"Zander, can you turn down the lights a little bit?"

He does, and the monitor screen glows. This is the moment I'm going to see my baby. Layers of anxiety stack inside me like bricks.

"Have you ever had one of these before, Romy?" she asks.

"No, I haven't." I eye the dildo-looking wand.

"That's for the ultrasound?" Zander asks, his gaze shifting from her to me.

"Yes." She squirts lube on it.

I remember Briar telling me a story about Emmett when he accompanied her to one of her OBGYN appointments and how lost he was.

Zander watches every move she makes, awe on his face, as she slides it inside me and turns toward the screen. All I see is a big black dot.

"I don't see the baby. There's no baby. You said she was pregnant." There's an edge of panic in Zander's voice as he squints at the screen.

Dr. Rojas points at a spot on the screen. "You see this little white dot here? The one that's kind of flickering? That's your baby."

"That's our baby?" Zander asks, surprise in his tone.

"Did you think it just grew the head and hands automatically? It's a process." I give him an amused smile.

"I get that it's a process, but it looks like a pea. That poster said it should look like a kidney bean at eight weeks. But that's a pea. Is there something wrong?"

"The baby is the size of a raspberry right now. If you want, I can send you home with a pamphlet and recommend some books."

"Yeah, I've already got some books on my phone I've been checking out. I trust you. If you say that's the baby, that's the baby." Zander doesn't remove his gaze from the screen.

But then, the heartbeat rings out in the room.

"Oh my god." My eyes widen, and Dr. Rojas gives me a small nod and smile.

Zander freezes, his gaze shooting to mine. Unbidden, tears flow down my cheeks.

"Heartbeat is strong. That little raspberry is doing great." Dr. Rojas takes some pictures with the machine while Zander and I look at each other.

"Holy shit," Zander whispers, gripping my hand tighter. "Goddamn... fuck." He pauses. "Crap. I've got to clean up my language. I can't have our baby's first word be fuck." He looks at me with conviction. "I promise you, Romy. It's not going to come out saying fuck."

I giggle. "I hope not."

We return our attention to the screen, listening to the heartbeat in awe. This all just got a whole lot more real.

Chapter Twenty-One

ZANDER

Walking from her house to her parents' place on the path along the lake is peaceful. Usually on our walks, quiet settles in my chest, and I get more and more relaxed. But tonight, I'm just a walking frayed nerve. I wasn't even this nervous the first time I performed at the Grand Ole Opry.

"I feel like I should warn you before we walk in there," I say to Romy.

"Warn me?" She tugs at her sleeve against the evening chill. She's bundled in a sweater and jeans, dressed down from the flirty dresses she usually torments me with when she's at work. The dresses are torture for me, so I'm kind of happy she's fully covered. That way I can concentrate on the dinner and her family and not that I want to get her into bed.

"I've never done the whole meet-the-parents thing."

She laughs, not fully understanding how stressful this is for me. "Well, good thing you already met them then."

"You know what I mean, Romy. I'm going to go in there, and after we deliver the news, your dad will know I've slept with you. We have to tell him you're pregnant, and we're not even a couple. He's going to hate me."

Why did I say I'd come? She wasn't expecting me to.

Because you weren't going to let her do this alone, you dipshit.

"Relax. I'm telling you right now, my parents are super cool. You don't have to worry. And my mom already knows. God, my dad probably already knows to be honest. He's just gonna pretend like it's a big surprise. That's the way they usually work."

She's so casual about it, but not a minute has gone by today that I didn't worry about how this was going to go down tonight. Family dinners? I thought that was television sitcom made-up shit.

"I know, but if I act weird or stutter or I'm quiet, please know it's just my nerves."

I stop on the path near the lake, and she halts beside me. She leans into me, resting her head on my shoulder.

"Zander, you're way overthinking this. We're just going to tell them I'm pregnant. Lottie's going to be sarcastic. Brooks will probably groan. Bennett's gonna shrug, more worried about chasing Wren or Leia than my situation. And Delaney will probably swoon, thinking it's the best thing ever. And my dad? He's not one of those 'I'm gonna clean my shotgun' dads." She squeezes my forearm. "I promise, you're good."

Her words should ease me, but the weight still presses down on me. I've thought a lot about why it's so important to me for her family not to hate me because of the situation we've found ourselves in, and I keep saying it's because they're my kid's family, and I'll be an active part in their lives. But I think part of it is also that I want them to like me for Romy. Think I'm worthy of being the father of their grandchild. How could they possibly though, when we're announcing Romy's pregnancy and telling them we're going to co-parent instead of be a couple?

"I don't want them to think I'm some jackass who left you

high and dry. It's bad enough that I was careless enough not to use a condom. That might say everything he needs to know about me."

"My parents know people have sex before marriage. And believe me, Bennett's story is a doozy compared to ours."

"Really, what?"

She shakes her head. "I'll tell you later."

Romy slides her hand into mine as if that's going to soothe my fears. Her thumb brushes across my knuckles, and surprisingly, her affection does calm me a bit.

We climb the steps to the back porch, and she walks into the house. I thought we'd have a few more seconds while we waited for someone to answer the door.

My nerves sharpen into a steel edge. I realize that I feel the same way I did the first time I stepped onstage in a packed arena, the spotlight burning down on me. Somehow it almost feels harder tonight, and it's just a table full of her family. But these people's opinions mean more to me than thousands of nameless, faceless fans in the crowd.

"Hey, Mom. Dad," Romy calls, leading me through the house.

The house is everything I'd expect from the Owens. Pictures of the kids at different ages. Christmases, Halloweens, school pictures, sports pictures all proudly displayed. Everyone smiling and posed. Laughing impromptu ones, too. Love seeps out of every wall and surface.

My throat tightens. I don't belong here. I'm never going to be a family member to them. I'm just going to be the dad of one of their grandchildren.

I hover behind Romy. She releases my hand, and I almost reach for it back like a lifeline. The love in this house crowds in from all corners. I'm glad that Romy had it, but it's a reminder of everything I wanted once upon a time that I never got.

Her mom is at the stove, lifting foil off a pan, while her

dad tosses a salad. Appetizers line the counter. Romy doesn't hesitate, sitting and digging into bruschetta. I stand stiffly behind her, unsure what to do.

Darla glances over her shoulder. "Hey, Zander, nice of you to join us."

She wipes her hands on a dish towel, taps Brad's shoulder, and crosses the room. I extend my hand, expecting a shake, but she walks right into my unopened arms.

"No handshakes here, big guy—just hugs."

Her arms are warm and steady and provide the kind of motherly comfort I've never known. She knows Romy is pregnant, yet she still hugs me when she should be kicking me in the balls. Romy was right, it might be okay.

Brad sets down the salad tongs. I met him at the cookout, exchanged a few words, but that was before he knew I'm the guy who knocked up his daughter.

He extends a hand. "Hey, Zander, nice to see you again."

I shake it, firm as if I'm trying to prove something, convey I'm not going to fuck over his daughter.

"She's the hugger. I gotta feel you out." He winks, and I'm unsure how to take that.

"Oh my god, Dad, stop." Romy takes another piece of bread and puts the tomato concoction over it. "Zander, want some?"

Brad kisses Romy's cheek, hugs her from behind, and winks at me again before walking back over to the salad. The ease between them is so foreign that witnessing it seems as if I'm staring into a snow globe.

The door bursts open, and a golden retriever barrels in.

"Mack, Mack, Mack!" Romy kneels, hugging the golden retriever. "Oh, I missed you, buddy. I haven't seen you in forever. Where are they keeping you these days?"

"We're keeping him in our house. Maybe you should

venture away from The Knotted Barn occasionally and visit your family," Lottie says, stepping into the room.

Brooks follows, still dressed in his sheriff's uniform. "He's driving me crazy. He's getting used to the new land, but I feel like he's trying to teach all the bunnies he's the sheriff." He shakes Brad's hand, then Darla hugs him.

"Hey, Brooks, keeping our girl out of trouble?" Darla asks.

Brooks chuckles. "Yeah, you might remember, but your eldest daughter finds her own trouble."

They laugh, and I shift awkwardly until Brooks turns to me.

"Zander, nice to see you. I heard you were going to join us this evening."

He shakes my hand, feeling firmer than necessary, but who am I to judge? I'm trying to prove who I am here too.

Then the chaos begins. The door bangs open, and two little girls dart into the room, sliding across the floor toward the dog. One of them has a tennis ball in hand.

"Mack, Mack, let's go!" they say in unison.

"Whoa, whoa, whoa, girls," Darla says.

"Say your hellos," Brad says, stripping away the tennis ball.

"Where are your parents?" Darla asks.

"They were taking forever, so we ran ahead," one says.

The girls hug everyone quickly, barely allowing each person to wrap their arms around them. Then they stop in front of me. They look alike but different. Clearly siblings.

"Who are you?" the one with darker hair asks.

"You know who he is," the other one says. "Don't act dumb."

"I'm not dumb."

"He's Zander Shaw. We were at the cookout, Wren. Don't you remember—"

"Girls!" Romy drops her half-eaten bruschetta on the

counter and bolts up. "Let me introduce you." She stands behind the darker haired one. "This is Wren." She shifts her body behind the next one. "This is Leia. Girls, say hi to Zander." She smiles over their heads, and my heart stutters because she introduced me as Zander and didn't use my last name.

"Hi!" they say in unison. Then they look at Brad and Darla. "Can we go now?" The slight whine in their voices makes me chuckle.

"Go." Brad tosses them the tennis ball.

They run off out the door, Mack following them with a single excited bark.

"Girls, careful! If the ball goes in the water, come tell us," Bennett calls, then he and Delaney enter. Bennett's arm is around her.

I glance at Romy because what must it be like for her in this family where everyone is coupled up, and she's not? And now she's pregnant.

"Oh, it's nice of you to join us," Lottie says.

Bennett puts out his hand. "Hey, Zander." Then he moves to the next person, saying all his hellos.

Darla calls, "Okay, dinner's ready. Let's go. It's lasagna."

Romy grins. "Oh, you're gonna love it, Zander."

We file into the dining room. Bennett goes to get the girls, but Romy asks him to wait a second.

Shit. This is it. She's gonna do it now.

I can't breathe under the weight of the silence.

Romy stands behind what I assume is her chair. "I'm just going to make the announcement now because I want to really enjoy—" Her voice wobbles, and she turns to me.

I step closer, as if we're a united front even if my heart is lodged in my throat.

Her voice steadies as she stands tall. "I'm pregnant. And Zander is the father."

Chapter Twenty-Two

ZANDER

My back is as stiff as a damn board as I wait for their inquisition. Every set of eyes drills into Romy and me.

Her dad turns toward her mom. "You knew about this?" She nods. "Thought so."

His chair scrapes along the floor as he stands, coming around the table without a glance in anyone's direction. I mutter something under my breath, bracing for impact. He's going to punch me, and I'm going to let him. I deserve it. I got his baby girl pregnant.

As he reaches Romy, my muscles tense, preparing for the impact, but he embraces her in a tight hug.

"Congratulations. Another baby. How exciting."

His eyes lock on mine over his daughter's shoulder. This is it—the moment I've seen a hundred times on TV. The whole "don't mess with my daughter, you break her heart, I break your jaw" speech.

Instead, he sticks his hand out, gives me a once-over, and says, "Congratulations, Zander." With our hands entwined, he pulls me forward into a one-armed hug. My body relaxes just as he whispers, "We'll talk later."

My neck prickles. Maybe Brad isn't as laid-back as his daughter thinks.

When Brad is done, the rest of the family comes out of their stupor, rounding the table to congratulate us. Lottie's up out of her chair, playing surprised even though she already knew.

"Oh, Lottie, relax," Romy teases. "Everybody probably figures you already knew."

"What do you mean she already knew?" Bennett asks, mid hug with Romy. He looks around the room. Darla's sheepish grin gives away that Lottie wasn't the only one in the know. "Everyone knew already?"

"I am her mother," Darla says.

"I'm her father," Brad adds and hugs his wife into his side, kissing her temple.

They really are happy about the pregnancy.

"No, not everybody knew," Romy says. "I just blurted it out to Lottie when I was spiraling, and Mom found the test. We didn't leave you out on purpose."

Bennett groans. "Oh my god, of course. I should've expected this. I'm excluded just because I'm the guy. If I was another girl, it'd be different."

Romy cuts him off, lifting her hand. "Those who kept a lot of their own secrets from us can't throw stones."

Bennett and Delaney share a look and nod as if Romy is right. I'm more curious than ever to know their story now.

Brooks and Delaney step up to congratulate us both, then Romy looks around the room. "And hey, we're not going to tell the girls. I'm really sorry."

Her smile fades for the first time tonight, and I hate that it's my fault. If I was an average Joe, everyone could know.

I clear my throat, wanting to step in so Romy's not in this

alone. "Listen, I'm sorry, but that's my fault. I don't want you to keep secrets from your family. That's not my intention. But unfortunately, Romy is right. We have to be careful. I don't know your girls, and I'm sure they're great secret-keepers. But in my experience, it doesn't take much to coax something like this out of anybody, much less a child. Please don't take this as me not trusting them. It's just safer for all involved this way."

Delaney bursts out laughing. "Oh my god, I totally understand. Leia told her teacher the other day that she saw Bennett and me wrestling in the shower. Kids talk. So, no worries. They won't be told until you're ready to tell everybody."

Romy and Lottie say in unison, "Eww."

Brad cuts in. "What about the rest of the family? When are we able to tell them?"

Guilt burns through my chest like a bullet hole. His daughter's pregnant, and I'm sure he wants to shout it from the rooftops. But because of me and who I am, he can't.

Romy touches my arm as if she's trying to save me. But I don't want to be saved. I don't want them thinking my life will be a burden on theirs, but I suppose it already is. There's no way my life doesn't have a ripple effect through their world.

"It's just for now," I say. "Eventually we'll tell everybody. But there will probably need to be NDAs signed. It's all very legal, and I apologize ahead of time for Beau. He's a little neurotic. As of right now though, the extended family can't know."

Darla purses her lips and looks at Brad. She's upset. She wants to tell her brother, her sister, their families who live on this ranch. Nieces, nephews. And because of me, she can't share this news. Her silent disappointment hits harder than any words.

"Listen, I'll go over it with Beau again. He was just in shock when we first told him," I add.

"Beau knows?" Bennett's voice spikes with anger. "Who

else knows? Does your whole crew know? Romy, I'm your brother. I'm your blood. How could you not tell me?"

"Oh Bennett, relax," Lottie shoots back. "Look at the secrets you were keeping all those years."

Bennett grumbles, and Delaney slides her hand under the table to his thigh, calming him instantly.

"Honestly," I say, needing to make them understand, "Beau is my family. He isn't blood, but he's my brother in all the ways that count. That's why he knew first. Yeah, it's his job with all the legal stuff too, but he's my family nonetheless."

Romy's hand slides into mine, and she squeezes. I turn to her, and she offers me a soft smile.

Brad lifts his hands. "All right, all right. Let's everybody just calm down. So, when's this happening? When's our new bundle arriving?"

Thank you, Brad.

Romy beams. "Oh, Dad, I just went to the doctor." She runs into the other room, digs through her purse, and comes back with the ultrasound pictures, spreading them out on the table like treasures. "Here's the baby. I'm eight weeks along."

Everyone at the table lights up. The pictures get passed around, smiles blooming on each of their faces.

And me? For the first time since I walked into this house, I breathe easy.

It feels good to share this with them, to see people smiling at the thought of a part of me coming into the world. But it also hits me hard, cracking me open in ways I'm not ready for.

Because looking around this table, one thing is clear—my child is already loved. Loved without anyone even knowing him or her yet. Unconditionally.

Just the fact that they're going to be born is enough for this family to be excited and anticipate their arrival.

And that... that's some heavy shit I'm not ready to unpack just yet.

Chapter Twenty-Three

ROMY

Zander and I walk down the hill from The Knotted Barn toward The Perfect Petal to pick out flowers. Finally, Delaney and Poppy have time to sit with us and go over everything. The store might not be open to the public at the moment, but they still have customers calling in orders and still have all the landscaping projects for clients to deal with.

The conversation at my parents' house went fairly well—although I can tell that my parents are a little perturbed they can't share this news with my entire family.

I'm not even sure Zander fully understands what it's like to try to keep a secret from my family because, unfortunately, he hasn't had the blessing of a family that has his back.

I understand my nieces to a certain extent. They're young, impulsive, and adults can easily manipulate them and get them to spill. So maybe waiting until I start showing makes sense. Although I want to share this with them. I want them to want to feel my stomach and talk about their new cousin. But it's okay. I'm going to let this go. This is part of what it means to be having Zander's baby.

"So, what were you thinking flower-wise?" Zander asks, cutting into my spiraling thoughts.

"I don't know. Honestly, Delaney is so good with flowers. She's going to know exactly what you're looking for just from you describing it. She's great at putting different combinations together."

"She seemed really nice at dinner the other night."

"Yeah, she's really sweet. She lived in town a long time ago. She and Bennett were high school sweethearts and then parted, came together again, parted, and what you're witnessing now is the getting back together again. It's a long, tangled story."

He nods, and I can tell he's listening, but he looks as though his mind is somewhere else. "I'd like to see Willow-brook. I've barely set foot outside this ranch since I got here."

I glance at him. He's in his typical black jeans, black T-shirt. He'd be like a walking neon sign if I took him downtown right now.

"Would you really want to get off the ranch? Everybody knows you're here, and I'm sure there are press just waiting to snap a picture of you."

I'd love the opportunity to show him around my town. To take him to Laurel's bakery or The Sprout House for the best chicken sandwich he's ever had. I could make him try a cheese-burger pizza.

"Beau would blow his gasket if I told him I was going into town. He'd give me every reason in the book why I shouldn't. But there's still a part of me that wants to. This ranch is amaz-ing, but I'm feeling a little cooped up."

"I can imagine."

He side-eyes me. "You understand that it's the life you're gonna get, right?"

"I know." I do. Maybe Beau thinks I'm naïve about it, but I know it won't be easy. "I mean, sure, I understand our baby will be stuck in the limelight, and people will follow them. God forbid, I hope he or she doesn't want a music career."

Zander laughs. "Shit, I hate that. When people just assume the kid of a sports star is supposed to come out of the womb already throwing one hundred miles per hour."

"I definitely don't want those expectations on our child."

He looks at the land to our right, an open field of flowers. "I'm happy our child will grow up here. I would've loved to. It must've been amazing."

I can't help but smile. "It was. All of this wasn't always here. My parents built this part. But my Uncle Bruce and the cattle ranch, that's been in my family forever. Then we had all this vacant land, and my mom and Aunt Bette wanted to stake their claim on their own piece of the property, because back in the day, only the son got everything."

"Right." He rocks his head back. "Old school."

I nod. "Everything was left to Uncle Bruce. But my parents, when they moved here, built their part. The Knotted Barn and The Getaway Lodge are theirs. The flower shop is Poppy and Bennett's—they started that. The Harvest Depot is my parents', and the vineyard is Aunt Bette's and Uncle Wade's."

"It's beautiful here." There's longing in his tone.

"Yeah, it was a lot of fun growing up here."

"You always had a playmate." He nudges me gently with his shoulder.

"That's good and bad though. I probably fought with my cousins like siblings. But I'm grateful for that childhood, and I want my child to have the same."

He turns to me, and our eyes lock. We pause just before the parking lot of The Perfect Petal. It's another question for us to find an answer to. What will our kid's future look like? We haven't discussed it, but I think we both know our child will grow up here. But will they also split time with Zander on the road? The thought of missing holidays with him or her is already agony.

So, I push away the thought. We're not there yet.

"Well, let's go pick out some flowers." I motion toward the building.

His lips slowly tip, but then he faces the shop, and we cross the parking lot.

We could have taken the UTV, but Zander seems to like walking. And walking is good for me, so I agreed.

We step inside The Perfect Petal, and the bell rings. It's one of my favorite places on the ranch because the rush of air that greets you inside is heavenly—like a unique floral perfume. Rows of vibrant flowers in vases and stainless-steel buckets cover the floor and worn tabletops.

Delaney is already there, wearing her usual cute overalls with daisy patches. "You guys made it. I kept waiting to hear the UTV."

"Oh, Zander likes to walk." I nod in his direction.

His shoulders raise to his ears as he stuffs his hands in his pockets. He's almost shy looking. "I don't get to walk many places without a camera in my face, so I'm taking full advantage while I'm here."

"This is the place to do it," Delaney says, smiling.

Poppy breezes into the room from the back. "Oh, I thought I'd missed you. I'm telling you, that queen bee is on my last nerve. Zander, you're missing out by not filming a scene at The Honey Pot."

I love it when she talks about the bees, especially how entitled the queen bee is. It's so clear how much she enjoys them.

"Never been stung by a bee, and I'm not taking my chances on going into anaphylactic shock," he mutters. "Done that once in my life."

"You're such a baby." Poppy gives him a cheeky smile to say she's joking.

"All right, guys, this is the deal." Delaney claps her hands together. "I want to go over some of the flowers we have available, and you can tell me about your vision for the video. I already have a couple things lined up from what we talked about at dinner. But I can probably bring in whatever we need if we don't already have it."

"Dinner?" Poppy's eyebrows rise. "Oh, when did you guys have dinner?"

I glance at Zander.

Delaney bites her lip.

"All the families have family dinners," I say quickly. "True, we Owens probably have them a little more often than most, but we all have them. It was just the weekly family dinner." I shrug.

Now I'm outright lying to my cousins, and I hate it.

"We Ellises are so bad at that. Scarlett's always somewhere, and Jensen's always working. The most we do is stand around The Getaway Lodge kitchen and try Jensen's cooking."

"Well, that's still a tradition," Delaney says. "Traditions are what families are all about."

My mind snags on the word *tradition*. What kind of traditions will I have with my son or daughter? Surely, they won't have any that involve both of their parents. They'll have separate ones with Zander and other ones with me. That is my reality, and I need to come to terms with that faster than I am. No matter how well Zander and I are getting on, the fact is that he's leaving, and we are not a couple.

"Weird that Zander was there though..."

He shrugs, playing it off. "I sort of invited myself when I caught wind of it. Figured it was as good a time as any to go over some things with Romy and Delaney."

Before Poppy can respond I clap my hands together. "All right, let's get on with it then," I say, changing the subject.

Delaney brings out some bouquets she's already arranged.

"We can also go out to the greenhouse and take a look at what we have there. What do you prefer, Zander?"

His eyes search the room as if he's looking for one specific flower. "Truthfully, flowers aren't my thing. I don't know much."

"Surely, you've sent them to a woman before. What did you pick out?" Delaney asks.

I do not want to think about Zander sending flowers to a woman. Going to a florist and picking them out especially for her. Writing poetic words on the card. The most I got was that he shared his king size Twix bar with me.

"I've never sent a woman flowers."

"Never?" Poppy asks, judgment in her tone.

"No," Zander admits, his gaze flicking to mine. I swear the tops of his cheeks above his beard are growing pink.

"Never?" she clarifies as if she heard wrong.

"That's what I said." There's a bit of an edge to his voice now.

"Oh." Delaney's voice is soft, almost sad, as though he's missed out on something. Her gaze flicks to me, as if confirming he never sent me flowers.

I want to ask her if she missed the memo the other night that I'm pregnant, but we're not in a relationship. Never really were in one.

"All right, well, that doesn't matter. Men don't know much about flowers half the time even when they do send them." Delaney quickly makes an excuse.

"Except your brother," Poppy cuts in.

Delany shakes her head, although I'm sure Bennett is very particular about what flowers he gives Delaney. "Yeah, but most men just point at something and say, 'Put something pretty together.' Not everybody's partner is a landscape architect."

Delaney smiles, her love for my brother clear. A tinge of

jealousy hits me, wondering what having that kind of certainty in your life feels like.

"Okay, let's just continue." I take a breath. "We're trusting you, Delaney."

"Just Delaney?" Poppy sounds offended.

"Oh, come on, Poppy, I'll go to you about bees and honey." I laugh.

Delaney shows us more flowers. I spot one in a vase higher than I can reach on the shelf, so I grab the step stool and stretch up to reach it. It's big, full, and white with the palest pink coloring around the petals. It's perfect.

I'm on my tiptoes, and I almost have the flower when an arm wraps around my waist, lifting my feet off the stool.

Zander plops me on the floor and steps up to grab it himself. "I'll get it."

"She almost had it," Poppy says from the counter. "She doesn't need saving."

I glance at Delaney with a questioning look, wondering what is wrong with Poppy today. Usually she's easygoing and fun, but today she seems angry.

Delaney shrugs.

"Overbearing much?" Poppy murmurs, but we all hear her.

"It's not overbearing. It's romantic," Delaney cuts in quickly, shooting me a smile.

"Romantic? It's controlling," Poppy snaps. "She's perfectly capable of getting a flower."

"Okay, Poppy, thanks for the opinion. We have the flower now," I say, desperate to defuse the situation.

"I'm just helping her," Zander mutters and leans in close. "You can't be climbing on stools like that," he whispers.

Poppy can't hear him, but she's eyeing me suspiciously.

This secret has no shot of staying undiscovered when he's doing things like that.

ZANDER

Beau and I are sitting and having breakfast in The Getaway Lodge dining room.

"I need a night out," I say to him.

Darla is flitting around, making sure all of my crew are happy. She's the most hospitable person I've ever known. The most considerate too. Neither she nor Brad has approached me with questions about my intentions for their daughter. It's kind of nice, I have to admit, to not have that pressure on me while I'm trying to figure out how I'm going to do this parenting thing.

The books Beau loaded onto my phone are good, and I've watched a few YouTube videos, but I still question whether I'll figure out how to be a good father or not, even as committed as I am to becoming one.

"I want off the ranch," I say again when Beau ignores my first request.

He glances up from his plate of egg whites, spinach, garlic, and peppers—everything nutritious, because that's Beau. He's the most neurotic person I know.

"No," he says with a finality that pisses me off.

"No?" I ask. "You can't tell me what to do."

"I can tell you when you're in jeopardy. You don't under-stand what's out there. You've been off the ranch once, to go to that doctor's appointment, and news has traveled tenfold since then. There's no way I can get you off this ranch and into any place secure where pictures won't be taken." He forks another bite of egg whites and sips his coffee. "Why do you want off so bad?"

"Because I feel cooped up." I wiggle in my seat like a toddler. "I feel caged in."

"Hmm..." he says and goes back to eating his eggs.

"Beau," I snap.

"Are you sure it's the ranch making you feel that way?"

"I don't need your psychoanalytical bullshit right now." I pick up my coffee mug and watch Darla smiling and talking to everyone. What must it be like to be a person like her? So free with her kindness.

"We're dodging the question. Gotcha. But I see you and Romy walking all the time. Seems like you guys really enjoy the fresh air."

My coffee mug thuds on the table from my annoyance at not having control over my own life. "I'm not sure what you're implying, but yeah, sure, I love the nightly walks I've been going on with Romy."

"Speaking of which, we need to talk. There's paperwork to be done. There're tests to be had. We've got to figure this out."

I slouch back in my seat and glare at my best friend. "There's nothing to talk about. I told you no to the paternity test. I'm not going to bring it up to her, and we're not having one."

His fork clatters onto the plate, and he leans back in his chair as if we're about to have a showdown. We've both got temper problems, and this was probably a long time coming.

"I'm telling you now, Zander, this is a big mistake. Get the paternity test. When we have proof, we can draw up paper-work. But you don't want to be listed on that birth certificate if you're not the father."

"I *am* the father." My voice is louder than I intended, and a few heads turn in our direction, Darla's included, so I lean in closer. "I am the father. End of discussion."

"You hired me a long time ago to protect you, and I think I've done a damn good job. Don't get me wrong, I like Romy. I like her family. Hell, this place is like fucking paradise. Who even knew families like this existed? Sure as shit, not us. But we've seen the other side of people, and you're ignoring that reality. You're ignoring how many people you've trusted who turned around and fucked you over."

"Not her," I say firmly. "She's not the enemy."

Beau's hard lines on his face soften, but he doesn't back off. "Listen." He straightens and picks up his fork again. "I know you have feelings for her. I know she is someone special to you."

I give him a scathing look. "You don't know shit."

He shakes his head. "Are we really playing this game?"

"I'm going to be a dad, but I'm not going to screw her again."

Beau smirks. "I guarantee you're fucking her within a month."

"Piss off."

"Come on, I know you better than that. I can already see it in these nightly walks. You guys are always together. Laughing and smiling and flirting."

"She's helping me with the video." My eyes narrow.

"She's helping you plan a video for a love song. A love song that—"

I point at him. "Don't fucking say it."

Beau lifts his hands in his usual calm down gesture. "I'm just saying, it's inevitable. You're going to have a kid, so we need to put some parameters in place. Because if you cross that line, Zan, and break things off again, it won't go as smoothly as it did before. She's not just going to disappear this time. You think she'll want to share custody after you hurt her again? A woman can only take so much. You've got to get this shit together now or stay the hell away from her."

I stare at my plate. He expects me to stay away from her? I can't. She's the mother of my child—she'll be in my life forever.

"Yeah, I see you're getting it now," he says. "You have a decision to make. Is she just the mother of your child, or is she something more? Either way, there's paperwork involved. Lawyers. Settlements. Child support. Visitation. You two can't just wander around thinking you're average people who can figure this out as you go. That's not your reality."

I take a moment and think about what he's saying. He has a point. "What you're saying is fair," I admit. "But I'm not going to ask her for a paternity test. That's where I draw the line."

"Fine. But I sure as hell hope that baby looks like you when it pops out. A test doesn't mean you think Romy slept with someone else—it just prevents problems down the road. It protects the kid. But whatever, we still need paperwork. You've got to start arranging things with her now because once the video is wrapped, it needs to be in place before you leave."

He has no idea what I've been thinking, and when he sees my facial expression, his imploring stare turns annoyed.

"Well, that's the thing..."

Beau blows out a long breath. "I already knew. I guessed it. I even told DeSoto. Shit, let's call him—he owes me a hundred bucks."

My forehead wrinkles. "What did you guys bet on?"

"That you'd stay here after the video."

"Well, where am I going to go?" I throw my hands up at my sides.

"I don't know. How about recording your next album? Do you want to do it here? Because if so, I've got to build you a damn studio."

"I thought this would be a great place for inspiration, but the pregnancy—it changes everything."

"Yeah, it does. But what are you going to do? You can't just hang around rubbing her feet for months on end. You need to work before the baby's born, so you can spend time with it after. Where are you going to live, Zander? You need to figure this shit out."

I run a hand through my hair and pull on the back of my neck as the chair beside me slides out. Darla sits down, coffee cup in one hand, phone in the other.

"Good morning, boys. Enjoying your breakfast?" She smiles at each of us, and we answer in the affirmative. "So how are the beds in The Getaway Lodge? I changed them last year. Aren't they so comfortable? Plush, right? I made Brad get us one of our own."

Beau smiles politely, but my head is spinning. He can always hide it well, but I know he's still thinking about everything we just said. All I can think is how my career keeps getting in the way of everything good.

Then Darla looks me straight in the eye. "So... this whole secret-keeping thing? It's not going well. Supposedly people are starting not to like you, Zander."

"What? Who doesn't like me?"

She leans in closer. "Apparently you pulled Romy off a step stool at The Perfect Petal. Poppy thinks you're controlling and that you aren't about girl power. And the other day, you brought Romy a burger when she was meeting with Ben and Gillian and told her that she needs to eat red meat."

"Because he brought her a burger, they don't like him?" Beau asks, always my ally.

"No, but they wanted to know why she needs to eat red meat." Darla tips her head, and Beau gives me a look like I'm a moron.

"And Jensen said the other day that you told her to watch how many pistachio cookies she was eating?" Darla cringes.

"What the fuck, Zan?" Beau asks, looking at me as if I told him I wanted to quit music and become a circus clown.

"Too much sugar. I don't want her to get gestational diabetes."

Beau's eyebrows are furrowed.

Darla laughs. "Someone's been doing some reading."

I shrug and pick up my coffee mug to block my face.

She pats my hand on the table. "Thank you for watching out for her." She winks, and warmth spreads across my chest at her approval. Then she turns her attention to Beau. "People are wondering. Some already think they're a couple. We need to nip this in the bud."

Beau sighs.

"I understand your reason for wanting to keep this to yourselves. You think you can't trust our family. If I'm honest, I think that's sad. You obviously didn't grow up with people you can count on." Darla's expression sharpens, and she continues before Beau can argue. "No, you don't understand, Zander, because you didn't have family love, people who have your back no matter what. That's what family is, and that's what our family is. So, I'm telling you—we're going to tell the rest of the family. You're family now, Zander, and we're going to protect you."

She holds my hand. Beau scoffs until she takes his too.

"You're an extension of Zander, so you're our family too. We'll protect both of you. We'll keep the secret as long as you think you need us to. But as someone older and wiser, I'm telling you—it always comes out. Better to be ahead of it than behind. You're too smart not to know that, Beau." She releases our hands, stands, and leaves the table.

"Fuck, I just got schooled by Romy's mom," I mutter.

"Yeah," Beau murmurs.

"Did she just say we're part of her family?" I ask.

"Yep."

I shake my head and blow out a breath. "Fuck. That's heavy."

"Yeah, it is."

But for some reason, it feels like maybe it's the good kind of heavy.

ROMY

Zander and I have started doing nightly walks around the lake. We talk about things, but nothing about the baby and all the questions we probably should be addressing. He tells me about life on the road and funny stories about him and Beau when they were younger. I tell him stories about growing up on Plain Daisy Ranch and the games I used to play with my cousins.

Before tonight, on all our walks, other than when we told my parents, we've never ventured over to my family's part of the land. Where my parents live, Lottie's finished house, Bennett's house that's under construction, and my vacant parcel of land.

I slow my walking when we come upon it. I'm not sure I've ever truly thought about the house I'd build here.

"So, this is my parcel of land," I say, signaling to the empty piece of land in front of us. "This is mine to build on whenever I want."

Zander steps up off the walking path, crossing the property line. "You have a great view of the lake." He turns, facing me and staring as the sun sets on the other side. "Why haven't you built here yet?"

"Finances for one. Second... I don't mind living with my cousins. You know, I'm not really big on being alone." It's the truth, as embarrassing as it is. I don't want to build a house, even if I could afford it, just to live in by myself.

"Why don't you like to be alone?" he asks, coming back over and holding out his hand. "Walk it with me."

I accept his hand and walk onto the land I've been ignoring until recently when I realized I'm the last one of my siblings to build here. "I'm a people person. I like to be around other people."

"I can see that. You're easy to talk to and enjoy sharing things with others." His hand stays secure around mine. "We're opposite in that way. I like being by myself, and I don't open up to anyone."

I knock my shoulder to his. "And why is that?"

He shrugs, his gaze not veering in my direction. "Probably because I've spent most of my life by myself. Most of it only being able to rely on myself."

"Would you ever want to talk about that? Growing up in foster care?"

He stops us and turns me to face him. "There isn't a lot to say. There are successful stories of kids in foster care. I've known a couple. But whatever you assume, you're probably right when it comes to my experience. And I'm not going to taint those rose-colored glasses of yours. I like that about you."

I wish I could change his mind, but maybe sharing makes him relive it, and he'd rather keep it in the past. "Well, I'm here if you want to talk about it."

He squeezes my hand. "I know. Thank you..." He lets out a long sigh. "Anyway, Beau is on my ass about us making some decisions."

I guess this is his way of changing the subject because he

doesn't want to talk about it anymore. "I can only imagine. What does Beau want now?"

He chuckles, and we walk along the perimeter from the road that the driveway would be off and then circle back.

"He wants us to decide on how we plan to be co-parents, and he wants us to get some paperwork done."

His Adam's apple bobs, and his shoulders seem more tense. I've suspected and wondered why I haven't been asked yet about a paternity test. He must feel uncomfortable bringing it up, so I might as well save him the trouble.

"You know, I mean it when I say I'll take a paternity test. I'm sure Beau's pushing you on it, and I'm fine with doing it. Please, just—"

"No, Romy. I don't need proof." He shuts me down quickly, his tone leaving little room for argument.

"You might not, but maybe Beau does, and I'm fine with taking it."

His hand slips out of mine, and he runs it along the back of his head, tugging at his neck. "It's unnecessary. I told him no."

"Why? It's a simple test. It's not a big deal."

"No, Romy. Jesus." He looks out toward the lake, then his gaze lands on mine, but there's something I can't read in it. "I just... I don't want you to have one. I believe you and trust you. If we're going to make this whole co-parenting thing work, then we need to have that between us."

Now I understand. "Okay. Okay then."

"I don't give a shit what Beau wants. I know that baby's mine."

"Paternity test is off the table then."

His shoulders relax, and the tension between us dissipates. "But as far as the other stuff, yeah, we need to figure some things out. I'm gonna start a bank account, and there'll be money in it for you."

I shake my head. "I don't want your money."

He huffs and turns his gaze away from me once again. "It's not a buy-off, or that I think you need it, but at this point, I don't know where I'm going to be living after I leave here. I just want to make sure you have everything you need."

I frown. "What do you mean? Won't you go home to Nashville?"

He laughs for the first time this walk, and it loosens something in my chest. "You think I live in Nashville in some big mansion or something, right?"

I shrug. "Isn't that where all country stars live?"

He laughs again. "No, Romy, they don't all live in Nashville." He grins. "And now I don't want to tell you where I live."

My eyebrows furrow. "Why? You worried I'm going to become some kind of stalker? Newsflash, I'm having your baby. You're kind of stuck with me for at least eighteen years." I try to joke because the reality that I am pregnant with a man's baby and I don't know where he lives is an uncomfortable one.

He sits on the ground and pats the spot next to him. "You can stalk me whenever you want."

"Well, you're welcome to stalk me anytime you want too. Then why?" I sit next to him, the solid ground cool against my behind, and cross my legs, picking at the weeds.

He sighs and runs his hand through his hair. "I don't have a home."

The weed slips through my fingers. "What do you mean you don't have a home? Everybody has a home."

"No, Romy. I don't. I don't have a home base. I don't own any real estate. I live out of hotels on tour or the tour bus. When I'm recording, I rent a house wherever I'm at. And if I have a short amount of down time between the two, I'll just go somewhere and do the same. I've never—I don't have a mortgage."

"You mean you have, like, no things that belong to you? No couches, no... no bed... no pillows, no dishes, or stuff like that?"

He chuckles, and I wonder if he's laughing at my naïveté. "I know what kind of pillows I like, and Beau just gets them wherever I'm at."

"Okay, but that's not the same, Zander. Everybody needs a home."

"I don't need one." He stands and walks to the path again, not helping me up, which is how I know I've struck a nerve. "Don't give me that sad fucking look, Romy. This is why I didn't want to tell you. It's my choice. My decision. I could afford ten houses in ten different countries if I wanted."

"I know," I say, getting up off the ground and dusting myself off. "I just... I'm not giving you a sad look."

He doesn't turn around, and I break the distance.

"I just... I want you to have a home." What I really mean is that despite myself, I want to be his home, but I'm never saying that. If I do, I might as well get used to the view of his back.

His gaze stays on the lake. "I don't need a home, but I do want my kid to have one. I want you to build a house on this land, and I want that to be our kid's home. I know that I'm the dad, and I'm going to want to spend time with him or her. And I'm hoping we can come to an arrangement on that. But I'll come back here, and I don't care where I stay. I'll stay in that motel down the highway if I have to."

"No. You would stay here."

He looks at me expectantly as if he needs more of an explanation.

I want to say, *You would stay wherever I am.* But I don't think he wants that. So, I quickly add, "The Getaway Lodge is always open. The honeymoon suite is yours for however long you want it."

My attempt at humor dies in the still air. He breaks the distance back to me.

"Romy, you're going to build a house on this land, and you're going to raise our kid here, and this is going to be their primary residence. I want them to have a place they call home."

As thankful as I am that he wants our baby to be raised here, the idea tastes sour without him.

"And where does that leave you, Zander?" My question is barely audible.

He runs his palm down his short beard. "I don't know right now. But I'll be a part of our kid's life. Don't ever think I'm going to dodge my responsibility financially or emotionally. I will be their father. I might not be able to wake up with them every morning or kiss them good night every night, but that's the thing about co-parenting, right? I mean, all parents who co-parent have to deal with those nights they're not with their kid. And their kid learns how to manage between the two parents. There's nothing wrong with that."

"No. There's nothing wrong with it," I agree.

Nothing at all, even though I want to scream that we haven't given *us* a shot. We don't even know what we could be. God, I'm so fucking foolish for letting these feelings creep up on me. To think that there is *something* here, that something could work between us.

"Zander, you're my family now. And I know that you might, like, find someone and marry someday…" I force myself to push out the words. "And she'll be a second mom to our child. But this…" I take his hand and put it on my stomach. "This makes us family. We are a family."

I swear wetness pools in his eyes, but he tears his gaze away from mine before I can tell for sure.

He straightens and removes his hand from my stomach. "It's a good piece of land." He clears his throat. "We should probably get going. It's getting cold, and I didn't bring a jacket."

I nod and step on the path with him.

Hopefully one day Zander will be truthful about what he wants with me, but most of all, I hope he can learn to be honest with himself.

Chapter Twenty-Six

ZANDER

Beau walks into The Knotted Barn, raises his arms in the air, and says, "Who's your daddy?"

I turn around. We've gotten almost everything done for the video. Zara is arriving tomorrow to start filming. The crew is already pretty much gone for the night, so it's just me and Beau. Romy went to lie down at her house, saying she wasn't feeling good. I told her I'd check on her on my way back, but ever since last night, I feel as if there's something off with us.

"That's creepy and weird. Try rephrasing it," I say.

"What's creepy? I made a huge deal today. I'm getting you what you want, and I want some kudos."

"Tell me what I'm thanking you for before I actually fall to my knees in gratitude."

"You're thanking me for renting out some bar called The Hidden Cave. Don't worry—you paid a pretty penny for it, but the crew and anyone else you want can go. There are only going to be two employees there, so we'll have to have some designated bartenders. But you'll be off the ranch. Happy?" His smug smile says he's pleased with himself. "But we cannot talk about the fucking pregnancy while we're there."

"I'm not gonna talk about the pregnancy. But I mean... she's going, right? Romy's coming? Did you tell her?"

He scoffs. "You sound like an adolescent boy asking me if I told the girl you like that you like her and want to know what she said."

I lean against the wall. I do sound pathetic, but I'm not ready to show my cards yet. "I just want to make sure she's going. It would be nice for her to get off the ranch too."

"Yeah, okay. Just keep telling yourself that." Beau picks up a donut from this morning from the box on the table. "I told Jensen this morning that he needs to go on one of those chef shows. He's wasting his talent here."

"Fuck, Beau, why would you say that? He's with his family."

He finishes the donut and licks the sugar from his fingers. "It's the truth. It was a compliment. What's up your ass?"

"Nothing," I grumble and turn back to what I was doing.

"Uh-huh. Sure. Lines are blurring, and you're gonna have to address it pretty soon. Is that why you're acting like a shithead?"

Beau is my best friend, and he's seen me through a lot of crap, but neither one of us is good with relationship talks.

"I don't need advice—least of all from you."

He puts his hand over his heart and pretends to stumble back. "I'm wounded. I give great advice."

I glance around the empty room. "Funny, you don't ever have a woman by your side."

"I have them in my bed, and that's good enough for me. That's the difference."

"Difference? Who said I wanted a woman?"

"Jesus Christ, Zander, look at yourself in the mirror. You're with her nonstop. I haven't really seen you in like a week. Don't get me wrong, I understand it. I know you've got to get to know each other, you're going to be parents. But we're still sitting on the fucking paperwork that hasn't been discussed, let alone signed. What exactly are we doing here?"

He has his points, but the thought of involving lawyers makes my skin crawl. It just isn't something I want to do. I don't want it to be like that with us.

"You're living in a fairytale. One day she's going to be just like the rest of the women who get pregnant by someone famous. She's going to see you on the red carpet with some pretty blonde on your arm while she's got a crying kid in her arms, and she's gonna be pissed and want to make problems for you."

Beau's cynical. I am too—that's the reason I pushed her away in the first place. No woman can be that perfect, that kind and sweet. Especially one who was such a big fan of mine.

"All I asked was if she was going to be there."

He quirks an eyebrow. "We're ignoring this, okay, got the memo. I don't know if she got the invite. That's up to you, buddy. Man up and ask her if you want her there."

When we stand in silence, I'm thankful to be alone with him. I walk out to the balcony, hoping the last of the sunshine will help me see the light in this situation. Beau follows me onto the balcony.

"I don't want to put her on the spot. I feel like she already thinks it's weird, me showing interest. I mean, I cut her off, Beau. Without explanation. There's no coming back from that."

He rests his forearms on the balcony. "Yeah, but things have changed since then. She wasn't pregnant with your baby when you blew her off."

"Still... I mean, I don't know. Shit. I don't have my life together. I'm not made for this. Romy's having my baby. She's turned from the woman I fucked into the one who's gonna raise my kid. I can't screw this up. If I fuck with her and things go bad, I could be screwed. I don't want my kid to be raised in complete chaos like we were."

"I give you shit because you pay me to. She does seem different though." He shrugs. "She seems... I don't know. But you definitely don't want to make this situation more complicated than it is. As legal advice—although I'm not a lawyer—I would say keep your dick in your pants."

"But my dick wants out."

"Well, yeah, of course the dick wants out."

"I really liked her back then."

"I know," Beau admits, his voice softer.

"You did?"

He holds a cocky smirk, staring at me from the corner of his eye. "The whole time. When you told DeSoto not to let her in, I knew you were a fool. You kept her hidden from almost everybody. You didn't flaunt her. You didn't make a big deal about it. You actually tried to hide out and spend time alone with her. That's not you. You used to entertain girls then take them in the back. They were never allowed to go from city to city. You broke the rule that we didn't leave a city with a woman in the back."

"I know." I knew I was breaking my one rule, but damn, Romy was different. Which was exactly what made me panic and push her away.

"But you flew her here and there—something you've never done for anyone before. Even though it was only three times, it seemed like your longest relationship ever—which is fucking sad, I might add."

"Let's see your long list of relationships."

He chuckles and nods. "So, I always knew she was somebody important to you. That's why I feel this whole pregnancy thing is interesting. It shakes up the playbook a little bit."

"Oh my god, you're not helping." I throw my head in my hands.

"You can't predict the future, Zan. You have to put yourself out there. I'm gonna shift from manager mode into best friend mode now. You ready?"

"Just say whatever you want to." I blow out an annoyed breath.

"Make your move," he says, as if it's so simple.

"As my best friend, you're saying I should see what we could be? I don't even think she'd entertain the idea."

"You don't know that. And I'm saying this as your best friend, I can see you want to. I have to play so many roles in your life, so let me get this right. As your manager, I'd say no fucking way, stay away from her. As your best friend, I'm saying fuck her. But as your brother, I'm saying take it slow. Feel it out. See where it goes. See if this thing has any legs or substance for the long haul."

I sigh. "How the hell do I know if a relationship has legs?"

Beau looks at me hard. "You're an idiot. If it does, you'll know. Look for the signs."

"What are the signs?"

"Oh my god, do I have to hold your hand? You'll know when you know."

"What if I don't?"

"Zander, you know when a girl likes you. You know the feeling it provokes. And when you feel something different from what you've always felt—that's your sign."

I nod and stand straight. I can do this. "All right. Okay. So, what do I do tonight? I mean, she can't drink, and we're going to a bar."

"You don't even know if she's fucking coming. That's your first step, buddy. Ask her to go to the bar first."

I grip the back of my neck with both hands. "My god, I feel like a thirteen-year-old boy."

"Well, yeah, you're acting like one. Time to man up, buddy. You've got big balls and a big dick now. Act like it." He pats me on the back and heads out of the barn. "Seven o'clock, the SUVs roll out!"

I've never even dated a woman, and somehow the first one I'm trying to win over is the mother of my child. If that's not messed up, I don't know what is.

Chapter Twenty-Seven

ZANDER

I never thought I'd be the type of guy who got nervous about knocking on a woman's door, but as I stand on Romy's front porch with sweaty palms and my heartbeat thrumming in my ears, I realize that's who I am. At least with Romy.

She doesn't want me here. What I did is unforgiveable. There's no way she'll trust me with her heart again.

I raise my hand to knock and lower my fist back to my side.

Come on, you're Zander fucking Shaw, of course she's going to say yes.

The problem with that thinking is that I don't want her to want me because of who I am to everyone else. I want her to want me for me.

I raise my fist another time, but the door swings open. Instead of Romy, it's Poppy.

"Gonna stand there all night?" She opens the door wider.

Judging from her glare, I'm still on her shit list. And it's hard to get off that list when I can't tell her that I didn't want her pregnant cousin on the ladder in case she fell.

"Hello, Mr. Country Superstar." Her voice drips with sarcasm. She leans against the doorframe, arms folded across her chest as though I'm the last person she wants to see tonight. "Here to pick out her outfit tonight? Tell her she can't wear lipstick?"

"I think you and your queen bee have some similarities." I nod toward inside the house. "Is Romy here?"

"Maybe." She shrugs, her arms crossed.

I hear a set of steps walk up the stairs behind me as Poppy's scowl deepens.

"I feel so honored to have two controlling men on my porch tonight," she says.

I slyly look at the man next to me. Nash.

"Fucking hell, Poppy. Are you ready?" he asks, then looks at me. "You're on her shit list, too?" He holds out his hand, and I shake it.

"Apparently."

Poppy stares at him as if he's her history teacher in high school, the most boring person she's ever met.

"Ready?" he asks, not entertaining her piss poor attitude. I like his style.

"Maybe I'm not gonna go with you," she says with an abundance of sass.

I feel as if I'm at a tennis match with my head moving back and forth.

"You are. Go get your sweater."

Fuck, these two are entertaining. My head volleys back over to Poppy.

"I'm only going because I don't want to miss out."

"Noted." Poppy disappears inside, and Nash leans against the porch railing, crosses his ankles, and stuffs his hands in his pockets as though he doesn't have a care in the world. "She's mad at me, not you. Actually, she's just mad at men in general because she's pissed at me. Don't sweat it."

Poppy comes out, sliding her sleeves into her sweater. "Romy will be down in a second." She shuts the door.

"Jesus, Poppy, let the poor guy wait inside." Nash pushes off the railing, waiting for her to head down the stairs.

"Superstar likes traditional roles where the man has to protect the woman because she's defenseless. He should wait outside to make sure there're no predators lurking about."

Nash shoots me an apologetic look, and they head down the porch stairs.

I open my mouth to say something back, but the front door opens again, and I forget all about Poppy. I'm here for Romy.

Romy raises her finger, her phone plastered to her ear. Then she waves me inside and holds the door open all the way. She's wearing panda pajama pants and a cropped T-shirt that shows just a sliver of her stomach. I don't see any sign of a baby bump, but she mentioned the other day that her clothes were getting tight.

I step in, and she disappears through an archway, but I can still hear her talking. "I'm not going. Why? You know why. I'll go over and walk Mack... do not come over here. Zander just got here, I gotta go." She groans and comes back in the room, holding the phone. "Sorry, that was Lottie. She's demanding I go to The Hidden Cave tonight." She smiles. "Way to work on Beau. You get to go off the ranch."

"You're not going?" I'm sure she can hear the disappointment in my tone.

"No. Then I'd have to explain to people why I'm not drinking. It's better if I just stay home."

I chew on the inside of my lip. "Your entire family is going, and you're going to stay here?"

"Yeah. If you and Beau want this little one to be a secret, I cannot show up there and not drink. And obviously I'm not going to drink." Her hand runs along her stomach. Every time she does that, a flicker of the caveman inside me lights up.

"So, if you weren't pregnant, you'd be going?"

She sits on the couch and tucks her legs under her. "Well, yeah."

No way am I going tonight without her. Either I stay here with her, or she comes with me. I think we both need a night off of the ranch to just have fun. Beau is supplying the most trusted spot he can right now, so we're doing this together.

"All right, get up," I say, holding out my hand.

"Not you too?" She groans.

"Come on. You're not missing out because you have to explain why you don't have a drink. Let's go."

"You're being bossy. Poppy would have opinions on that." Her cheeky smile says she's joking. Thank God she has a better opinion of me than Poppy does.

"I don't give a shit. Now get your sweet ass upstairs and get dressed to go dancing." I gesture with my hand out, using a little more force this time so she'll get the point to grab it.

"Zander, they're going to notice."

"So what?"

At this point, I don't give a shit. She's already going to miss out on so much just because she's the mother of my child. I'm not going to let her miss out on stuff like this before she's even had the baby. Romy seems entirely confident that if her inner circle does figure it out, it won't pose a problem. I want to build trust between us, so maybe I need to trust in that.

"Beau will be upset."

"Screw Beau. He'll deal with it." I take her hand in mine, slowly pulling her up off the couch.

She humors me, and I lead her to the bottom of the stairs.

"I'm going to wait here like a good boy while you go get dressed." I release her hand.

She steps on the first stair, and I grab her wrist to stop her.

"What?" she asks, turning back around.

"I just want to ask... will you go with me to The Hidden Cave?"

Her eyes narrow. "I thought we already established I was going."

You're fucking this up.

"Well, yeah, but I wanted to ask you though. If you'd go with me."

She laughs and turns all the way around to face me. "I'd assumed we would be, no?"

"Yeah... yeah, of course."

She studies me for a second, and sweat pebbles along the back of my neck. I'm terrible at putting myself out there. "Are you okay?"

"Yeah." Did my voice crack? "We'll leave when you're ready."

Her lips tip up. God, I love her smile. Especially when she's excited. It was the first thing I noticed about her that night I picked her out of the crowd after she showed up on the Jumbotron.

"Okay, I won't be long. The remote is on the coffee table." She walks up two stairs and turns around. "There's no beer, but there're energy drinks in the fridge. They're Scarlett's. I don't drink them."

I chuckle and motion her forward. "I'm good, go."

"Okay." She jogs up two more stairs and turns back to me again. "Snacks. The chip cabinet—"

"Romy, go."

"Okay, okay. Be right back." She scurries up the stairs.

"And stop going up and down the stairs, you're giving me a heart attack," I call.

Her giggle carries down the hall and stairs to me.

I go sit on the couch, tapping my fingers on my jeans.

Faster than I expected, Romy returns. She's changed into jeans and a sweater, hair out of her ponytail and brushed out. Her makeup is barely there, but she still has what I know now is a pregnancy glow. She grabs her coat from the hook and looks at me with an expression I can't quite read.

"Ready?" she asks.

I nod and get up off the couch, relief flooding me. "Let's go."

DeSoto waits in the black, tinted SUV. It's a clear giveaway of who is probably driving off this ranch. We'd be better off driving a beat-up Chevy truck.

I wave off DeSoto and open the SUV's back door for her. She pauses right before she climbs in.

"Hi, DeSoto, I hope you can have at least one beer tonight." She climbs inside.

I shut the door, and my hand stays on the handle for a second before I round the back to get in my side.

The road stretches out ahead of us, dark except for the glow of the headlights. I can't stop stealing glances at her. She's nervous based on the way her hands twist together in her lap. A memory of those hands tugging me closer flashes through my mind. Feeling them sneak up the hem of my T-shirt and explore my chest as she stared into my eyes.

I feel her hand touch mine and turn to see her looking at me.

"Thank you," she whispers.

"For what?"

"This." She gestures between us. "I know it's because you feel guilty, and you shouldn't—"

"Guilty?"

"Well yeah, but still, thank you."

I should tell her I didn't go get her because I felt guilty. I came to her house because I want to spend the night with her. I want to walk into The Hidden Cave with her by my side. I want to make her laugh and smile and be the reason she has a good time. It's all selfish reasons, and guilt has nothing to do with it.

"Romy, I don't want you missing out on anything more than you have to because of me."

Coward.

The rest of the drive passes, and by the time The Hidden Cave sign comes into view, my chest is filled with a mix of nerves and anticipation.

And with that, we step out of the truck together, the night air cool against my skin.

I offer her my hand, and she accepts it. We walk to the front door with DeSoto right behind us. Maybe we can move past what happened and have a new start. I sure as hell hope so.

ROMY

The Hidden Cave is packed. Zander and I are the last to get there, which means we'll be making an entrance.

We walk through the main bar inside toward the door leading outside, and I try to wiggle my hand free of Zander's, but he grips me tighter.

I stop and tilt my head in his direction. I haven't questioned why he wants to hold my hand sometimes on our walks because it feels natural, and I'm just desperate enough to take what I can get, I suppose. But walking out there holding his hand makes a statement, and even I'm not delusional enough to think he really wants that.

He releases my hand and reaches past me, pushing the door open for me to go through first. Laughter and country music fill the cool October air.

Sure enough, my entire family is huddled around the same four tables we usually take here. The girls are together at one end and the boys at the other.

We walk in the direction of my family, but someone pulls Zander's attention away. I'm prepared to leave him to talk, but his hand wraps around my wrist. I circle around, and he tugs me closer to him, his hand warming the small of my back, so I'm tucked into his side.

Zander leans down, and my heart beats out of my chest as his mouth lowers to my ear. "Sorry, I have to talk to Cal. I'll be right there," he says loudly enough that I can hear him over the music. He draws back as if he wants to see my reaction.

I nod, and a smile pierces his face, and my damn heart disobeys, pitter pattering. Then he releases me, leaving only the chill of the air.

Oh boy, I need to get a hold of these feelings because this man doesn't want commitment. He's only being this way because I'm having his child.

Scarlett slides off her stool and opens her arms. "Lottie said you weren't coming. Are you feeling okay?" She grips me tightly, and from her outfit, I see she came straight from work.

I look at Lottie over Scarlett's shoulder, and she raises her eyebrows at me as if she said what she could without lying.

"I'm feeling better and—"

"Mr. Country Superstar came over to get her," Poppy says from across the table.

I glance at the guys' table and see Nash talking with Jensen. She was cursing Nash up and down earlier.

"There's an empty seat near me." Scarlett leads me over, and I slide onto the stool.

"I'll get you a drink," Lottie says and shifts to move away from the table.

"She can have some from the pitcher." My cousin Jude's wife, Sadie, holds it up and reaches for a plastic cup.

"Is that margarita?" I ask. She's already pouring it. "Oh, I... um... I think I just want..."

Fuck, spit something out, Romy, they're all staring at you.

"She likes strawberry better." Lottie leaves the table before anyone can stop her.

Sadie lowers the pitcher to the table and shrugs. "I always forget everyone's favorite."

My cousin Emmett's wife, Briar, slides in beside me. "Saw you walk in with Zander..." She raises one perfectly arched eyebrow, stirring her drink.

I shift in my seat "Yeah."

"Here you go!" Lottie slides the drink in front of me.

"Thanks." I shoot her a look of appreciation. Maybe I was wrong, and we can pull this off.

"Briar, you took my seat," Lottie says.

I'm sure Lottie wants to stay by my side tonight, make sure no one suspects anything because, although she doesn't agree with the secrecy, she'll honor it for me.

"Sorry, I haven't seen Romy in weeks. Someone's been stealing all her time," Lottie says.

"Yeah, what's the story there?" Gillian asks.

My cousins stare me down from all sides of the table, so I say, "We're just... I'm helping him with the video."

They all look at one another and laugh.

"Okay," Sadie says. "I saw the way he pulled you to him when you walked in." She nods toward the area where the crew is all hanging. "Even now, he hasn't really stopped looking at you."

Everyone at the table turns and looks over, but I keep my back straight. "I'm sure he's just looking around."

Lottie offers me a sympathetic smile because she knows. I think Scarlett assumes I hooked up with him at some point, and Briar keeps glancing at my untouched drink. I feel as if I'm in a boiling pot of water with the lid on.

"I'm pretty sure he's only looking at you." Sadie pours herself another margarita and holds the empty pitcher. "Jude, can you get us more?"

He comes over and takes it from her, kissing her cheek and murmuring something in her ear before he walks away.

"It's amazing how much men can change for the women they love," Scarlett says. "If I asked Jude to get a refill, he would've flipped me off."

The whole table laughs.

"Daisy is having a sleepover at her grandpa's tonight, so we're making the most of the hours we have." Sadie waggles her eyebrows.

I turn to Briar. "And Colter?"

"Aunt Bette and Uncle Wade have him for the night."

The group turns to talking about how Aunt Bette and Uncle Wade are the only ones without grandkids. Poppy and Scarlett say their parents don't care, but they think they're secretly hoping for one of them to get pregnant by accident.

Poppy shakes her head and laughs. "Seriously, if I told them Nash knocked me up—"

"Nash?" Gillian asks, eyebrows raised.

"I'm using him for story purposes only." Poppy flits her hand in the air.

She can claim they're friends all she wants, but I have a feeling about those two. Poppy's emotions toward him run hot and cold too much for her not to care. I get that he's like a brother since he's Jensen's best friend, but I'd bet money on it they are more than friends.

"One night stand, drunken fling... she wouldn't care, my mom would be over the moon." Poppy rolls her eyes.

My hand slips to my stomach. I'm the fling. Not the drunk part, but I'm the careless one who allowed a man to not use a condom. But I can't seem to care about that anymore because every day I fall more in love with my baby.

Briar glances at my hand, and I retract it right away, my cheeks heating. But then she stares at my drink again. "Do you not like it?"

"Oh, no, I do. My stomach..."

"Is growing?" A tiny smile tips her lips with an expression

to say it's okay, I was there too. My eyes widen, and she places her hand on my knee in reassurance. She shakes her head. "You should stop by sometime. We see you and Zander walking around the lake a lot. Emmett told me to mind my business, but we have a great porch and would love to get to know him better."

I give her a wan smile. "Thanks. Yeah, I'll message you."

She squeezes my knee. "Great. Can't wait."

"Where's Jude?" Scarlett asks, looking at the bar since her glass is now empty. "Let me try your strawberry margarita while we wait. You don't mind, do you, Romy?"

Before I can stop her, Scarlett snatches my glass.

My heart shoots into my throat. "Scarlett—"

She takes a long sip and hands it back over with a look of disgust. "I think they forgot the alcohol."

"I'm sure it's there. Tracey just did an excellent job of making the drink," Briar says.

"I saw the bottle in her hand," Lottie adds.

"Let me see." Sadie, who I think is a little tipsy, grabs the cup from in front of me and sips the drink. "Yeah, I think she forgot it. I'll tell Jude to get you a new one." She raises her hand. "Jude!"

Panic rises in my chest. "You guys, it's fine. My stomach isn't right anyway." The lie tastes bitter, but what choice do I have?

"Huh. A stomachache and your drink doesn't have alcohol..." Poppy's eyes widen then zero in on my stomach. "Oh."

"Oh what?" Scarlett asks, following her sister's line of sight. "No way."

"No what?" Gillian asks. "Let me grab Ben. We're getting you two shots in the next drink, Romy, you need to catch up." She slides off the stool, but Sadie grips her arm. "What?" Her forehead wrinkles.

"Stomachache and no alcohol. Lottie got Romy's drink," Sadie fills her in, and everyone's eyes shift to Lottie.

She holds up her hands. "It's not my fault that Tracy's so overworked she forgot to put alcohol in it."

Their eyebrows shoot up because Lottie has a hard time lying, and she can't look any of them in the eye.

I can't put Lottie in that position, so I lean forward, look over my shoulder, and say quietly, "Yes, it's what you're thinking."

They all shout and cheer, making spectacles of our table, drawing attention.

"Shh..." Lottie says. "It has to stay quiet."

"Why?" Poppy asks, but she glances over my shoulder. "Oh..." Her eyes widen. "Ohhhh!!!"

I nod.

"What?" Gillian asks, not making the connection.

"The mystery man is... him?" Poppy connects all the dots.

All of their heads turn, and I don't have it in me to see if Zander now sees half my family staring at him with their jaws dropped.

"Way to make it obvious," Lottie says.

Heat creeps up my neck as the floor tilts under me.

Once everyone is done looking, I chance a glance over my shoulder and find Zander leaning against the bar, hat on backward. He's laughing and smiling with the people around him. This must feel really good to him—no pressure, no cameras, free to relax a bit.

His gaze lifts and catches mine. The ease he just displayed vanishes. His smile falters, and something flickers across his face as if he knows me well enough to figure out that something's wrong.

I push up from the table. "I'll be back."

Briar frowns. "Okay."

My eyes don't stray from his as I weave through the crowd. Zander straightens, his brows pulling together as he pushes off the bar and removes himself from the people he's chatting with.

He meets me halfway and places his hands on my upper arms. "What is it? Is everything okay with..." His gaze darts down to my stomach.

"Dance with me?"

His mouth opens as if he's about to ask why, but then he grabs my hand and leads me onto the dance floor just as the music shifts into a love song. Couples sway close together, bodies pressed tightly.

Zander twirls me in front of him, slipping his hand into mine and his other around my waist. He pulls me against him, and my breath hitches, the heat of his body burning through my sweater.

"What's going on?" he murmurs low enough that only I can hear.

I swallow hard, trying to find words. His thumb runs slow circles along my hip, and it makes it impossible to remember why I asked him to dance in the first place. All my attention is drawn there.

I shake off my stupor. "They know."

"That was fast."

"Yeah, I'm sorry."

I expect him to stop, to let me go, and push away to go find Beau to figure out the plan. But he doesn't. Instead, his hands tighten, pulling me flush until there's not even an inch between us.

"Scarlett tasted my drink, and it snowballed from there."

He exhales slowly, his breath warm against my temple. "You trust them, right?"

I nod against his chest, resting my chin there to look up to him. "Yes."

His hand slides up my back, steady and protective. "Okay. Are you relieved?"

"Yeah." And I am. It's nice not to have to hide it in front of my family.

"Good."

He doesn't let go or pull away. We sway together as though there isn't a storm about to engulf us.

The thread between us pulls taut, and I can't tear my eyes from his as his gaze lingers on me, softer than usual. His thumb grazes the small of my back like a caress.

"Are you sure you're not mad?" I whisper, more to myself than to him.

"They were all going to find out eventually. I knew what bringing you here might mean." He spins me so we're away from the other couples. "Let's just enjoy the dance."

His hand is splayed on my back, and he nudges me so there isn't a millimeter of space between us. The music swells around us, drowning out the pounding of my heart.

It feels so intimate. So right. My emotions and my desire expand in my chest until I can barely breathe.

"Zander..." I whisper.

He dips his head, lips hovering so close to mine that our breath mingles. My knees weaken, my body aching to close the distance.

It would be so easy for me to rise on my tiptoes and press my lips to his. Find the comfort in his body that I always found with him.

Then I remember reality—he doesn't do relationships. I have more than me to think about now.

I press my hand against his chest, pushing back just enough to break the connection. "We can't do this." Although my voice doesn't hold the conviction I wish it did.

His eyes search mine, yearning swirling in them, but he

doesn't argue. He nods once and steps back, allowing more space between us.

The song ends, and we separate as people shout out drink orders and laughter echoes through the open air.

Even though we didn't kiss, the almost part might haunt me just the same. It's a stark reminder that no matter how hard I try to push him away, part of me still wants him.

What if that never goes away?

Keeping my distance from him romantically might be the hardest thing I'll ever have to do.

Chapter Twenty-Nine

ZANDER

Plain Daisy Ranch has brought a peace to my life I haven't had in a long time, maybe ever, but even as quiet as it is, I need to get out of here again before I go stir-crazy.

The last few days leading up to the actual filming, every time I step outside the lodge, there's some crew member waiting with a clipboard full of questions. Thank God I had decided to bring Jack on as co-director. Romy is proving to be a big distraction. A good one, but I still need to make sure the bases are covered as far as the video goes.

After breakfast, I let Beau go do whatever he does during the day, and I head to The Knotted Barn.

Romy is in her office as usual.

I've been trying not to think about our almost kiss, but that feels impossible now that I'm standing in her doorway.

She looks up from her computer. "Oh, hey."

I grab the trim of the door above me, needing to do something with my hands so I don't head across this room, pull her up from her chair, and tell her she made the wrong decision last night. That she shouldn't have pushed me away.

"I need a really big favor."

She leans back and runs her hand over her stomach. "I feel like I'm already doing you a big favor."

I chuckle, staring at her stomach. God, I can't wait to see that swell. "This one's much easier, I promise."

"Good, because the one I'm doing for you now is giving me horrible heartburn." She opens a drawer, takes out a bottle of antacids, pops two in her hand, and puts them in her mouth.

"What do I have to do to get you to take me out of here?"

"Take you out of where?" she asks, mumbling around the antacids.

"I need to get off the ranch."

"Again? Oh, well, I'm not—"

"No, no, no, listen to me. I know we can do it. I have a hat and sunglasses."

She laughs. "I was told a hat and sunglasses would not disguise the magnificent Zander Shaw."

I cross the room and sit in the chair across from her, resting my clasped hands on her desk. "I want to see Willowbrook. I want to see what everybody's always talking about. I keep hearing all these stories about a bakery with pumpkin spice cream cheese cupcakes, some donut place with apple spice."

"Shouldn't it be me who has cravings?" She grins at me, brown eyes alight with amusement.

"Fair, but some chicken place was mentioned? The Sprout something? And people showed me pictures of the gazebo in the town square."

She stares at me long and hard. "Zander, you're not missing out on anything. It's a small town. You've seen plenty. It's like all the rest."

"It's not just any small town. It's the small town where my kid is gonna grow up."

She releases a slow breath and stares at me, hand resting in her lap. "You're asking me to somehow hide you and take you into town. We'll get caught, and then Beau will kill me—"

"You let me handle him. But we're not gonna get caught because I have a hat and sunglasses." I wink at her.

She chuckles. "I don't think you realize… I was out last week. I had to run to the post office. And honestly, I'm not joking, Zander, there is so much press outside of these fence lines. So much."

"It doesn't matter. I want to see everything. I don't even care if they see me at this point."

"Beau cares," she argues.

"I'm the one who matters. My well-being matters. So, I'm asking you—take me to Willowbrook. Let me see where our kid's gonna grow up."

That same look crosses her face, the one she always gets whenever we come close to broaching the topic that she'll be the one primarily raising our child. It kills me to know I'll be flying in and out of his or her life. But what choice do I have? I have to support my child, make sure they're set up for life and never want for anything. That means I have to travel. Plus, I don't want my kid to grow up with cameras in their face and people pestering them. They deserve to have a normal childhood on a ranch like this, surrounded by family.

She sighs. "Fine. Let's go. But you're gonna have to be on your best behavior. And I want to see the hat and sunglasses."

I smile and stand, feeling victorious. "Awesome, let's skedaddle."

She eyes me. "I don't see a hat or sunglasses."

"I'm gonna stop by The Harvest Depot and pick some up."

"You're just going to swing by The Harvest Depot where people are loitering to catch a glimpse of you?" Her eyebrows raise as she stands and goes to a cabinet in the corner.

"What choice do I have?"

She hands me a pink Plain Daisy Ranch baseball cap, over-sized sunglasses, and a green scarf with the logo for Plain Daisy Ranch on it.

"Man, you really like your logo, huh?" I look at the green winter scarf. "Not sure it's cold enough for this yet."

"Yeah, well, it's kind of cold. I figured you could cover up around your neck and half your face."

"You don't think that will draw more attention? Me looking like I'm going to rob someone?"

She shrugs one shoulder and grabs her purse. "It's either that, or I don't take you. I don't want to face Beau's wrath."

"Fine," I grumble.

We leave The Knotted Barn and walk to her house, where we get into her small SUV that doesn't do shit to hide me. I put on the hat and sunglasses, hoping no one looks too closely. We get out past security, her smiling and waving, distracting the guards from me.

The minute she drives us under the iron arch that says *Plain Daisy Ranch*, I strip off the hat and sunglasses and ridiculous scarf and let out a huge breath.

"Thank you." I roll down the window and stick out my head.

She laughs. "You're like a dog on its first car ride."

The breeze flows through my hair. "You have no idea how good this feels."

"You're fine on these country roads, but once we get into downtown, you're gonna have to roll that window up and put that stuff on again."

"The scarf too?" I whine.

She smirks. "Yes, the scarf too, you baby."

We reach downtown, rolling down Main Street. I do as she says—window up, hat on. The heart of Willowbrook unfolds around me—a barber shop, a hardware store, a bakery. People are strolling down sidewalks and there's a big gazebo in the center. It's life, and I've missed it. It's everything small-town America is supposed to be.

Then I spot a pastel blue storefront with flower boxes spilling over with daisies and a sign for The Sugar Cottage.

"Is that the cupcake place?" I point at it.

She laughs. "Yeah, that's Laurel's. She wasn't allowed to come to your private party the other night, but she's Gillian's best friend."

"Which means we can trust her?"

Her stare sharpens. "Zander, I promised you one car ride up and down Main Street. That's it. You got to hang your head out the window, and I'll even let you hang it out on the way home. But we are not stopping. We are not getting out."

"I like your mom voice. It turns me on."

"Oh my god." She looks away, and I'm pretty sure it's to hide her smile.

"Come on, if she's Gillian's best friend, surely, we can trust her. You've been going on and on about how trustworthy the people in your life are." I lean over the console really close to her. "I'll even wear the scarf."

"You're gonna get me in trouble."

I glance at her stomach. "I think I already managed to do that."

She laughs. "True story. All right, here's what we'll do. I'll park, and we'll walk in casually and go right to the back."

"Sounds like a plan. I kind of like this. It's kinda like MacGyver stuff."

"It's not MacGyver stuff."

"Why not?"

"Because MacGyver fixes problems, and I have a feeling we're about to create one."

"So, maybe more like *Mission Impossible*."

She shakes her head and pulls into a spot. "We're gonna

get out nice and calm, go straight inside, and walk right into the back of Laurel's bakery."

"I like this side of you. We could've had some fun together had I known you were like this."

"We had fun together, and our prize comes out in six months or so."

I laugh, adjust the scarf, hat, and sunglasses, then we exit the car and slip inside.

A blonde woman glances over her shoulder. "Romy?"

"Hi, Laurel." Romy waves and keeps walking.

"Should I call the police?" a woman sitting at one of the tables says.

"Did he have a gun?" another woman asks.

Romy tugs me into a corner, and the blonde who greeted us walks around the corner, holding up a pair of tongs.

"What's going on?" She raises the tongs.

"What are you going to do? Pinch my nose?" I ask, which was probably the wrong decision, since the woman is now annoyed. And I like my nose a lot. It gives me character.

"Sorry." Romy pulls the hat and sunglasses off me.

Laurel's eyes widen. "Oh." She glances toward the front area, then back at me. "Why are you bringing trouble into my store?"

"We're not bringing you trouble," Romy says. "Zander just heard something about your cupcakes and…"

"Oh, you did?" She smiles, and her hand covers her heart. "What did they say?"

"Romy's doing me a solid. I wanted off the ranch. People keep raving about your pumpkin spice ones. After some swindling, Romy agreed to sneak me in here."

Laurel laughs. "It's not really the best time. I'm expecting about fifteen little visitors in"—she checks her watch—"three minutes. If you look at those tables, it's all set for them. So, I'll grab some cupcakes, put them in a box, and bring them to you. Then you're going out the back door."

"Thanks, I really appreciate this," I say.

Laurel gives Romy a look, then disappears to the front of the place.

The bell above the door rings, and suddenly kids' voices flood the bakery. Romy's eyes widen.

We hear Laurel panic in the front area, saying, "No, no, wait, wait, wait!"

But it's too late. The kids have already walked into the back room.

And lo and behold—Leia and Wren are two of the fifteen visitors. Both squeal and scream at once. "Zander!"

Romy shoots me a look that says *I told you so.*

Chapter Thirty

ROMY

I grab Zander's arm and pull him close, whispering in his ear, "I told you so."

All he does is laugh and hold up his hand. "Leia, Wren, give me high fives."

Of course, they run to him, with expressions on their faces that say, *Isn't this great? I know Zander Shaw.* They both jump up and slap his palm.

A little kid my nieces refer to as Peyton pipes up, "I want a high five! I want a high five!"

So, Zander gives him one too.

Laurel turns the corner, still empty-handed. She nods for me to go out the back door. Now I'm thinking there's someone in the front room who isn't just a customer. Someone who's part of the press.

"Okay, guys, time to start your class," I say, clapping. The teachers join the kids in the back with us and help, although they keep glancing in Zander's direction. "We have to get going."

"Noooo," Wren says. "Are you coming to dinner Wednesday?"

"Yeah, are you coming?" Leia waits anxiously for his answer.

I haven't had Zander over since the first time because it feels weird. We're not a couple.

"Are you inviting me?" he asks, side-eyeing me.

He seems different today. Lighter almost. It's refreshing.

"Yes, you can come. Grandma will love it," Wren says, taking the lead.

I smile at the two innocent girls who have no idea the complicated situation I've gotten myself in.

"Okay, girls, we have to go." I kiss the tops of their heads. "I love you."

I grab Zander's arm again, tugging him away as the kids scream and cheer, making their way to the tables. I manage to drag him around the corner and open the back door, but two men are walking down the back alley. I slam the door shut and peek around the corner. Laurel is standing in front of the opening to the back part of the bakery with a woman and a man holding a very expensive camera trying to look over her shoulder.

I grab Zander's hand and shove him through the first door I find, slamming it shut behind us.

What I didn't realize is that it's not Laurel's storage room —it's Laurel's janitorial closet. The cramped space barely fits us both.

"We shouldn't be doing this with little kids in the other room," Zander mutters, voice low.

"Stop thinking with your dick right now," I whisper, my ear to the door.

"That's hard to do when I'm around you."

I let out an exasperated sigh. "Stop flirting with me."

"I'm not flirting," he says, voice rougher now. "I'm stating a fact."

I roll my eyes, which is a waste because he probably can't even see them in the almost complete darkness. We're quiet for a beat, and it dawns on me that the people who say your senses are heightened during pregnancy must be right because the scent of his cologne or soap or whatever it is makes him smell delectable. Plus, the cramped space, I feel his presence too. "You're impossible."

"And yet"—he leans closer, his breath warm against my cheek—"you dragged me in here with you."

I press my back to the door. "Had I known it was this small, I would've just let you be spotted."

He chuckles in my ear. "I like you looking out for me." His voice is flirtatious and sweet.

I want to grab the back of his head and press my lips to his.

"What do you want, Zander?" I'm confused after that almost kiss the other night at The Hidden Cave and him acting this way now.

"Is *you* not the answer you want?" His hand brushes over mine fisted at my side. The touch is light, but deliberate, and my pulse trips.

I swallow. "Zan."

"Say it again."

"What?"

"My name. The way you just did." His pinkie strokes along mine as he weaves our fingers together.

"What?"

"Still not the word I wanted." His thumb strokes my knuckles.

The walls of the closet feel as if they're closing in on me, the air becoming heavy. I should push him away, but instead, I tilt up my chin. And he's there, as if he was waiting for me in the darkness.

"I never forgot you," he says softly.

His mouth catches mine before I can talk myself out of it. Soft and hesitant at first, as if he's waiting for me to shove him away. When I melt into him instead, he deepens the kiss, his hands cradling my jaw.

For a few blissful seconds, it's just us again. No crew. No press. No small-town gossip. No complications. Just Zander and me, pressed together in a janitor closet, stealing a kiss that feels so right. I inch up on my toes, my fingers tightening around his dark strands.

Then light floods the small space.

We jerk apart and stare through the open door, eyes squinted.

Peyton stands in the doorway, eyes wide. "Kissing!" He points at us.

Then a bunch of other little faces come into view.

"Zander and Romy sitting in a tree…" one of the children starts singing, and they all join in.

Zander laughs and mutters, "Busted," with his hand still on my ass.

All I want to do is shut the door and slam my lips on his again.

"You can come out now. Zara Sloane was spotted at the gazebo, so they all ran over there." Laurel pushes past the kids and shoves a box of cupcakes at us. "Here you go."

So, Zara is in town. Zander had mentioned she'd be coming to film the video. The butterflies in my stomach are replaced with anxious insecurity. Zara is a model and rumors swirled in the press once that she and Zander were involved.

"Thanks." I take the box and hand it off to Zander, stepping out of the closet. "You worked hard for these, so enjoy."

He opens the box, takes one out, and engulfs it in a huge bite.

Laurel says a quick goodbye and heads back to the kids at the table.

"Worth it?"

His gaze flicks to my lips. "Definitely."

I wish I knew if he was talking about the cupcakes or the kiss. With him, you never know.

Chapter Thirty-One

ROMY

We had to wake up early to film and catch the best light. I'm hanging around because Zander asked if I could so I can give him my input when needed and make any changes necessary to the set dressing once we see it on film.

I hug my clipboard at the edge of the field, trying to look like a professional taking notes as my stomach twists into knots watching Zara Sloan tilt her chin up to the sky while Zander tucks a strand of hair behind her ear with natural ease, causing havoc in my brain.

Rumors are that they were a couple once upon a time. They've remained friends obviously, since she's the one sprawled out on a plaid blanket with a wicker basket as if she stepped right out of a country magazine.

Her smile is soft, and Zander doesn't use his cocky smile. No, the infuriating grin is nowhere on display, but rather, she gets one that looks almost real. The one I've only ever gotten sparingly.

One of the camera guys shouts something, and the clapboard snaps shut. Zander lies beside her on the blanket, the brim of his cowboy hat shadowing his eyes, but not enough because I see his eyes catch hers. They laugh at something I can't hear.

The thread I'm holding onto snaps when he rolls on top of her.

Relax. It's all choreographed.

I know this, yet it doesn't stop my chest from caving in. Especially when Zara's hand slides up his arm as if she's familiar with the map of his body.

The crew murmurs their approval behind the camera, and I overhear someone whisper, "God, they look good together."

I flinch. But they're right. He's broad and strong, and she's soft and delicate. They fit perfectly together, and I'm not the only one who sees it.

I force my attention back to my clipboard, scribbling notes that are nonsense, to block anyone from witnessing my unraveling.

The co-director yells cut, and laughter ripples through the field. Zara pushes up on her elbows, and Zander offers her his hand, tugging her up in a way that looks effortless. He says something to her, and she laughs, tilting her head back as though he's so funny.

He's not funny. He's a grump most of the time.

One of the crew says, "You two could sell a million records on looks alone."

I'd like to meet him in a back alley.

I click my pen so hard Zara notices. Her attention flicks my way as she laughs as if she's already part of the crew. It doesn't sound forced at all, as though she's been here this whole time.

They take a break, and Zander grabs a bottle of water from the cooler, twisting the cap off before handing it to her. A gesture that is gentlemanly and shouldn't mean anything, but I feel sliced open by it.

It's just his job. All an act.

Zara walks toward me with effortless grace and stops right in front of me. Her smile is open and welcoming.

I hate her.

"You must be Romy. Zander mentioned you," she says, holding out her dainty hand.

I blink.

Before I can answer, Zander comes to her side and gestures toward me. "Zara, this is Romy Owens. She manages The Knotted Barn, where the ceremony will be held. She's done amazing stuff up there."

Huh, interesting introduction.

I guess I'm a nobody beyond a set decorator. Guess I'm not the one he kissed in a dark closet yesterday and then said nothing about it after.

"Pleasure," Zara says.

I take her hand, gripping it firmly, but I'm sure my smile isn't sincere. "Welcome to Willowbrook."

Her eyes flash, clearly catching the bite in my voice, but she doesn't call me out on it. Instead, she giggles, leaning toward Zander as she says, "Everyone's been so welcoming. Honestly, it feels like I've been here longer than a day."

"Yeah," I murmur, pulling back my hand. "You fit right in."

Zander watches me. I force myself to look away, flipping my clipboard open as though my notes are the most important thing in the world.

His gaze stays on me a little longer until they get called back to the blanket.

"It was good to meet you," Zara says.

I offer her a tight smile. "Keep up the good work."

Zander tilts his head, but when I return my attention to my clipboard, he follows Zara to the blanket. Zara laughs at something one of the cameramen says. She tips her head, dark hair shining, and Zander grins at her.

The ache in my chest spreads like a disease.

They set up the next shot, and the director mutters something about how natural the chemistry is while another crew member agrees. Zander helps Zara smooth out the blanket, his fingers brushing hers.

I snap the clipboard shut. I cannot do this, so I turn around to leave.

"Romy," he calls after me.

I'm surprised he even noticed I was leaving. I glance up, and Zander is striding toward me, a sheen of sweat glinting at his temple.

"How does it look?" he asks, nodding at the clipboard as though I have any meaningful feedback written on it.

I arch a brow, channeling every ounce of composure I can muster. "Like a romantic picnic."

Something flickers in his eyes, but he doesn't bite. He smirks that slow, half smile that leaves me off balance. "That's good, right?"

I shrug and jot a note that's probably gibberish. "If the goal was chemistry, you and Zara nailed it."

He studies me, peeling back every layer I'm trying to hide.

"You okay?" he asks quietly.

He sounds genuine. I should snap out of this. I know it's just a music video, but there are always so many doubts with Zander Shaw.

I shut the clipboard. "Fine. Just need to get back to work. Ben and Gillian's wedding has taken a back seat with all this." I wave dramatically at the surrounding production.

His jaw clenches, but he doesn't push. Which makes this worse. Because if he wanted to know, he could lean in, drop his voice low enough, and remind me of what it felt like when his mouth covered mine in the dark.

But he doesn't. He lets me walk away.

My heels dig into the grass as the crew's laughter rises up

behind me. Someone repeats for the fifteen millionth time how good Zander and Zara look together, and I deny myself the urge to whip around and scream, *We all heard you the first fifty times.*

Whatever happened in that closet at Laurel's was a mistake. And judging by the fact that he didn't stop me from leaving, Zander Shaw thinks so too.

Chapter Thirty-Two

ZANDER

The scene is perfect. The crew has outdone themselves. Fairy lights are strung on low branches around the lake. A canoe sits halfway in the water, like something out of *The Notebook*. A blanket is spread out with grapes and champagne glasses. Even the sun is cooperating and hanging low in the sky, giving us purple and pink streaks in the sky. Every element is completely ready and staged for this to be a picture-perfect scene.

But it all feels wrong.

The woman standing across from me is wrong. Zara Sloan is gorgeous—there's no argument there. Any man would love to be with her. Her long, dark hair, skin that looks airbrushed to perfection, even her laugh. She's got flirty smiles, leaning just close enough for the camera to catch the suggestion. She tosses her hair back like a perfect perfume ad.

And I hate every second of it.

I hate this fake, manufactured version of love. The fact that a music video romance is built out of camera angles and stage directions. There's nothing authentic about it.

I hold Zara in my arms at the edge of the dock. And all I can see—all I can wish—is that it was Romy.

The co-director calls, "Closer, Zander. Look like you want her."

I grit my teeth. I've done lots of music videos. Usually, they're heartbreak songs. This one is supposed to be about hope. But tonight, I can't flip the switch. I can't see Zara as somebody fictional, because I feel as though this is Romy's ranch, Romy's spot. Like I, somehow, am Romy's, even if I'm not.

Still, I tilt closer to Zara to get this over with. My stomach twists. I think Zara notices my stiff posture and inability to play the part I need to.

Once upon a time, rumors spread that we were dating after we were seen on a red carpet together. We hung out one night, and suddenly people claimed we had an affair for six months. It never happened. We talked once or twice, realized we wanted different things, and went our separate ways. She's really nice, though. Beau was the one who thought she was perfect for the part, so I made the call and asked her.

"Hold it," the co-director calls. "Zara, I want you to laugh. Zander, pick her up. Zara, wrap your legs around him."

I go through the motions. Pick her up. Hold her gaze. Rock my head back in laughter.

Finally, my co-director yells, "Cut!"

"Well, that was fun," Zara says as she lowers herself from me. There's sarcasm in her voice, and I don't blame her. I wasn't into it, and I'm sure she felt it, which makes her job ten times harder.

I glance toward the edge of the set where Romy was watching earlier. Yesterday, something was wrong. I don't know if she's mad about the kiss. I don't know anything anymore, and it's pissing me off. My head is a fucking mess.

I head over to Beau, who's behind the monitor, talking to the cameraman.

"Where's Romy?"

Beau shrugs. "I don't know. Haven't seen her in a while." He turns his attention back to what he was doing.

"That's not an answer."

With a sigh, he turns to face me. "I don't know, man. Maybe she went to deal with something for her cousin's wedding. She's been juggling both events."

A niggling feeling stabs like the twist of a knife between my ribs. I have the bad feeling she's upset after seeing me with Zara. I've heard the crew and Jack saying how great we are together. I should have addressed this yesterday.

I'm a fucking idiot.

"You fucked up, didn't you?" Beau asks, walking us away from the cameras.

"I think so."

"This is why you get the paperwork." He glares at me.

"Fuck the paperwork." I stalk off and slide into the first UTV with keys inside.

"What the hell, Zander? We might need reshoots. You haven't even looked at the tape yet."

"You got the take. It's fine. Jack, you good?" I shout to the co-director.

Jack gives me a thumbs-up. "We're good."

"See, Beau?"

He blows out a breath in frustration. He thinks I don't know what I want, but I do. I've just been too chickenshit to go after it until now.

I check The Knotted Barn, and Romy's not there. She's not at The Getaway Lodge either. Finally, I knock on her door at the house. As I'm walking down the porch steps, trying to figure out where else Romy might be, a yellow Jeep with giant daisies on it pulls up.

Great, this is not what I want to deal with right now.

Poppy climbs out of the Jeep. "Hey, Mr. Country Superstar. What's up?"

"Do you know where she is?"

She sighs as if I just ruined her night. "All right, you'll probably only hear this once from me, so pay attention. I'm sorry. I didn't know Romy was pregnant. I get it now, and it's a little endearing, I suppose. But don't treat her like a baby bird who needs you to survive, okay?"

"So, you don't hate me anymore?" I raise my eyebrows.

Poppy rolls her eyes. "She's at Uncle Bruce's, helping with Ben and Gillian's wedding. She's putting the arch up today."

I jog toward the UTV. "Is this your way of making up for hating me, Poppy?"

"Maybe. But I'll tell you this, Zander Shaw. If you fuck with her emotions, you'll have me to answer to. So before you drive off, I suggest you know what the hell you want."

"Believe me, I do. You don't need to worry, Poppy."

"I hope so. I'd hate to kick your ass and get arrested for breaking your nose."

I point at my nose. "That's all right. It's been broken twice before."

"Yeah, it looks a little crooked," she says.

I floor the gas pedal, speeding down the path toward Romy's Uncle Bruce's place.

When I get there, Romy's in the yard in front of the arch, standing on a step stool—which she knows will piss me off. She's putting up the flowers for Ben and Gillian's wedding that's in two days.

"Romy."

She doesn't look at me, attaching flowers to the arch.

"Romy," I say again, walking closer.

She finally glances over her shoulder and pops out her AirPods. "Sorry. Didn't hear you. What are you doing here?"

"Why did you leave the set again?"

"Everything looked great. You and Zara—chemistry for days. You didn't need my help or opinion."

I step closer. The distance between us suddenly feels unbearable. My voice drops low. "You know it's just a video. It's not real."

"Yeah, I know." But she looks away from me.

I laugh bitterly. "Doesn't seem like you know."

Her jaw tightens. "I don't know what you want from me, Zander. I have to get this done for Ben and Gillian. I know you're used to things revolving around you, but this time, it doesn't." She bends to get more flowers to attach.

"Goddamn it. Do you think I want her? You think I'd rather roll around on a blanket with her than you?"

With glassy eyes, she whispers, "Just let it go."

My patience snaps, and everything I'm holding in feels primed to break through. "Christ, Romy, don't you get it?"

She whips around and throws her arms in the air. "What am I supposed to get, Zander?"

"That I fucking want you. That I made a huge mistake ghosting you. I only did it because... fuck, Romy, you scare me. You scare the shit out of me." My voice raises, and I hate myself for allowing my emotions to be so uncontrolled.

She steps off the stool to square off with me. "And what, you think I'm not scared? You think I'm such a believer in true love and fate and kismet that what I felt when I was with you didn't scare me? It did, Zander. I signed your stupid NDA. I hid us from my family. I did that because I believed in us and what I felt. Maybe some people would say I was naïve, but they weren't on that bus with you. You're the one who didn't believe in us. Who still doesn't believe in us."

Chest tight, I inch closer. "I was an idiot."

"Yeah, you were."

I take the flower in her hand and drop it in the bucket of water. "And now? What do you want?"

She scoffs. "God, if you think I'm going to say it, you're a fool."

"Come on, Romy. Trust me. I swear you can trust me."

She crosses her arms, cheeks red. "You first."

I blow out a breath. "Fine. You were the first woman I ever thought about having more with, and it scared the shit out of me. I've never felt deserving of love like that. Never thought I would know how to hold onto it. So, I pushed you away. I told DeSoto not to let you through. I figured you'd go away, forget about me and find the right guy, settle here, and have kids. Live happily ever after."

"Why do you think you know more than me? Don't you see the problem with that?"

"What's the problem?"

"I don't want anybody else."

Her words send a rush of adrenaline through my veins, and I can't get her in my arms fast enough.

I lean forward to kiss her, but she places her finger on my lips. "But, Zander, I can't be your toy. You can't play with me when you want and set me on the shelf when you're done and think I'll be there the next time you're interested." She places her hands on either side of my face. "I know you struggle with your demons, but I want to be the one who proves to you that you're worthy of love. But in order to do that, you have to promise not to run off or push away when you're feeling over-whelmed. If you can't do that, this won't work."

I stare into her brown eyes, eyes that haunted me the entire time we were apart.

"Goddamn it, you're not a toy, Romy." I grip her waist tighter. "You're everything. I'm trying my hardest to tell myself I deserve you. I want you. I want us. I want to try. But I don't know how to be a boyfriend. I don't know how to be—"

"Well, you're not going to learn by pushing everyone away, Zander. Letting me in is your first lesson. You have to try." Her hands don't leave me, and her eyes don't waver. "I need you to promise before I can even entertain this."

I swallow past the baseball-sized lump in my throat. She's right. I know she is. And even though the ghosts of my past are trying to scare me off, I'll try. "For you, I promise, I'll try. Only ever for you."

"Okay," she says as if I just asked her to go for coffee.

"Can I kiss you?" I inch closer.

"You sure as hell better."

"Fuck, Romy, c'mere." I wrap my arms around her waist and tug her to me, my lips crashing to hers.

Chapter Thirty-Three

ROMY

Our plan was simple.

Zander drops me off at the side of the lodge and parks the UTV.

He walks in by himself and goes up into his honeymoon suite.

I follow ten minutes later.

It's the longest ten minutes of my life.

We could barely stop kissing in the UTV, and now as I stand on the side of the building, watching the time tick down on my phone, all I can feel are his hands and lips on me.

Finally, the ten minutes pass, and I walk around and up the steps, trying to act as if I'm not on my way to have sex. My saving grace is that my mom isn't here. And the staff are distracted by the crew loitering around the reception area. I slide right by them, and once I turn the corner to the stairs up to the rooms, I finally breathe.

I tiptoe up the stairs, peeking around the corners like some stealthy hitwoman. Thankfully, the hallway carpet muffles the sound of my boots.

When I reach his door, I hesitate. I look down at what I'm

wearing, pull at my sweater and smooth out my hair, wishing I was dressed up rather than in jeans and a sweater.

The door opens, and a hand grabs my arm, pulling me into the room. Zander shuts it and cages me against the back of the door in one fluid motion. I did always love his moves.

"You're wasting time out there." He steps up to me, leaving one hand plastered above me against the door and the other holding my hip.

"Who says?"

"You will be once I'm done with you."

"You sure are doing a lot of talking." I set my hands on my hips, trying to be cool when I really want to jump him.

He laughs and leans in closer, his breath feathering my cheek. "Tell me what you want, Romy," he whispers.

Goose bumps scatter up my spine. "You're such a cocky bastard."

My fingers curl into his T-shirt, and I pull him toward me, lips locking with his. His tongue sweeps into my mouth, stealing my breath and every ounce of self-control I naïvely thought I'd come here with. He breaks away from our kiss long enough to drag his T-shirt over his head.

My gaze traces his broad shoulders, muscled chest, and the trail of hair that leads down past the waist of his jeans.

Zander smirks when he catches me staring. "See something you like?"

"Maybe." I bite my lip as if I can play the role of sex kitten.

His hand skims under my sweater, his palm hot against my stomach. "I want to get one thing clear before we continue." His fingers bend, and he cradles my stomach.

"Zan," I whisper.

He shakes his head. "I want to be clear about something." There's conviction in his voice, so I lift the hem of my sweater and cover his hand with mine. "I'm not doing this because of him or her. I went to you tonight because I want *you*."

I tighten my hand over his. "Thank you for telling me." I lean forward to kiss him, but he dodges my lips.

"I want to be sure you understand."

I chuckle. "I do. The baby is just a bonus."

"Yeah, just a bonus." He kisses me again, both of us losing ourselves once more.

We close the kiss and heave for a breath.

He lowers his forehead to press against mine. "You're overdressed."

"Am I now?"

He inches up my sweater, and I lift my arms, letting him pull it over my head. His gaze drops to my bra, and his tongue slides along his bottom lip.

"Jesus, Romy." His thumb brushes against the swell of my breast.

"Clasp is in the front," I offer, wanting to be naked with him.

He growls, his fingers dipping down and manipulating the clasp, so my breasts push the fabric to the sides. Then I'm bare for him, my breasts on display. He makes quick work of the bra, tossing it somewhere in the room. Leaning down, his lips close around my nipple, sucking and licking.

I gasp and clutch his hair. They're so much more sensitive than normal. "Zander—"

"Yeah, baby?" He flicks his tongue on my nipple, and my core tingles. He continues to savor me, and I squirm under his manipulation.

"Bed?"

"Good idea." He laughs, and in one motion, he scoops me up, then he places me on the mattress with care. He stands at the edge and stares at me.

"You are joining me, right?" I flick the button on my jeans, and his eyes follow the movement, watching me. I lower the zipper and hook my fingers into the sides of my jeans, wiggling them off my body. "I could use a little help."

He swallows audibly and grabs an ankle, tugging off one leg then the other. Again, his gaze coasts over my body. "Damn, Romy."

"You're terribly overdressed. Want me to undress you?"

He flicks the button of his jeans, and they hit the floor beside mine before I can even get up onto my knees. "Next time."

He crawls toward me, pinning me to the mattress with a mischievous grin.

"When did you become the bossy one?" he asks.

"When you became all touchy-feely." I run my fingers across his shoulder blades.

"Get used to it."

I giggle, but it dies quickly when his thighs nudge my legs apart, and he situates his hips between them.

"Yes," I pant, dragging his mouth to mine. "Just don't cry after sex, okay?"

"No promises."

We both chuckle until he presses me down with his pelvis, his hard length sliding against my slickness, and my whole body arches for him.

"Condom?" I manage, though my voice shakes.

"I haven't had sex since I've been with you. Got tested. You?"

I shake my head, staring into his dark eyes. "No one after you, and I got tested when they ran my bloodwork. All clear."

"And you can't get pregnant again, so..."

"No condom?"

He grins. "Fuck yeah."

The first push in steals my breath. He's big, stretching me inch by inch, filling me. My nails dig into his shoulders, needing something to hold onto.

"Jesus, you feel good," he groans against my ear.

"You too," I whisper, legs locking around him, desperate for more friction.

He moves tortuously slowly at first, and I beg as he moves with a maddening patience, dragging out each stroke. Then he drives deeper, harder, faster until all I feel is him, all I can hear is our ragged breaths and the rasp of his stubble against my skin.

"Finally, Romy," he practically growls. "Tell me you're mine."

I should roll my eyes at the caveman possessiveness of his words, but it strikes me deep, right in the sore spot where I've been so scared he'd never choose me. "I'm yours. Only yours."

He kisses me with a hunger that can't be abated, but it's tender all at once. My body clenches, pleasure barreling down on me.

"Fuck, you feel so damn good. Like you're made for me. I'm gonna take you again tonight. Tell me I can take you again."

"You can," I pant, pushing my orgasm back, not wanting this to be over.

"Romy." He groans my name like a prayer and a curse all in one, and my orgasm tumbles over.

I strip my mouth off his, crying out.

Zander follows seconds later, his breath hot and heavy in my ear. "Fucking Christ."

I feel the jerk of him and the heat between my legs as he explodes. After, he collapses on top of me, careful to keep too much of his weight from pressing down on me as we catch our breath.

"Remember that whole promise about our kid not coming out and saying the word *fuck*?"

"I'm doing a piss poor job. I know." He pushes my damp

hair off my forehead and kisses me. "New deal, I watch my language everywhere except when I'm inside you."

My head tips back, and I laugh. "Deal."

"You want my dirty mouth, huh?" His lips cast little kisses along my shoulder. "Say it."

"You weren't that dirty," I egg him on.

He picks up his head and looks down at me. "Challenge accepted."

I have no doubt he's going to meet that challenge and conquer it.

Chapter Thirty-Four

ZANDER

I'm not sure if it's the sliver of light streaming in through the drapes or the scent of her vanilla lotion, but I stir awake. For a moment, I don't open my eyes because if this is a dream and Romy's warm body really isn't next to me, I don't want to be dragged out of it.

Then she shifts beside me, her leg running along mine, and she lets out a little sigh. And damn, she's real. Romy Owens is naked in my bed, and I'd have to be such an idiot to screw this up again.

Her hair is a mess on the pillow. I brush a strand off her cheek, and her eyes blink open.

"Morning," I say before giving her a quick kiss on the lips.

Her lips tug into a half smile. "Morning."

God, I could live my life like this. What was I ever thinking, letting her go in the first place?

Her stomach growls, and I grin. "Want some food?"

"It is customary to feed someone after you make them expend so much energy."

I chuckle. I took her three times last night and could get

lost in her so easily again. But instead of kissing her the way I want to, I pull back. "We should talk."

The sheet rustles around her body as her brows lift. "That sounds... serious."

"We have some issues we have to face," I say, then kiss her one more time.

She watches me, doubt swimming in her eyes. I take her hand and place it flat against my chest.

"I don't know what kind of man I'm going to be, Romy, but I want you to know I want this to work. I'm going to try."

She swallows, looking at her hand over my heart. Then she looks away, rolls onto her back, and stares at the ceiling. "I want us too. But what does this mean?"

I let out a breath. "I thought I was pretty clear last night that I want you."

She turns on her side, her lips curving. "I know you want me, and I want you. But there's a lot that makes it complicated, Zander. Like... how do I get out of this room? Are you going to order breakfast for two? That'll invite gossip. At some point, we have to figure out what we want people to know." I open my mouth, but she continues. "I don't want to be sneaking in and out of your life. If this is going to work, I need to be part of it."

I chuckle, and she narrows her eyes. "What?"

I slide her toward me. "Can I talk now?"

"Sure."

I nuzzle my head into the crook of her neck, inhaling her scent, and as always, it makes me feel centered. "I want that too. I want it more than anything." I nod. "So, I say we order room service... for two people." I draw back to look into her eyes. "Or if you want to make a real statement, you get dressed in last night's clothes, and I'll escort you into that dining room holding my hand."

She smacks my arm, but her eyes sparkle. I want to tell her

I want that. I want the entire world to know she's mine. It's not my confidence in us holding me back but my worries that once she experiences everything that comes along with me, she won't want it.

"My god, can you imagine? Beau would go ballistic." She laughs as I kiss the hollow of her throat.

"I don't care," I murmur along her skin. "Beau is hired to consider my best interests, and he's done a damn good job of it all these years. But now…" I pause, softening. "I love him for it, but you're right—in order for this to work, I can't hide you away in a closet."

"I don't mind as long as you're in it with me." Her hands run up and down my back.

"Oh, if I had you in that closet again…" I slide my thigh between her legs, and she sighs.

"Damn, Romy."

I apply pressure to her core with my thigh, and she grinds against it. It would be so easy to let this conversation die and have her again, but I want this all out on the table before we move forward.

"I need something from you."

She leans back and stares into my eyes. "You know, you're asking for a lot. Carrying your baby, sneaking you off to town, now what?"

I place my hand on her stomach, enjoying the liberty of being able to do that at any time now. Her laughter dies, sensing this is serious.

"I don't want the pregnancy to come out yet. Not because I don't want the whole world to know you're carrying my baby, or even that I'm having a baby. I wish I could scream it to everyone I know. But, Romy, if this gets out, you have no idea how much your life will change. And you shouldn't have that stress on you when you're pregnant. So, let's… I'm happy to come out as a couple, but let's keep the baby under wraps a little longer. It will only make the attention you're already going to get that much worse."

She stares at me long and hard, and I worry this could be a sticking point for her. She's not the type of person to keep secrets, but if she's going to make it in my life, she has to learn. "Okay, but we're safe here on the ranch, right?"

She's so innocent, and it makes me love her even more. I hate that I'll probably taint that side of her over time. One day she's going to learn that being with me is so much stress, and she might not think it's worth it in the end.

"I don't know, Romy. I mean, we hope so. They all signed paperwork. I trust my crew for the most part. Nothing's come out yet, and I'm pretty sure people see that something is going on between us, but you never know. You can never be too sure. I just really want us to be careful, okay?"

She nods. "But as far as us, we can..."

I laugh. "Yeah, definitely."

"So that means you're going to order room service for two?" There's such a hopeful expression on her face that if I were standing, it would bring me to my knees.

"If that's okay with you."

She bites her lower lip and nods. "Yeah."

"And you're okay with your family knowing we're together?"

She laughs and falls against me, her arms winding around my neck, her bare breasts pressing to my chest. "Yes, of course. Why wouldn't I be?"

"Because I'm the bastard who pushed you away."

She shakes her head. "If you want us to move forward, Zander, you need to stop feeling guilty for that. Yeah, it was terrible, but it's in the past. So now we start fresh."

"Fresh." I let the word settle. God, when's the last time I had a fresh start anywhere?

She chuckles. "My god, there's such a thing as a fresh start,

Zander. Okay, so why don't you pick up that phone, order some room service for two, have it delivered, and then you can take me again before we face the world hand in hand?"

"God, you're the perfect woman." I kiss her and roll over to call down for breakfast.

A half hour later, we're still in bed, tangled in the sheets. She may have dozed off again, so I roll out of bed, tug on my sweats, and open the door.

Jensen holds out a tray for me.

"Ah... thanks." I quickly take it.

He doesn't say anything and wears no expression to say whether he knows that Romy's in here or not. I shut the door.

When I come back to the bedroom, Romy pulls the sheets tighter around herself, sitting up. I set the tray on the small table by the window. It's filled with eggs, bacon, French toast, coffee, tea, fruit—then my eyes stray to one item.

I lift the tray of cookies. "I think our secret might already be out."

She laughs and falls back against the headboard. "Of course. Pistachio cookies. My family. I swear they have cameras implanted in me where they can see everything I do."

"God, I hope they don't have cameras. Your father might never speak to me again."

"So, everybody probably already knows I'm in your bed. This is a little embarrassing."

I sit on the edge of the bed. "It's not embarrassing. Let them talk. Who cares? This is what we want, right? We want to be out in the open." I lean in to kiss her slow and steady.

Then we forget about the cookies and the breakfast tray. Because the second her mouth parts under mine, I'm only hungry for one thing.

"Enough energy for another round?"

She laughs against my mouth. "Always."

Then she's tugging off my pants, I'm lowering the sheet,

and we're right back where we were—two people who can't get enough of each other.

The sunlight streams through the curtains, catching a glint in her hair. I swear she's never looked more beautiful. Here and now, when she's smiling and flushed and *mine*.

She closes our kiss. "You do know what this means?"

"What?"

"Another family dinner." She laughs.

If I thought admitting I was the father of their grandchild was hard, now I've got to prove I'm actually worthy of their daughter. Hell.

Chapter Thirty-Five

ROMY

We're parked outside the softball field in the back of Zander's SUV, with DeSoto outside after he's done a perimeter check to make sure there aren't any wild bulls ready to chase us down. We're here early, so my legs are swung over his lap, and his hands are lazily massaging them.

"All right, so explain this to me again. Grown men and women are playing softball?"

"I don't know why it's such a big thing to you. Ranches play against other ranches. We have a really big rivalry with Wild Bull Ranch." I remember that when Zander was trying to get out of being at Plain Daisy Ranch, they were going to go to Wild Bull Ranch. "And just so you know, Wild Bull Ranch does not have a Romy. You should count yourself lucky you filmed your video at Plain Daisy Ranch."

He laughs. God, I love hearing his authentic, genuine laugh. And the way his head rocks back makes me a goner for him.

"Nobody has a Romy. Believe me, I know how lucky I am." His fingers slide higher under the hem of my shorts, brushing the inside of my thigh.

I press my hand over his. "Hey, you have a game to play. And I'm really sorry about where you are in the lineup. I'm not that strong of a hitter." Zander is taking my place on the team for this game.

"No problem. I don't need the pressure of trying to get a hit." He shifts, bringing me closer, his hand sliding under the denim waistband. His finger thrums against my panties, and I gasp.

"Zan," I whisper, knowing we shouldn't but not having it in me to fight him too hard.

"Goddamn it, Romy. Tell me you're wet for me right now."

"You're starting the dirty talk a little early, aren't you?"

"Are you?" He ignores my question.

He pushes past the edge of my panties, his finger coasting under the elastic. My head falls back against the window with a sigh.

"That's my girl. Wet and warm for me," he whispers.

"God, Zander..."

He withdraws his finger and brings it to his mouth, rubbing his bottom lip before snaking his tongue out and licking. "Open those jeans, Romy. Pull them down so I can see your pussy."

I straighten in the seat. "Oh my god, no! DeSoto is standing at the back of the truck. Are you crazy? We cannot do this here."

"Oh, yes, we can." His hands go to my hips, and he eases me back into the position I was in. "I might not be able to get off, but you sure as hell can."

"Then you're going to be sporting a hard-on in the middle of the game. That's not the bat you're supposed to be playing with out there."

He laughs, but God help me, he pops the button of my jeans, and I don't stop him. His fingers dive under the waistband, gliding along my stomach. That's all it takes. I slide the zipper down and scoot them low enough.

"There you go." His voice is laced with seduction, and I am here for it. He pulls my panties aside and stares, his teeth locking down on his bottom lip. "Shit. So perfect. So fucking perfect. And all mine."

His thumb lazily circles my clit.

"We should not be doing this." But there's zero fight in my voice.

"What do I have to do to get you to pull your shirt up and slide down those bra cups?"

"I am not going to sit in this car half naked for anyone to see."

My words don't stop Zander, and his thumb's lazy pace makes my heart race.

"That's a Zander Shaw perk. Tinted windows." He quirks his eyebrow.

"Oh, the perks." I chuckle low in my throat.

"Come on, baby. Show me those tits." He applies a little more pressure, and with it, the promise that I'll be coming soon if I cooperate.

God help me, I do what he asks. I tug my shirt up and pull down the cups of my bra.

"Just as perfect as your pussy." He leans forward and captures one nipple in his mouth, his teeth scraping along my sensitive skin, before he kisses the valley between my breasts. "I need you."

"You can't have me yet. You have to wait. Maybe we put a little wager on this."

He draws back and looks at me in the eye. "A wager? Sounds interesting."

In the meantime, his fingers work me over, sliding, circling, pushing me closer to the edge.

"These hormones make me lose the ability to fight you on this."

He withdraws completely, staring me in the eye. "Don't blame your hormones, baby. I'm getting you hot because I'm your boyfriend, and I know exactly how to get you off."

He plunges a finger inside me, and my head rocks back against the glass.

"There you go." His voice goes back to a seductive low tone.

Another finger joins the first, his thumb pressing just right. His tongue swirls over my nipple, every nerve ending sparking and traveling right down to my center.

"Come on, baby. I know you're close. Don't hold back." He shifts to my other breast, sucking hard, his pace between my thighs quickening.

I grip his forearm as though I'm afraid he's going to stop.

He lifts up and kisses my neck, his breath in my ear causing goose bumps to explode over my skin. "Squeeze my fingers. And after you come, I'm going to suck you off my fingers, so I have the taste of you on my tongue the entire game. And I'm going to play really good, baby. So good that you'll want to suck my cock tonight. You want that, right, baby?"

"Zan," I pant, my thoughts a jumbled mess.

"But I'm not going to come in that mouth, no. I'm going to come deep inside your warm, wet pussy." His voice is so low in my ear that I clench again, not wanting this to end. "That's it. Yes, I can feel how close you are, Romy. Now give it to me." He plunges deeper and sucks my earlobe into his mouth.

I close my eyes as he rockets me over that cliff. Stars burst behind my eyelids as I tense, then collapse against the seat as he slowly withdraws his fingers, the wet sound echoing in the small space.

True to his word, he brings his fingers to his mouth, eyes closing as though he's never tasted anything sweeter.

God help me. This man is going to be the death of me.

A bang on the window jolts me upright with wide eyes, but not Zander. He just leans back as though he knows no one will open the door until he says they can. I scramble, yanking my bra back in place, shoving down my shirt, and yanking my jeans back up.

Zander laughs the whole time. "Shit, baby. Calm down. Don't worry about it."

Then we hear DeSoto shout, "Emmett, get away from that fucking door!"

"It's game time," Emmett argues.

"They'll be ready when Zander says he's ready."

Knowing that DeSoto won't let anyone open the door without Zander's word, I straddle him. "Good luck today. I feel like I should've been the one giving you the orgasm for taking my spot."

"That's okay. I'm just playing for my reward later."

"I never actually promised you a reward."

"Baby, you'll be on your knees later tonight. Every time I'm at bat, I'll be thinking about impressing you more and more, so you'll want my cock tonight."

I laugh and kiss him one last time. "Good luck. Don't take it too seriously."

He grabs my ass, pulling me against him. "What do you mean, don't take it too seriously?"

"It's just a regular softball game against another ranch. Well... it is competitive. We're not playing Wild Bull Ranch tonight, but still. I think it's the second-best team."

He kisses my neck, then pats my ass. "All right, all right. We better get going."

We climb out of the SUV.

Emmett is halfway to the field by now. He must hear the

car door because he swings around. "Hey, Zander. Why don't you sing the national anthem?"

"Fuck no," Zander shoots back, laughing.

Almost everyone is here. Which means everyone knows I was in the SUV with Zander the whole time—probably saw it rocking.

I kiss him once more before heading to the bleachers, while he joins the crew in the dugout with Emmett.

Sadie, Gillian, and Briar stare at me, wearing their matching shirts—Jude's girl, Ben's girl, and Emmett's girl. Daisy is playing in the dirt with Wren and Leia in front of the fence. Colter is on his mom's lap.

Sadie nudges me when I sit down. "So it's true."

"What's true?"

"That you and Zander Shaw are a thing."

Heat rushes to my cheeks. I see now why Zander doesn't like the whole first and last name. It makes him sound more like a thing than a person.

Gillian rolls her eyes. "Please. You two are all anyone is buzzing about. Just confirm it for us."

I glance toward the field. Zander is throwing the ball back and forth with Emmett, muscles flexing, and then— God help me—his eyes catch mine, that half smile tugging at his lips.

"Yeah. We're together," I say.

The squeals erupt. Sadie fans herself while Briar swoons.

Finally, Briar says, "I was starting to think we'd have to lock you two in the barn until you admitted it."

Before I can answer, Beau drops onto the bleacher beside me. "Grown men playing softball. This is what happens when you have too much free time."

"You don't sound impressed." I chuckle.

"Yeah, well. Why would I be? I've lived through this."

"You played baseball?" I ask.

"Fuck no. Foster care picnic every year. Zander was the strikeout king. Couldn't hit the ball for shit."

I glance at Zander again. "No way. He hasn't said anything about that."

"We used to bet on how many swings it'd take."

"Well, I'm sure he's going to do great." I straighten my back.

Beau laughs. "Said like any good girlfriend."

I turn toward him. I assume Zander has told Beau, but we haven't talked about it. Is Beau happy or upset about the status of our relationship? He's smiling, smug and cocky, but still smiling, so maybe he's okay with it?

The game starts, and we all face the diamond. It takes the second inning before Zander gets up to bat, and after Beau's insight, I'm more worried than I was before.

Zander steps into the batter's box. The pitch comes. *Crack.* The ball soars over the shortstop's head and skips into the outfield. Zander sprints out of the box, rounds first, and slides into second. When he stands, his eyes seek me out.

I clap and cheer for him along with the other ladies.

"Well, looks like his strikeout days are over." Beau shakes his head. "Must be the Romy effect."

Something warms in my chest.

The game passes in a blur of banter, laughter, and cheers. And when it's over, we've won. Zander went three-for-three.

Beau is still shaking his head. "I can't fucking believe it."

Later, as the bleachers clear, I turn to Beau. "Hey," I say, pulling him aside.

He puts his hands in the pockets of his slacks, smirking.

"You know?"

"Yeah, I know." He rolls his eyes.

"And?" I bite my lip and fidget with my fingers.

He chuckles and shakes his head. "Listen, Romy, my friendship with him comes first. He's my best friend. My brother. I want him to be happy. I want him to have every-thing he wants. You make him happy, so that makes me happy. Will there be more bullshit to deal with as a result of this? You bet your ass. You and him and…" His gaze falls to my stomach. "Complicates a lot of shit. But I'll do it with a smile because I love the guy."

"Can I help with any of it?"

He smiles and shakes his head at me. "Yeah, I get why he fell for you. Just don't argue about your security detail."

"What? Oh my god, that's not going to happen."

He sobers and tilts his head. "Romy, you don't know this world yet. You only saw a small percentage while you were on the bus. You're important to him. Which means you're impor-tant to me. So I need to make sure nothing happens to you."

"But it's just the ranch."

With a sigh, he opens his arms. "Let's take this slow, but don't think for a second that I don't welcome you into our pseudo family with open arms. That means as long as you're with him, you're stuck with me. I'm Uncle Beau. And good luck with him. He's not the easiest guy to deal with, so if you ever need someone in your corner, call me." He pulls me into a hug, and the warm feeling in my chest spreads further.

Zander leaves the dugout with the rest of my cousins and family.

Beau breaks away from me and slaps Zander on the back. "Way to go, buddy. Didn't live up to your reputation today."

I lean back, watching them laugh together, and I'm thankful that if Zander didn't have an easy childhood, at least he had Beau.

Then Beau's words echo in my head—security detail, a world I don't fully understand. I think we're in for a bumpy ride, but it's all worth it to see that smile aimed at me.

Chapter Thirty-Six

ZANDER

"We stick out like a sore thumb," Beau mumbles in my ear.

I've never been to a farmers' market in my life. I never thought I ever would. But I don't hate it. Booths line the main street, and families are talking with other families. Kids run around.

"Did you pay them or something?" I mutter to Beau.

Not one person has approached us. I told Beau about wanting to go into town, so people know I'm with Romy, and here we are. It's a coming out of sorts, but also because in order for me to feel secure leaving her when I go to edit the video, I want to experience the town a little more.

"No. You told me you wanted to come without any interference from me." His voice still holds a small amount of agitation.

The paps hover at the edges, pretending to browse jam jars and homemade soaps while their shutters click slyly. Or so they think. My security detail fans out—four men in dark jackets who stick out more than blend in—but DeSoto's the only one who stays glued to us, his gaze constantly roving.

And then there's the entire reason I'm here.

Romy walks slightly ahead of me, hair loose, one hand brushing over a basket of apples, talking to the vendor as if she's her best friend. Maybe she is her best friend. This is Romy's element, where she lives and shops. I never want to take her out of this town. I want her to remain in her innocent Willowbrook bubble.

"Stop it," Beau whispers, picking up a jar of carrots with a bemused expression.

"What?"

"She wants to be with you. And sure, she doesn't know exactly what it all means, but she's going to fight for you. So, wrestle those fucking demons and stop staring at her like she's about to turn around and tell you she's changed her mind."

Romy waves, and someone crosses the path to flag her down. Beau and I stand to the side, taking in a scene neither of us ever thought we'd be part of.

"What am I supposed to expect? That she'll be okay being chased down for a picture? That the shitty keyboard warriors—"

"Yes. Because that's part of being with you. It might take some time for you guys to figure it out, but you will. Stop feeling guilty about it."

Romy glances over her shoulder and smiles mid-conversation, then eventually she hugs the person goodbye and nods for us to follow her.

"Go and keep your head out of dark places." Beau slaps me on the back.

I head up to walk alongside Romy, and the crowd presses close near a stall selling candles. My hand skims over the small of her back, just a light brush, fingers spread wide enough that I feel the heat of her through her sweater. She relaxes into my touch, and her back rests against my chest as she picks up and smells a variety of candles.

"Smell this," she says and holds it up to my nose.

I bend and smell. "Doesn't smell nearly as good as you," I whisper in her ear.

Romy doesn't look at me, but I see pink creep up her neck. She puts the candle down, and we continue to walk down the road, stopping at different booths.

Every chance I get, I touch her. A brush of her fingers here. A graze of my knuckles there. My hand rests against her hip when we step aside for a family with a double stroller.

Nobody stares for too long. A few smile politely, some nod. One older man selling honey gives me a firm handshake and welcomes me to Willowbrook. It's strange, as if I'm camouflaged or something. Everyone acts as though I'm not who I am while the paps keep taking pictures.

I catch DeSoto's tight jaw. He hates crowds. They're too unpredictable. But I'm... weirdly calm. Maybe because the only thing I'm focused on is Romy.

She leans over to smell a bouquet of flowers, and I nearly lose it. The way her hair falls forward, the soft curve of her neck exposed. My hand twitches at my side, itching to cup the back of her head and kiss her in the middle of the market.

Instead, I step closer, my arm brushing hers. She glances up, eyes flicking to mine for half a second, and the corner of her mouth lifts.

Yeah. I could get used to this life.

"Zander?"

I look up and see Zara Sloane walking toward us. Her hair is in two pigtail braids with oversized sunglasses perched on top of her head. She holds three different bags, looking like she's lived here her entire life and fits right in.

"Wow, small world!" She laughs at her own joke. "How adorable are these little vendors? Did you see the macramé booth? And the vegan donuts! They're giving samples, you have to try one." Her attention finally lands on Romy, and she says Romy's name as if they're best friends.

"Hi, Zara." Romy lifts her hand and eyes Zara's bags. "Man, you've really done well today."

I step closer to Romy, putting my arm around her waist, and Zara's eyes flick from my hand to me with her eyebrows raised. A small smile tips her lips. "You didn't find anything?" She frowns.

"Well, I live here, so... but I saw a lot of cute things." Romy shrugs.

"It's great here. I was telling my friend we should do a girls' trip here sometime. I was talking to..." She looks toward the sky. "She's blonde and has a baby on her hip a lot."

"Briar," Romy answers.

"Yes! And she was telling me they can put together a whole thing for us. And we can maybe camp outside."

"You're going to camp?" Beau says, joining us.

"Yes, Beau, I'm not one of those high maintenance girls." She rolls her eyes at him.

"If you say so." He laughs.

She narrows her eyes at him and turns back to Romy. I have to admit, I love that she's giving all her attention to Romy, but I'd like us to get out of this conversation so I can have Romy all to myself.

I open my mouth to end it, but Zara claps. "Let's grab lunch! Someone said The Sprout House has the best chicken sandwich." She slides her arm through Romy's and escorts her away from me.

I stare at Beau in disbelief, but he just laughs.

The Sprout House is packed, sunlight streaming through big windows onto reclaimed wood tables. It smells like roasted vegetables and fresh herbs, and the hostess can't take her eyes off me but composes herself enough to lead us to a booth in the back.

I slide in next to Romy. DeSoto and the four others take seats at a nearby table, scanning the room. Beau sits across from me, next to Zara, who can't stop gushing about the farm-to-table feel of the restaurant. Beau looks as if it's taking everything in him to pretend he's interested.

I tune Zara out, turning my focus to Romy.

Romy's thigh presses against mine, and I don't move. Neither does she. My hand drops casually to my lap. Then over a bit. I brush my fingers against the outside of her thigh. She picks up the menu and turns to me, giving me a *stop it* look.

Beau looks up from his menu. "Everything good over there?"

"Fine," Romy says quickly, cheeks flushed.

I smirk and slide my hand higher. She remains rigid.

Zara puts her finger on the top of Romy's menu and pulls it down. "Do they have kombucha?"

"Why don't you look at your own menu?" Beau says.

My hand slides higher. My palm settles firmly just beneath the juncture of Romy's thighs. Her breath hitches, and her body tenses.

Beau gives me a look, telling me to stop doing whatever it is I'm doing. I bite back a laugh, leaning closer so my shoulder brushes Romy's, covering the movement under the table. Her hand drops to her lap, fingers brushing mine, and I wait for her to push me away. She doesn't.

My pinkie strokes the inside of her thigh, and I slide my fingers to weave between her thighs. She presses her thighs together, trapping my hand, and it's the hottest damn thing that her pussy is only inches from my fingers.

Zara and Beau talk about the video and wrap up and when we'll be editing. She says she's going back to Nashville too and that we should all get together for dinner while I'm there. Romy must be too distracted because she doesn't question me about Nashville. We haven't had that conversation yet. The one where I tell her I gotta go away for a little while.

God, she's beautiful flustered, and I try to stay composed. She lets me push just far enough that she's squirming, but not as far as I wish we could go.

I lean in, my lips brushing her ear. "Relax. You look guilty."

"Because I am," she whispers back, barely moving her lips.

"Good."

The waitress comes over, and we give her our orders. I leave my hand on Romy's leg the rest of the meal, stroking lazy patterns against her thigh, keeping her on edge. She doesn't move it. She doesn't tell me to stop. And every time Zara goes on another tangent, I swear Romy opens her thighs a little wider.

The reputation of this place is well earned. It is indeed the best chicken sandwich I've ever had.

We leave The Sprout House with Zara going on about starting a pop-up goat yoga class in town. DeSoto ushers us through the door, scanning the sidewalk. The paps are still there, cameras clicking, but the townsfolk keep pretending not to notice.

Romy walks beside me, chin high, pretending I didn't spend lunch making her squirm. I slide my hand in hers, weaving our fingers together.

She turns to me, looking surprised, but then she relaxes and leans her head on my shoulder for a moment. I take the opportunity to kiss the top of her head.

I'm sure the cameras are buzzing, but I don't care. I want the world to know she's mine because this is my future. Her and the baby growing inside her.

Chapter Thirty-Seven

ROMY

I t's almost midnight when my phone buzzes on the nightstand. I know it's him before I even roll over.

I swipe the screen, and sure enough, his name lights up.

You awake?

I grin in the glare of the phone screen, biting my lip.

Yes.

Naked?

I laugh quietly.

Nope. Pajamas. Very unsexy pajamas.

You look sexy in everything you wear.

I glance down at my flannel pants and the oversized "Harvest Depot Fall Festival" tee with stains on the front.

Believe me, you're wrong.

Only one way to end this argument. Take them off.

Please tell me you're not going to ask me to send you a pic.

Nah, too chancy. I don't want anyone seeing what's mine.

I shake my head, unable to stop smiling.

You sure like to stake your claim.

Three dots blink.

Do you not like it?

Heat licks through me, which is ridiculous given he's not even here. He knows exactly how to push me.

I didn't say that.

Good. So back to the pajamas…

I drop the phone to my chest. I'm falling so fast for him, those fears are prickling to surface even though he's given me no reason to think he isn't my future and my forever. After the farmers' market and the pictures that surfaced of the two of us, he's only doubled down.

Beau is busy making sure things don't get too crazy. I've stayed off socials like they both told me to, but I heard Beau talking to Lottie and Poppy the other day about how they need to stay out of the comments sections and that they aren't my protectors. I can only imagine what they're saying to people on there.

I finish typing my message to Zander and hit Send.

> You have a good imagination. Use it and put me in something really sexy. Where I don't feel bloated and huge.

My stomach has grown, the baby bump starting, and I'm addicted to placing my hand on it.

> Look out your window.

I frown, heart hitching. I push off the covers and walk across the room, then tug back the curtain.

"Oh my god," I whisper.

Zander is climbing up the side of the house on my mom's old trellis that we haven't done anything with in ages.

I fling the window open, and the cooler air rushes inside. "Are you insane? Beau is going to murder me if you fall."

"Well, you refused to strip, so I figured I should offer a hand." He hauls himself up another couple of feet.

"I should shut the window."

"But you won't." He hoists himself onto the sill with alarming grace, sliding one leg over. His boot slips against the siding, and my stomach plummets, my arms reaching for him.

"Zander!"

But he catches himself, laughing under his breath, and tumbles into my room in one piece. He straightens. "See? Perfectly fine."

"Get ready for Poppy to storm in here any minute with something to beat you with."

He laughs, and I shut the window.

I fold my arms, trying not to smile too big. "We're adults. I would have opened the door for you."

"Nah, this is romantic." His gaze flicks down my body. "Sorry to start this argument again, but you were wrong. You're sexy in flannel."

I glance at myself and shake my head.

He steps closer, hands finding my hips. "Baby, that shirt is hiding everything I want to see."

I roll my eyes. "You're impossible."

His fingers coast up under the hem of my shirt. My pulse skitters, and his eyes remain on mine as his fingers inch up.

He dips his head, and his lips graze my ear. "Take it off, Romy."

"You came this far. I'd hate to ruin your quest."

He tugs the fabric upward. "You're too kind to me. We'll do it together. Arms up, baby."

I raise my arms, letting him peel the shirt off me. He drops it onto the floor.

His gaze drags down me as though he's memorizing every inch. "See, so damn sexy." He slides his hand down the slope of my waist, dipping beneath the waistband of my pants.

"Are we having a sleepover?" My breathy voice gives me away.

"Hell yeah we are, but I forgot my pajamas, so I guess I have to sleep in the nude."

"Too bad." I give him a mock frown.

Then he kisses me. Hard and fast with a hunger I'm growing addicted to. Our banter dissolves, our mouths clash, his hands roam. My knees hit the mattress, but he holds me steady.

He pulls down my pants. "Commando? You forgot to mention that in your text."

"Sorry."

"It's okay, we're even." He unbuttons and unzips his jeans, pulling them down his body, and his dick springs free.

My hands grapple for the hem of his shirt, tearing it off his body.

"Can you be a good girl and keep quiet? You'll wake the whole house."

I swat his shoulder. "Good girl?"

He brings me flush to his body, and his hard length hits my stomach. "No?"

I shrug. "I don't hate it."

He laughs and nudges me onto the bed, climbing over me. He's already lowering himself, placing kisses along my stomach. "Say you missed me."

"I missed you."

"Good girl." He quirks an eyebrow with that half smile on his lips. He pauses at my stomach and kisses it again. "You're showing."

I nod.

"This makes you so damn sexy, you have no idea." He presses his hands gently on my belly. "Mine," he says. Not in the possessive way he does during sex, but more to himself as though he still can't believe we're his. He inches down, his shoulders nudging my thighs open. "Say it."

"I'm yours," I affirm, and he smiles right before his mouth slips between my legs.

His mouth is hot and soft, his tongue sliding up and down as his hands grip my hips, holding me still as though he's not about to let me get away.

"Shit," I whisper, my head falling to the pillow.

His groan vibrates along my skin, and his tongue circles my clit in measured strokes, as if he's taking his time.

"Zander, oh my god—" My hands whip down to his head, fisting his strands, and he growls, dragging his tongue lower, plunging inside me.

He pulls back and smirks, lips glistening. "Look at me. I want your eyes on me when my mouth makes you come."

I tremble from the command in his voice, and I drag my gaze down my body to meet his gaze. Seeing his messy hair and his lust-drunk eyes undoes me, taking me halfway there already.

His mouth closes over me again, sucking my clit, and my world tilts. Pleasure floods through me.

"Zander—" I cry out, crashing hard.

But he doesn't stop until I'm whimpering and weakly pushing his shoulders, trying to clamp my legs shut because I'm so sensitive. Then he pulls away, resting his chin on my stomach and licking his lips.

Why is that so hot?

"Always so sweet," he says hoarsely, elbowing over me until the tip of his dick nudges at my entrance. "I'll never get enough of you."

He kisses me deep and thoroughly, and I taste myself on his tongue. It only spurs my desire.

"You're—" I moan when he slips the tip inside me. "You're insatiable."

"And yet..." He thrusts deep, and my words and thoughts collapse in an abyss of pleasure.

We move together as though we've been doing this forever, and he whispers the filthiest things in my ear, making me flush and tremble.

When I come, it rips through me so hard I'm certain Poppy or Scarlett must've heard. He follows, collapsing against me, his laughter muffled against my neck.

"You gave us away," he whispers.

"Because of you." I swat his shoulder.

The banter fades, and for a while, we just lie there, tangled limbs, catching our breath.

He strokes my hair, softer now. "You drive me insane, you know that?"

"Good," I whisper.

His lips brush mine in the most tender way, and tears sting in my eyes. I could stay here forever.

He pulls back, eyes shadowed. "Romy..." A chill rushes over my body from his tone. "I have to leave to go edit the video."

My heart stutters. I knew the time for him to leave was coming, but I didn't realize how soon it would be. "When?"

"Couple days," he admits.

I stare at him, trying not to show how upset this makes me. We knew his job wouldn't make this easy. "Okay. Does this mean that I have to invest in sexy pajamas?"

He chuckles and kisses me briefly. "No, I like your flannel ones."

His arms wrap around me, and I hold him. I'm going to be strong, and we're going to get through this.

Then he slips down and kisses my stomach. "Don't grow too fast, little one. And be good for Mommy."

Tears sting my eyes, but I push them back when he crawls back up and moves my hair off my face.

"We're going to be fine," I say, trying to reassure him I can handle this, and I'm not going anywhere.

He doesn't say anything, but he holds me the rest of the night as though he worries I'm the one running off.

Chapter Thirty-Eight

I lean back in my chair, the glow from the monitors making the room feel like a cave. It's dark and suffocating, and I've never missed Romy more. Saying goodbye was the hardest thing I've ever done, but I have to do my job in order to give her and our child everything they need. I never want her to think about or worry about money. There's no fucking way the two people who mean the most to me are ever going to feel how I did growing up.

I rub the stubble on my jaw, my eyes bloodshot from staring at the same damn timeline for hours—weeks, really. I thought I could knock this out much faster than apparently is possible. I mean, I've never actually edited a video before, but I didn't think it would be this hard to capture the perfect visual rendition to match the words.

It's been a constant argument with Jack. All the footage is there. The lake, the ranch, the picnic, the horse riding. Zara did an amazing job at my side. But something is off.

Something doesn't fit when I place the track over the video. It just seems... jarring. It feels wrong.

"Fuck," I mutter, and I slam down my mouse. The sound echoes through the cramped room.

"You're gonna break the equipment," Beau says. He leans against the doorframe, arms crossed, giving me that look—to calm the fuck down before I have a stroke.

I spin in my chair. "Everything's off. The lighting, the timing. It's just not right."

"It looks fine. Hell, it looks more than fine. You're driving yourself nuts over nothing."

"It's not fine. Something's wrong, and I can't figure out what it is."

But that's a lie. I know what it is, and my chest tightens because it's more than that—

How can I do this when it's the first song I've ever written for a woman? It's the first thing that's ours—mine and Romy's. It's proof that she wasn't a secret, that she meant more to me back then, before I pushed her away.

We built this together. And it feels wrong that she's not the one in this video with me. It won't be perfect otherwise.

Beau pushes off the wall and drops into a chair. He studies the screen, frozen on the lake scene with Zara in my arms. "You've been at this for weeks. You need air. You need food. Sleep. Hell, a shower would be nice."

I don't even chuckle at his attempt at humor. "I just want to be done. If I'm done, I can go be with Romy. I can go back to the ranch."

"It doesn't need to be perfect. Hell, nothing ever is."

There's truth in what he's telling me.

"I don't know. I just feel like it needs to be... I need to do the song justice." I run my hand through my hair.

"Please don't tell me you're thinking what I think you're thinking." He gives me that look he always does when he knows I'm about to cause him stress and cost myself a shit-ton of money.

"What do you think I'm telling you?"

"That the wrong girl is in that video." Beau nods at the screen.

"She hasn't heard the song yet," I admit. I've been keeping it from her because I wanted to present it to her in a perfect package, at the perfect time.

"I figured you'd already serenaded her in some broken-down barn on their property one night." I look at Beau, and he smirks. "Come on, not my best line, but you're clearly head over heels in love and willing to do that kind of sappy shit for her."

I shrug because I can't really argue. I would do that for her.

"Once she hears the song, she'll know. It's pretty damn clear." He leans back in his chair, crossing his ankle on the opposite knee.

"You knew the song was about her this whole time?"

He gives me a *you're an idiot* look. "Fuck, man. I'm your best friend. Of course I knew. Why do you think I haven't given you any shit for this long-ass process?"

"Goddamn it. I knew you knew." I guess to a certain extent, I thought I was hiding it. And that's why I look him square in the eye. "Either I cut Zara out entirely, or I refilm it."

Beau's face sours as if he ate bad fish. "I figured we were on our way to the latter option. You do realize this pushes everything back, right?"

I hadn't really thought about that. To film the video over with Romy, I would first have to get her to agree to it, and I'm not sure she would want to do it pregnant. So we'd have to wait for the baby to come, then film the entire thing over.

"I don't know. It just looks so commercialized. There's nothing authentic about it. Nothing real. Nothing natural."

"Because it's the wrong girl," Beau says matter-of-factly.

"Yeah. And I don't know what I'm supposed to do about that."

"Listen. Take the weekend. Clear your head. Shit, go back to Willowbrook. Spend the weekend with your girl and come back refreshed and see what you think."

As much as I want to see her, I don't want to go for a weekend and leave again. It will only make this harder. "No, I'm not doing that. I just want to finish this so I can get back to her for more than a weekend."

"So you're gonna try to force something to happen with this when you don't even feel like it's the right thing?" He quirks an eyebrow and lowers his leg, resting his forearms on his thighs, staring at me like he does when he thinks my ideas are stupid.

"Like you said, it's a waste of money—"

"It is, but if you can't live with it, let's just do it."

I stare at the screen and figure maybe I can make this work. Just so I can get back to her and not spend another couple million.

"All right." He stands. "Well, I'm leaving for the night. I suggest you do the same. I'll see you back at the house."

"Yeah. All right."

He leaves with a clap on my shoulder. I don't suspect he'll be home when I get to the house we rented because he's been gone every night we've been here. I haven't asked where he's been going. If he wanted me to know, he'd tell me.

I stare at the clip I'm supposed to edit. I think I can do this. We have some solos of me in the barn. I can't cut Zara out completely, but I can probably do enough to make it work.

But as soon as I think it, I spot Romy in the background on a shot that's not meant for the video, and she's laughing at something Beau said. My insides feel as if they've split in two.

Before I can talk myself out of it, I grab my phone. It's late, but she picks up on the second ring. It's dark, but I can make out that she's lying in bed.

"Hey." Her voice is soft, a little scratchy.

"Did I wake you?"

"No," she says. But she's not nearly as convincing as she hopes.

I shut my eyes, imagining her alone in her big bed. "I think it might be a little longer. I need more time with the video."

There's a pause and a quiet, "Oh."

The weight of that one word layers on the guilt.

"You don't sound thrilled." I try for a light tone that I know neither of us feels.

"No. It's fine. I understand. You know I understand. It's just... the ranch feels so empty."

"Without me?"

"Beau... and the crew." She chuckles.

I grip my phone tighter, my knuckles aching. I want to crawl through the line and slip into bed with her and press my face into her hair, smell her, and remind myself that she's who I'm doing this for.

"I'm just kidding. It's you. It's lonely here without you."

"It's lonely here without *you*." I try to push away all the emotion clogging my throat. I change the subject from longing because that's not going to change. "Show me."

She laughs softly. "Show you what?"

"You know."

She makes a sound. There's a shuffle, then suddenly the camera flips, and I see her curled on her bed. She flips on a lamp, and I catch her tired eyes. She adjusts the phone, angling it toward her tummy, and the air gets sucked out of my lungs.

She's showing the gentle curve of her stomach that I haven't touched in weeks. My entire body aches with regret for missing her stomach growing inch by inch.

"God, you're beautiful."

She makes a face, embarrassed. "I feel like a balloon."

"You look—god, you're gorgeous. No movements yet, right?" I panic, feeling as if I've been gone for six months.

"No. No movement. I did feel a flutter the other day, but I'm not sure if it was the baby or something I ate."

The silence that follows is thick between us, and my chest feels as if it's cracking open because I'm not there to lay my hand over her warm skin.

"I wish I could touch you," I say.

"I hate this distance."

"Me too."

"Hey," she says.

In her tone, I hear it. I knew this could be coming. I had hoped it wouldn't, and I probably should've dealt with it head on, but I didn't want to upset her if it wasn't on her radar.

"I saw something online," she says.

"You're not supposed to be online, baby."

"I know. It just popped up. I wasn't trying to find it. We went out to dinner. Some woman in Nashville—"

My blood spikes. "Please don't believe what you read. Ever. We talked about this." I sigh.

The edge of my voice is sharp and protective and filled with anger. Not at her, but them. At anyone who would make up shit and upset her.

Her eyes search mine through the screen. "Was it true?"

I rake a hand through my hair. "No. It was Jack's wife. She tripped, and I was the one who caught her. He was there too. It was a late dinner after editing."

Beau brought me the picture the next day and said he thought he'd gotten it squashed. Said I should tell Romy just in case. And I didn't want to bring it up, so it's my fault she's questioning me now.

The longer her silence lasts, the harder the knot in my gut twists and tightens.

"Romy, you are the only one. You know that, right?"

She nods, but her smile doesn't reach her eyes. "I just... I don't like being so far away. It makes it easier to believe things I shouldn't."

Her honesty stabs me clean through like the blade of a sword. Panic flares through my bloodstream, afraid that I'm going to lose her because of who I am.

"Please don't let doubt creep in. Not about me and not about us." There's a pleading note to my voice.

Her eyes glisten, and I can tell she's fighting back the tears.

"Just hurry back," she says.

"I'm trying."

We talk for a while. I tell her about Beau riding my ass, trying to act like a parent, on me about my diet. She tells me about how pistachio cookies don't taste the same without me there.

When the lull in the conversation comes—when I know the conversation's going to have to end soon so she can get some sleep—I blurt out, "Come with me."

"What?"

"When I start the interview circuit, the promo stuff for the single. Come with me."

Her lips part, surprise etched across her face. "You're serious?"

"Deadly. I don't want to be away from you. Can you get time away from The Knotted Barn?"

For a moment, I let myself imagine having her by my side, her waiting just off stage for me to be done.

She studies me for a beat. "I think I can pull it off. I— we're going into the slow season, and I'm sure my mom would handle things for me for a little while. But I mean... I'll be showing."

Right. So far we've kept the pregnancy quiet, and with the colder weather, Romy wears a lot of sweaters, so thankfully, no one in Willowbrook has caught on. But on the press tour, it will be harder to hide the bump.

I'm not sure if she can hear my thoughts.

"I'd have to hide out probably, but—I think I'd like us to try," she says.

"Really?"

"I mean, this whole you being gone thing isn't working. At least for me. Not that I won't do it. Don't think that, but I miss you so much. Maybe we see what it's like if I go with you for a little while."

"I'd love for you to be with me."

She smiles. A little soft. A little hesitant.

I'll have to find a way to protect her from all the noise, the rumors, the spotlight that is my life.

"Okay, I'm gonna go get some sleep. You know, I *am* growing your baby."

"They're never gonna want to come out," I say.

"Oh, I think... we're gonna make them come out." She laughs again.

"God, I can't wait to be with you."

"Hey," she says before we're about to hang up.

"Yeah?"

"What about that single? I haven't even heard any of it yet."

"You will. I promise."

"Okay. Good night, Zander."

"Night, baby."

I hold onto the phone, the silence stretching between us. I don't want to hang up. I don't want to stop hearing her breathe. I don't want to stop closing my eyes and imagining that she's right next to me.

"Okay, you gotta hang up," she says.

"So do you."

She giggles. "Good night, Zan."

She hangs up, and I stare at the screen, thinking of her laughing. Yeah, time to figure this out and get home to my girl.

Chapter Thirty-Nine

ROMY

I'm pacing around the barn as if I'm trying to get this baby out—which I'm not. We've still got about four months to go, this baby and me.

I run my hands over my belly that has grown pretty well. Strings of pastel-colored balloons hang along the rafters, and the table where cupcakes are lined is half blue, half pink. Everywhere I look, our family's laughter bursts around the room. But we're missing one important person.

My stomach is tight, and my palms are damp, and it has nothing to do with the baby. It's the anticipation because Zander should have already been here.

He's been gone for the last week, back in his studio. He was able to come home for a little while after the video editing but has had to leave for shorter trips. This has been our life— him coming and going and me staying behind.

But the interviews are next, and in two weeks, we're gonna leave this ranch together. I'll hide out as much as I possibly can, which I realized would be even more important when I woke up one day, and my stomach had popped.

We're still keeping our secret from the world.

The public knows that we're dating, and there have been stories in the press every time Zander even seems to run into a woman. Even if he's just getting coffee and opening the door for a woman, it turns into *they went there together, it was the morning after*. They accuse him of stepping out on me—his sweet little small-town girl, as they like to refer to me.

"Oh my god, stop pacing, Romy." Sadie picks up a blue-frosted cupcake. "You're making me dizzy."

"I'm not pacing." My hands automatically rest on my belly. It's become their favorite resting place.

"You're nesting. Like, in motion." She grins, blue frosting smeared along her upper lip. "His plane landed, didn't it?"

I swallow hard. Because yes, it did. And obviously, we'll wait. But I still wish he was already here—because I miss him. This whole week, as with every time he has to go away, it's felt like torture being away from him.

Clearly, we are not meant to be in a long-distance relationship. The ranch has felt so empty since he left. And not only him—I mean, the whole crew left with him. Turns out I wasn't ready for my reality to go back to normal.

The barn doors open.

I hear murmuring, the buzz of voices, and someone says, "Zander." My heart launches into my throat.

There he is.

He and Beau walk in, while DeSoto stands at the edge of the barn. Zander strides in wearing a black button-down and black jeans. He takes off his ball cap that had been pulled low and searches the large room. He says hi to everybody, shaking hands, slapping backs. But his gaze keeps moving over everyone.

I watch for a second, so happy he's actually here.

Then I walk toward him.

Our eyes catch, and he says a halfhearted goodbye to whoever he's talking to. He crosses the room, ignoring the other handshakes, and catches me in his arms. He spins me once, my burgundy dress trailing around after me. I hug him as tears streak down my face.

"Jesus, I missed you," he murmurs into my neck, his breath hot and ragged. "I feel like your belly has grown so much in a week."

I swat him, tears still running down my face. "I know. I told you I felt like I was getting bigger."

"Yeah. But seeing it…" He places one hand on my stomach and the other on my cheek. "I'm so happy to be home. So happy to be with you. And I'm so fucking happy you're coming with me the next time I leave this ranch."

Brooks claps him on the back, and Beau makes some smart-ass comment about what a grumpy ass Zander has been all week. My mom hands Zander a drink, and suddenly every-one's around us. They all want to ask how it's going, and he gets swallowed up by my family.

He's smiling and laughing, but he keeps his hand tucked in mine and squeezes it every once in a while, as if he's saying, *I'm yours. Always remember, I'm yours.*

He's done a great job of squashing all those fears inside me, and I can't wait until I can go away with him—to see what it would be like if I dared to change my life. If I dared to leave The Knotted Barn and stayed with him on the road.

Because that's what has to happen if we're ever going to make this work. I know that now.

I lean up to his ear and say, "You're mine tonight."

He turns to me and locks me in his arms, moving us away from the others. "I'm always yours."

A grin tugs at his mouth, but there's a promise in his eyes of the sinful things he's going to do to me tonight. And I cannot wait. The hormones that come with being five months pregnant are hard. I've heard other women talk about it, but I can't believe how horny I am all the time.

We're interrupted by someone clapping.

Emmett tells everybody it's showtime. He's going to do the gender reveal.

He has the canisters set up outside that will blow up and release the color that will indicate the gender of the baby. We all go outside on the snow-dusted balcony.

Briar comes up to me and says, "Emmett's been worried, so I hope you love it."

I nod. "I'm sure I will. I gave him the envelope the doctor gave us last week."

She shrugs. "I hope so. You know, he had to rework his plan. There was a shipping problem, so he had to get the canisters through Amazon."

I smile and squeeze her shoulder. "I'm not worried."

"Let's go, Emmett!" Ben shouts down. "It's freezing."

"I'm the one freezing my balls off," he calls up.

"Oh, come on. Just do it," Lottie says.

"We're working on it!" Bennett shouts from beside Emmett.

All the cousins are pestering him to get going with it.

They're looking down at one of the canisters and talking intently as if they're trying to figure something out down there, but I don't really know what it is. Zander looks at me, and I mouth, "It's fine. It'll be fine."

"He does the gender reveals for the ranch," I say. "I'm sure he knows how to work these powder things, right?"

Emmett gives a thumbs-up and walks into the vineyard where he has the rest of the canisters set up.

Then someone uses the audio system to start a countdown. "Three... two... one..."

A big puff of purple smoke shoots out.

We all kind of stare at each other.

"Is that supposed to be pink?" my mom asks.

"I don't know..." I frown.

Then green smoke shoots up to the sky.

"I was afraid of this," Briar says next to me, covering her face with her hands.

Poppy mutters, "Oh, Jesus Christ. I can't believe we left these two buffoons in charge of it."

Then Bennett shouts, "Hold on, hold on, hold on! Just wait! There's more."

"More?" I look at Zander with wide eyes.

A shot of blue comes out.

"That's three," Zander whispers.

Then pink right after.

"Four." I rub my hand over my forehead.

"What does this mean?" my dad asks. "Wouldn't four colors mean four—"

"Oh my god! Are we having quadruplets or something?" I scream down at Emmett.

Zander and I stare at one another, then we both look at my stomach. Are there four babies in there?

"They would've told us if you were having four babies," he assures me.

"Four cousins!" Wren screams, and she and Leia dance around in a circle.

"Is this Emmett's idea of a joke?" I ask. "That he thinks we're having quadruplets and didn't know what colors to pick for each kid so he's just doing all of them? Like purple would be a girl, pink would be a girl, blue and green would be boys—"

Then a yellow one shoots off into the air, interrupting all of our thoughts.

"Oh my god. Five—what is five? What is the word for five babies?" I ask no one in particular.

"Quintuplets?" Briar cringes.

I stare at my belly. "There's no way. I'd be bigger if we were having quintuplets."

Zander just stares at my stomach, his face turning a shade whiter.

Briar passes Colter to Uncle Bruce and shouts, "Emmett! Get out here and tell us what's going on!"

Emmett comes out from the vineyard, and he and Bennett jog up the hill while a mix of colored smoke still lingers in the air.

"Wait, wait, wait, wait, wait!" Emmett pants as he finally makes it into The Knotted Barn.

Everyone goes back inside because we're freezing, but Zander's still standing on the balcony, staring at the sky and the smoke fading away. I return to his side.

"Five," he says. "Five."

I turn toward him, and Emmett blurts out, "No! I'm sorry. They sent me the wrong thing. They were supposed to be five of the same color. I don't know how it got mixed up."

Zander and I go back inside with everyone else.

"So, there's only one?" I ask.

"Yes! Yes, you're only having one baby." He laughs to himself but catches Briar's eye and sobers quickly.

"Emmett, tell us what it is," I say.

"I'm really upset about the surprise. I'm sorry. They're gonna hear from me, so don't worry."

"Emmett!" we all shout.

"Crap. A boy. You're having a boy!"

We all erupt into cheers and screams.

Zander pulls me into his arms, his face buried in my neck. "Oh, thank fuck. I mean, I want to have five kids with you, but I'm not sure I want to do it all at once."

I whisper into his ear, "It's a boy. We're going to have a son."

His voice cracks as if he might be crying, but then his tears spill hot onto my cheeks, and he kisses them away. We share a special moment right before my family presses in—hugging and clapping and shouting and giving us their congratulations in one big group hug.

By the time all the excitement dies down, my cheeks hurt from smiling and Zander's hand is welded to mine.

We carry on celebrating through the night, and it's so nice to see everyone loving on us so much. But the second we get inside the honeymoon suite at The Getaway Lodge, his mouth crashes onto mine.

Although I'm tired, I want him more.

My hunger for him aches. My back hits the wall, and his hands frame my face, his body flush against mine.

"God, do you have any idea how much I've wanted you this past week?" He's practically panting.

I claw at his shirt. "I hate sleeping alone. Have I told you that? I hate sleeping alone."

His laugh is low and vibrates through my chest as he helps me out of my dress. "Well, you're not sleeping alone tonight."

Our clothes come off fast and frantic, as if we're burning alive and the only way to put it out is to be with each other. His hands are everywhere—on my hips, my thighs, the swell of my stomach—and when his palm rests there, he pauses long enough to look at me.

"You, me, and him," he whispers. "You're everything I ever wanted and didn't think I could have."

I cup his face, my tears blurring the sight of him. "You have us. You always will."

Then there's no more talking.

His mouth claims mine as his hands guide me down to the bed. Our rhythm is frantic at first—desperation clawing at us from the starvation of being apart. But then it slows, and it turns into something that spurs more emotion out of me than I thought I'd ever have.

"I missed you," I gasp, my nails digging into his back. "God, I missed you."

When we finally collapse, slick with sweat and tangled in the sheets, his arms lock around me as though he'll never let go.

Then he places his head on the swell of my stomach, and at first, it's just a hum—a tune. But then his words slip out, low and tender.

Tour bus wheels roll down the highway,
Never cared if someone wanted to stay
But with you it's different, with you it's right,
One smile got me seeing the light
Got me wishin' I could be someone I'm not,
Someone who deserves you, who loves you a lot
A man without a temper, without all this pride,
Who ain't got some scared kid buried inside

I imagine it's the chorus of the single he's recording.

His hand covers the swell of my stomach as his voice seeps through my skin, reaching the teeny life inside.

And for the first time in weeks, I feel completely whole.

Chapter Forty

ZANDER

The hotel door shuts behind me with a soft click, and I rest my head against it for half a second. My cheeks hurt from making sure my charm was on display for every interview, and my jaw aches from all the talking and joking.

The interviews were fine. The same old recycled questions get asked—a bunch of *what's next for you* and *anything you want to share with us*, as though the entire world has a right to the blueprint of my life. As suspected, there were questions about Romy—who she is, how we met, what she means to me. I was quick to shut them all down and make it clear I wasn't there to discuss my personal life.

I should be used to it by now. I guess I am, kind of. But the questions hit differently when Romy is waiting for me. Every answer I gave today made me feel fake as hell because I was leaving out a big portion of the truth. Not telling anyone that the best thing in my life is holed up in a hotel room on the other side of the city, hidden away from cameras and waiting for me, felt like shit.

I run a hand over my face, scrubbing at the stubble, and

toss the key card on the table near the door. The suite is quiet and dim with only one lamp lit in the corner.

I step into the bedroom, assuming Romy will be asleep, but she's sprawled across the bed like a fantasy wrapped in black lace and silk. Her legs are crossed at the ankle, one knee bent, teasing me with what's underneath. Her belly, round now, rises beneath the delicate fabric of her lingerie.

She props up on her elbows, smirking because she knows exactly what she does to me.

"This is a welcome surprise."

"Long day, superstar?" she asks with a low purr.

I freeze for a second, caught between exhaustion and the sudden spike of lust. "You trying to kill me?"

"Like it?" She shifts, and the lace cups over her breasts shift, showcasing the pronounced swell of her breasts. "You were gone all day. Thought I'd remind you what you've got waiting for you back here."

I toe off my boots, never stripping my eyes off her. "Trust me, sweetheart. I didn't forget. I could never forget—even if I tried."

She tilts her head, lips quirking. "I bet you smiled your perfect smile, answered all those intrusive questions, and didn't even give me a second thought."

I tug off my jacket and toss it on the chair. "The whole time I was thinking about how fast I could get here. How fast I could get you on that bed." I nod to the bed she's lying in. The one I can't wait to join her in.

"Well, you are a superstar. They're expecting you to tell them how you swept me off my feet."

I lean on the edge of the dresser, crossing my arms. "Did I?"

For a second, the air tightens between us. She swings her legs over the edge of the mattress and stands.

"You know you did. Now, you worked so hard today…"

She walks toward me slowly, hips swaying, looking like a fucking sex kitten. "You deserve a little reward."

My pulse kicks up the closer she gets. Then she stops in front of me, tilting her head back to look me in the eye.

I brush my knuckles over her cheek. "You're gonna spoil me for sitting through six hours of questions about whether I'm secretly married?"

"You aren't, are you?" she teases, lips curving into the cutest smile.

"Smart-ass." I grip her chin gently. "You know damn well you're the only woman I want standing in front of me in lingerie, which make note of, is about two seconds away from getting ruined."

Her breath catches, then she smirks. "Well, that will have to wait. I have other plans."

My hand flexes at her hip.

"Sit," she orders softly, pushing at my chest.

I let her move me until I drop onto the edge of the bed. She falls to her knees in one smooth motion, hair spilling over her shoulder, eyes locked on mine.

My throat grows so tight it's hard to get out any words. "You don't have to—" I start, even though my body is already betraying me.

"I want to," she interrupts firmly. "I've missed you all day, Zander. Let me show you how much."

Her fingers work my belt before she tugs it free and pops the button on my jeans. I swallow hard, gripping the edge of the mattress, watching her every move like a man starved. She drags the zipper down, her knuckles brushing over my bulging cock begging to be let out, and my head tips back on a curse.

"Impatient," she murmurs.

I help her get my pants off, then she slips her hand inside my boxer briefs and wraps it around me.

My hips jerk at the contact of her hand. "Fuck, Romy. You're evil."

She smirks, pulling me free, stroking slowly and deliberately. "The best kind of evil."

"Fuck yeah."

She leans forward, pressing a kiss on the tip. My vision blurs at the edges when she slides her tongue along the length of me. I groan, fisting my hands in the sheets, every muscle in my forearms tight and straining.

Her lips close around me, and her hot, wet mouth makes me nearly bust a nut right then.

"You're killing me," I rasp. "You know that, right?"

Her eyes flick up with a mischievous glint, and she takes me deeper. My head falls back, a guttural sound tearing from my throat. Every nerve in my body is strung tight, wound up over the sight of her on her knees, the feel of her mouth on me.

The thought that she's mine. She's mine—even if she doesn't deserve everything that comes along with me.

I thread my fingers into her hair, guiding her gently, but she sets her own rhythm. A tortured, slow pace at first, then faster. Her hand works in tandem with her mouth, and I can't help it, my hips raise, chasing heaven in her mouth.

"Romy, baby... I'm close."

She hums around me, the vibration shooting sparks down my spine. Every muscle trembles as I come hard, spilling into her mouth with a groan that could shake the walls. She swallows every last drop and pulls back, licking her lips as if she's straight out of one of my wet dreams of her.

I collapse back on my elbows, breathing hard.

"Feel better?" She grins.

I laugh and pull her onto my lap. "So much better. But now... it's time for me to reward you for being such a good girl."

I nuzzle her in my arms, recovering for a minute before I

repay her for her excellent blow job. "So, tell me how boring your day was."

"Do you really want to know?"

"Of course I want to know." Even I can hear the edge of concern in my voice.

"Okay," she says. "I'm just getting tired. I'm just... growing tired."

My chest seizes, and it feels as if the oxygen has been ripped from my lungs. "Of us? Of me?"

She runs her palm over the scratchy surface of my beard. "I'm tired of living in a hotel. I'm going stir-crazy, Zander."

Relief that it's not me she's tired of barrels through me. I can fix anything as long as it's not me. "The hotel life's not glamorous enough for you?"

"Please." She rolls her eyes. "The walls are closing in on me. I miss fresh air that isn't from a balcony. I miss walking through The Harvest Depot. I miss grabbing a cider and not feeling like I'm sneaking around." She shifts off of me so she's beside me on the mattress. "I miss normal."

The word twists something inside me. *Normal.* I can never give her normal.

"You're telling me room service and Egyptian cotton sheets aren't enough for you? Some women would kill for a life like this." I try to keep my voice light, not knowing what to do with her confession.

She narrows her eyes playfully. "I'm not some woman. And besides, the pancakes downstairs are dry."

"Maybe I'll fly Jensen in to make you pancakes."

My joke falls flat, and she doesn't say anything.

"All right. We'll get you out. I'll talk to Beau. Maybe we can sneak you out somewhere."

Her eyes soften, and I'm grateful I can make her day a little bit better, but there's a niggling worry at the back of my mind that it won't be enough.

She nestles against me, her belly pressing into my stomach and her head tucked beneath my chin. And for a long moment, we just breathe together.

Her warmth. Her scent. The feel of her curves in my arms.

It's the only place I feel steady anymore. The only place that feels like *home*. I've been chasing home my entire life, never feeling like I had one.

But even as I think it, as I hold her, reality seeps in.

The world outside this room is waiting. The cameras, the headlines, the fans who think they own me.

And she's right.

We can't stay in here forever.

Sooner or later, she'll see what it really means to be with me.

The thought guts me because the minute she realizes what it really means, she'll run. And I'll have no right to stop her.

So I hold her tighter, bury my face in her hair. I'll lose her before I let my world destroy her.

Chapter Forty-One

ROMY

My phone vibrates on the nightstand, and I slide across the bed to grab it, the soft glow from the screen the only light in the room. The curtains are still drawn tight, even though it's well past noon, and I've been sprawled across the hotel bed—tangled in sheets and pillows—ever since Zander left this morning.

I can't find anything decent on TV anymore. I've binge-watched every show I can imagine. I don't bother turning on the lamp and just slide my thumb across the screen to answer.

Lottie's voice crackles through the speaker—chipper and happy—and I'm instantly homesick.

"Hey! How are you?" she says.

"Bored out of my mind." I lay my head on the pillow and stare at the ceiling. The only view I've had of whatever city I'm in now.

"How can you be bored? You've literally been touring the country. Where are you now?"

"I think we're in Chicago... maybe? But then tomorrow is Milwaukee or Indianapolis. I have no idea." It's all the same to me. A bed, an uncomfortable couch, a desk with a complimentary notepad and pen. Sure, the hotels are way fancier than I've ever stayed in before, but I spend most of my time in them alone, so the shine has worn off.

"So..." Her voice dips lower.

I sit up. My sister never stalls. She's more the spit-it-out type. "Lottie, what is it?"

I worry something is wrong back at the ranch. My parents? Uncle Bruce? One of my cousins? What's going on back home that I'm missing by lying around in a hotel room?

There's a beat of silence. I can practically hear her biting her lip.

"I really wanted to tell you at the family dinner, but I don't know when you're gonna be back. The process is starting, and I don't want you to be the only one who doesn't know. We haven't told anybody yet—other than Mom and Dad."

I grip the phone tighter. "Okay... what is it? What's wrong? Is something wrong with you and Brooks? What's going on?"

"No, no. We're fine. We're fine. But... I just want to let you know that..."

"Lottie!"

"We've started the surrogacy process."

My breath catches. "Surrogacy?"

"Yeah," she says softly. "We've talked to the doctors and some lawyers. We're really serious about it. And I really wanted to tell you in person. I'm sorry it's over the phone."

"You're sorry? I'm sorry. I wish I was there. I want to hug you. And I want to tell you how proud and excited I am that you're taking this step."

I flop back against the pillow, staring at the ceiling. Again. My chest aches because I want to be there. I want to be with her. I want to hug her and have her tell me everything.

"God, Lottie, that's huge."

"I know."

"You're going to be amazing parents," I whisper. "And I'm growing one great cousin for that little Watson."

She laughs, and guilt washes over me that I'm not there. But more than that—I miss home.

"You okay?" Her voice is soft, something you don't get a lot of with my sister.

"Yeah, I'm fine."

"No, really. Tell me, Romy. Are you okay?"

"Yeah."

"Then why do you sound like someone stole your puppy?"

I sigh. Loudly enough that I'm sure she hears it. "I don't know. I just... I miss the ranch. I miss the family. And you know, we're trying to keep the baby a secret—keep it out of the press—so most of my time is spent in a hotel bed waiting for Zander to come back."

My throat knots. I don't even want to loosen it. I'm finally opening up, and it feels good to admit to someone that this life isn't all that. Zander refuses to entertain people because of his fear that the paps will get information and that things will get worse for me and my family at the ranch.

"Have you talked to Zander about it?"

"A little. I don't want to ruin... this is what he wants. And being apart wasn't an option. I'll take the few hours I get with him a day, rather than not seeing him for a month at a time."

"I get it... but still. I mean, Romy, this doesn't seem very fair either."

I trust Lottie. She's my sister, but I don't want to waste our time talking about something I don't see changing anytime soon. "Anyway. Tell me what's going on—how are the family dinners? Anything interesting happening there?"

"Oh my god," Lottie says, letting me change the subject.

She knows there's no changing what I'm going through.

I'm not miraculously going to pop this baby out and be public-ready. I have no idea when Zander will feel safe telling anybody that I'm pregnant. And I haven't really broached the subject because he seems so busy and stressed with all the interviews.

"Well... let's see. Everybody's asking about you. Wren and Leia can't stop begging me to FaceTime you at every dinner. They keep saying Auntie Romy owes them souvenirs, so I hope you have a big duffel bag of things you've collected from all the places you've been to."

"Oh my god, I haven't bought them a thing," I admit.

She laughs. "It's fine. Just buy them something sparkly, and they'll be happy. You know Bennett and Delaney won't want you to spoil them anyway."

"I know. But still..."

She tells me how big Daisy is getting and how Emmett and Briar are exhausted from chasing after Colter because he's such a busy boy. For a moment, I can pretend we're still back on the ranch, on the couch and talking face-to-face.

We chat for a little longer, and it fills up a small space in the empty hole that is me missing home.

"Well, I guess I should let you go—" I say.

"Yeah, I gotta run anyway. There're a bunch of customers and stuff. But you are gonna come home soon, right, Romy?"

"Yeah, yeah. We're due home in... I think a couple weeks or so. And once we get closer to delivery, you know I have to be home. So, I'll be there for a while."

We're both quiet for a moment.

"I miss you," Lottie says.

"I miss you too. I miss everybody. Please tell them I said hi and that I'll be back soon." My voice comes out wobbly.

"I will. Love you."

"Love you."

We hang up, and the quiet of the room rushes in too fast. I

toss my phone on the bed and feel as if my whole world has shrunk to four beige walls.

I could send someone to grab gifts for the girls—Beau or DeSoto—but the thought of either of them trying to pick out something for two eight-year-old girls who mean so much to me but they barely know? I can see them coming back with coffee mugs. Besides, I don't want to pass off a gift to my nieces that I didn't personally pick out for them.

I get up off the bed, walk over to the window to pull the curtains to the side, and open them. God, I want to be out there on those streets.

I check the time. Zander isn't due back for at least two hours. I can definitely slip out, and he wouldn't even know.

And why would he have to know?

He doesn't have to know.

I'm an adult who doesn't need permission from her partner to run out for twenty minutes to find her nieces a gift.

I need to breathe some fresh air.

I walk over to the mirror and look at myself. My reflection looks... horrid. Pale skin. Messy bun. Zander's sweatshirt—it's the only thing that still fits lately.

I could get out and back without him even knowing. He's not due back for hours.

And when I get back, I'll tell him I was able to do it. I'll prove to him that it's possible.

I dig through his bag and find the baseball cap he left behind. I put on oversized sunglasses. A scarf knotted at my throat. A plain gray coat that Beau bought me when we got to the colder states. I'd already busted three buttons on mine.

This is harmless. A quick trip in and out. Nobody will notice. Nobody will recognize me.

I'm still a nobody except when Zander is by my side. By myself? I'm just like anyone else walking down a busy city sidewalk.

I leave the room, walk softly across the plush carpet to the elevators, and press the button. My pulse ticks as if I'm a thief or a fugitive and not an aunt going to buy toys for her nieces.

I tip my head low and move quickly out of the lobby, hoping everyone is too busy to give me a second glance.

As soon as I'm out on the city streets, I stare at the world and relish it. The cars honking. The voices overlapping. The cold air tinged with exhaust.

I hesitate at the curb, tugging my coat a little tighter, and scan the sidewalks. Then I walk steadily until I reach a souvenir shop and duck inside. I hunt the aisles quickly, grabbing two snow globes. Two keychains. Anything glittery. A couple teddy bears.

I pay in cash. Avoid eye contact with the cashier. Then step back out onto the street. My heart is racing, but this stolen sliver of normalcy is exactly what I needed.

Either from my adrenaline or the heated store, suddenly I'm overheated. Underneath my coat, sweat gathers at the small of my back, and my disguise feels suffocating. I'm so hot that it makes me feel a little nauseated.

I glance around. Nobody's watching. Nobody cares.

I unbutton my jacket, letting the cold breeze seep in through the sweatshirt. The relief is instant. Cool air slides across my overheated skin.

Click.

The sharp noise might as well have been a gunshot to my ears.

My head jerks in the direction of the sound.

A man stands across the street, lens aimed squarely at my stomach and me.

I freeze.

He lowers the camera, smirking as though he's already cashed the check for the shot he just scored.

Heat floods my cheeks. I yank my jacket closed, but it's too late.

I've been seen.

And no matter how fast I walk back to the hotel, no matter how tightly I shut the door behind me, the damage is done.

Tomorrow... or probably even tonight... hell, within minutes, the world will know that I'm carrying Zander Shaw's baby.

Chapter Forty-Two

ZANDER

Beau and I, with DeSoto behind us, step off the elevator.

"Thank fuck that was over early, right?" I shift the bouquet of flowers in my grip.

"Yeah, I'll be happy when these are over, and I think Romy will be too." Beau shoots me a look. "Rapunzel can finally be set free."

"I told you to find me somewhere I can take her that's private and safe."

Beau's been on me about Romy staying sequestered in the hotel rooms. We haven't gone to any restaurants, surviving on takeout and room service.

"I'm not a magician, Zan. Getting in and out of the hotel is hard enough. Sure, I could rent out something romantic for you, but there would still be employees we have to trust. You're so stuck on the world not knowing about this kid."

"Need I remind you that you were too? You were the one who pushed it the most."

His opinion on the matter has changed over the months. He's loosened his grip, while I've only tightened the reins. The closer Romy and I become, the more she means to me, and the bigger her stomach grows, the more desperate I feel to protect her from the hazards of my life.

"I get you're scar—"

"Fuck yeah, I am." I run a hand through my hair.

"Okay." Beau steps away from his door and walks across to mine. "Let's not argue about this now. Go give your girl the flowers and have some hot sex. It's been another long day. We can talk tomorrow."

He walks back to his door and DeSoto takes up his spot outside mine.

"You know I'd love for the world to know, but—"

"I do. I'll see you at breakfast tomorrow." Beau swipes his keycard and disappears inside his room.

I'm not sure what he expects me to do. If anyone finds out we're pregnant, shit will get nasty. Rumors will fly, and they'll pick apart every little thing about Romy more than they already do, make her think I'm only with her because of the baby. They'll be at the ranch again, bothering her and her family. She won't be able to go anywhere in Willowbrook without a photographer in her face.

Swiping my keycard, I try to think about some stupid line I can say when I deliver her the flowers. Something poetic, which should be easy since I'm a songwriter, but I'm mentally exhausted from constantly worrying that I have this wonderful person in my life and won't be able to hold onto her.

I push the door open, and the first thing I see is that the drapes are open, which is a good sign since she's been sleeping more lately. I'm assuming the baby is making her tired. I'm sure having a baby growing inside you does that.

I walk into the bedroom area, finding the bed empty. The sheets are rumpled and twisted, and her phone charger is still plugged into the nightstand. Her finished lunch plates sit on the table in the corner.

"Romy?"

I search the bathroom. Nothing.

A sense of dread coats my skin like poison seeping in.

I toss the bouquet on the desk and move through the room again, thinking maybe she's playing hide and seek, and I'll find her in a set of lingerie as my reward. I yank open the bathroom door again, but it's just my reflection in the mirror.

Closet. No.

I dig out my phone and hit her name. It rings but goes to voicemail.

Hey, it's Romy. Leave a message.

I hang up. Call again.

Same thing.

My pulse blares in my ears, like an alarm sounding that something is very wrong.

Think rationally. There are a hundred harmless reasons she could've slipped out. Maybe she went for ice.

But we've told her not to go anywhere, especially without security.

Beau's right, I've kept her locked in here like some kind of prisoner. What the hell did I expect? She's sick of it and has left me.

I pace the length of the room, dragging a hand through my hair, calling her again and again, trying to breathe, trying to remind myself it's fine as my chest gets tighter and tighter.

She'll come back.

She will.

Romy's not like everyone else who's left me behind.

I continue to pace until I spot her suitcase. That's a good sign, right? If she left me, she would've packed that.

So, what the hell happened to her? God, what if she opened the door, someone figured out she was here, and they took her? There are desperate people in this world who would see her as prize money.

My mind whirls with a million what-ifs, and I drop to the

edge of the bed, elbows braced on my knees, staring at the phone, willing it to ring.

Every second that ticks by is another chance that something awful has happened to her. That she's out there, scared and alone, and I'm not with her. I'm not there to protect her. I should've been wrapped around her like a guard dog.

I hit her name on my phone again.

Voicemail.

My throat burns, and I squeeze my eyes shut.

My thumb hovers over Beau's number, and I'm about to press the call button when the door clicks open.

I shoot to my feet.

The doorknob turns and opens.

Romy fills the doorway.

Sunglasses too big for her face. My black hat pulled low over her eyes. Her cheeks pink from the cold. Her coat open, showing her swollen belly under my old sweatshirt.

Relief crashes into me so hard, my knees nearly buckle. My lungs finally remember how to work.

But the storm inside me only shifts.

Because I want to grab her and hold her and never let her go. I want to scold her until she promises not to scare me like that again. Does she have any idea how empty my life would be without her? I want to kiss her until she knows exactly how much she undoes me.

She pauses in the doorway and tilts her head at me.

I cross the room and pull her into me, hugging her as if she's my fucking security blanket.

Chapter Forty-Three

ROMY

I pause in the doorway. Zander's standing in the middle of the hotel room, his jaw tight, hands clenched into fists.

His eyes cut to mine, and I see the storm brewing in them. I almost drop the bag dangling from my wrist. But before I can say anything, he's across the room. He pulls me into his chest, arms caging me tight and desperate as though he can't believe I'm actually here.

I sink into him for a second. He feels like home, and I missed him, even though it's only been a few hours. His heartbeat is pounding, his breath uneven against my hair.

Then he jerks back, holding me out by my upper arms. "What the hell were you thinking?" His voice is sharp. "You can't leave without me. Where'd you go?"

The whiplash from his emotions takes me a moment to find my thoughts.

"You can't do that. You can't—you know how dangerous it is for you. There are cameras everywhere. People everywhere —" He cuts himself off and turns and rakes both hands through his hair. "Jesus, Romy. I called you a bunch of times. I thought something had happened to you."

Guilt tugs at my gut. I'd never want him to worry about me, but my guilt tangles with the anger of feeling like a caged-up animal. "I'm sorry, my phone is on vibrate in my purse. I just went to buy souvenirs for Wren and Leia, not to run off to join the circus."

His eyes flash, and the storm there gets a little darker. "You think this is a joke?" he says incredulously. "If one person recognized you... one picture. That's all it takes for them to rip you apart. To rip *our baby* apart."

My chest caves at the word *our*, but my anger doesn't abate. I cross the room and toss the bag on the couch. "I can't live like this! I can't be locked in a room like your dirty little secret you get to play with whenever you get time."

He blinks, looking stunned for a beat. "This isn't about keeping you a secret."

"Yes, it is." My voice cracks. "You don't trust anyone to know about us unless it's on your terms. And I just can't do it, Zander. I can't do this if you're going to hide us all the time." I push out my stomach for emphasis.

His face twists as if I stabbed him in the heart. "You don't understand. I've lived this life a long time, you haven't. You don't know—"

I throw up my hands. "Then make me understand."

The air between us is electric and charged with everything we've been keeping in during this time on the road. His mouth opens to argue again, so I cut him off, making sure it's all out there.

"Someone got a picture of me."

A flash of panic crosses his face. "What?"

"I'm sorry. I was in the store, and I got overheated. I thought I was going to pass out."

"This is what I'm telling you. You shouldn't be out there in the first place." Desperation lines his face.

I hate that I'm the person who put it there, but we're

going to get nowhere by ignoring the problem here. "Will you just listen to me for a second?"

He huffs and sits, then stands again.

"I was overheated. I unbuttoned my jacket, and... and the guy was across the street. I didn't see him. I looked around before I did it."

"See, Romy? They're everywhere. They are everywhere. You cannot... this is why you need to stay in the hotel room."

"I can't be in the hotel room anymore! I'm losing my mind!" Tears of frustration prick at my eyes.

He swears under his breath, pacing across the room. "Fucking hell. I told you—one picture is all it takes. They're going to be on you like vultures now. You think *this* feels like a prison? Just wait until you find out that you can't even walk on the—hell, you can't do anything. Anything, Romy! Now they're going to be all over you. All over the ranch. All over the baby. Your entire life just blew up."

Beep.

A keycard swipes at the door, and Beau comes in with a concerned look, shutting the door behind him. "What the fuck is going on? You guys can't be heard screaming at each other. You want even more rumors to come out?"

Zander throws his arm out, not even looking at Beau. "Get the fuck out, Beau. Right now." His voice is as sharp as broken glass.

I turn to Beau. "I went out to get Leia and Wren souvenirs. Somebody got a picture of me."

Beau looks me up and down. "Are you sure they knew it was you?"

I nod. "Yeah. He knew."

His gaze falls to my exposed stomach. "Shit. All right. I'll handle it. I'm on it now. I'll try to squash it before it gets any legs. Maybe we can buy it before someone else does."

I raise my hand. "No."

"Romy, let the man do his job," Zander grits out.

"No. I don't want to keep being a secret. I don't want to hide in a hotel room for hours on end and go from town to town and not see one goddamn landmark anymore." I look at Zander, wishing he'd look at me, but he keeps his gaze anywhere but on me. "Zander, I can't do this anymore."

I don't know if it's what I said, but Beau looks at me—and I can see it in his face. He knew this would happen. That this would become a breaking point.

I've gone along to get along, but I'm taking control of my own damn life now. I'll suffer the repercussions of it, and I know Zander will too. And for that, I'm sorry. But I cannot keep doing this.

"Beau... let the story leak."

He sighs. "Romy, Zander has a point. If we're going to do this, let's do this right."

"What's right? What do you want me to do? This isn't a life. I don't have a life anymore. I mean sure, the hours..."

I look at Zander. He sits down and puts his head in his hands. I've never seen a man more stricken.

"Beau, can you just give us a second?"

Beau nods. "Yeah, of course." He steps out of the room, the door shutting behind him.

I go over and sit next to Zander. "I love the hours when we're here together. I love spending every minute with you that I can. But I can't live like this. I miss my family. I miss the ranch. I miss fresh air."

All he does is nod.

"This isn't working, Zander."

"I know." His voice is raw, and he doesn't pick up his head to look at me.

But does he really understand? I'm not sure.

Is he willing to take the few hours he has with me here because he's too afraid of losing me?

"I think I need to go home. You finish this out, and then we can talk."

"Romy..."

I place my hand on his thigh. He doesn't flinch, doesn't pull away, but he still doesn't look at me.

"I'm sorry. I don't want to put you in this position, and I would never ask you to choose me over any of this. I want you to have everything this world has to offer you. You deserve all the success in the world. But... we need to figure out something else." He still says nothing, so I continue, "Maybe we can try where I stay on the ranch, and you travel without me again. I don't know. Maybe there's a compromise somewhere."

He lifts his head.

Finally.

"I get it, Romy. You can stop now. I get it. We'll get you on a plane back to the ranch."

"Zander—"

"No. It's fine. It's what's best for you."

Zander stands, crosses the room, and opens the door, ignoring my objections to talk. Beau must be waiting outside, forever the protector and faithful friend, because Zander speaks.

"Get a private plane for Romy to go back to the ranch. And DeSoto goes with her."

Beau steps back into the room. "Whoa, whoa, whoa. Zander, DeSoto stays with you. I can get her someone—"

"No. DeSoto goes with her. End of conversation."

I stand, and Beau's eyes flash to me.

"Zander, what are you doing?" I ask.

"You want to end this, right, Romy? It doesn't work for you. My lifestyle doesn't work for you."

"No, I want to talk."

"No." He shakes his head. "I get that you don't want to

live the way I'm asking you to live. I get it. I understand it. But... where there is no choice—"

My heart splinters. "What are you... you're breaking it off?"

He turns to me, finally looking me in the eye. The storm is gone, and all that's left is a barren landscape of cold tundra. "What's gonna change, Romy? I'm still going to be Zander Shaw when we wake up tomorrow morning. I still have to do interviews. I still have to work to pay all these people under me. I can't just stop working because I fell in—"

"What?" My voice is a whisper.

He shakes his head, and I swear there are tears in his dark eyes. "Nothing. Just... just go. Pack your bag and go."

Zander grabs his hat—the one I'd taken off and set on the table—and he walks out the door.

"Zander," I call after him.

Beau calls, "Zan, come on. Come back here." His gaze shoots to me, then the other way down the hall. "DeSoto, get Michaels on him now."

I crumple onto the couch, and tears sting my eyes before they pour down my cheeks.

A body sinks down next to me, and two arms wrap around my shoulders and tug me into a hard chest. Beau makes sure I'm not alone. Just like Zander would want.

Chapter Forty-Four

ROMY

I step off the airplane—the private plane that Zander paid to take me home because apparently, he's done with me as soon as I challenge him.

DeSoto takes my suitcase, and I walk toward the small terminal where the private flights come in. But Lottie springs out the door and barrels toward me, hugging me so hard I stumble back. I look over her shoulder to see Poppy and my mom right behind her.

"Finally, you're home. You know how boring this ranch has been without you?" Lottie says.

She's dodging the reason I'm home. Someone called her because I sure as hell didn't. And my guess is it was Beau—making sure somebody was here to pick up the pieces that Zander crumbled under his boot.

"I'm sure you survived fine. I'll bet Brooks kept you busy."

"Barely." She pulls back and looks me over. "How are you doing?" Her eyes turn grim, and I guess she's done. I give her credit for trying though.

"I'm fine." Tears sting my eyes again, and I wipe them away. Poor DeSoto had to sit next to me the entire plane ride, handing me tissues and disposing of the old ones when they piled too high. "I don't want to cry anymore, so let's just... like... not talk about it."

Poppy steps forward, giving me a big hug. "Just when I was starting to like him. Now I gotta go bash him online."

"Don't you dare go be a keyboard warrior," I say.

"Some of those people are so nasty, they need to be put in their place."

Beau had a whole conversation with Poppy and Lottie about staying off the comments sections last time he was at the ranch. He told them they're just making it worse, but neither one has stopped telling off people who say shitty things about Zander or me online.

"No, Poppy," my mom says in her motherly tone. "We're thinking about changing all the Wi-Fi passwords and cutting her cell signal."

Poppy shrugs unapologetically.

"How are you, sweetheart?" My mom steps forward, swallowing me in a hug. "It's okay." She runs her hand over my back, and the tears I've been pushing back set free. "I know it's hard. Heartbreak is never easy."

Once I collect myself, we all file out of the airport.

At the curb is a black SUV—tinted out—another thing Zander's paying for. DeSoto opens the door for all of us to get in, puts my bag in the back, and sits up front with the driver.

Memories of being in the back seat of a similar SUV with Zander so many times surface. How easy and carefree it was. How I fell in love with him. And now it's over. Because we can't braid our two lives together.

We drive back toward Willowbrook. The Nebraska land is pretty much the same—stretching wide, winter fields. Nothing growing. Everything dead, just like me on the inside.

"So, you're never gonna believe what happened," Lottie starts a story, trying to lift my mood.

I'm only half paying attention because I'm staring out the window, wondering where Zander is right now and if he's okay. I want so badly to message Beau and ask where they are and how he's doing.

My stomach twists, and I have no idea what conversation is going on around me. It could be about pictures of me pregnant hitting the media for all I know. I haven't even looked at my phone to see the fallout of my impulsive decision.

But I don't regret it. I couldn't live like that anymore. I couldn't live in secret, hiding all the time. I don't care if paps bother me. I don't care if they know. I don't care about anything except what I've lost.

I know that's probably naïve of me. Zander would think I'm being foolish. But at this point, I can't find it in myself to care.

I run my hands over my stomach, thinking about how I'm ever going to make this work with him. How I'll ever do normal drop-offs and pick-ups for our son with him and not think to myself, could we have made it work? We could have had one hell of a life together.

I'll still want Zander every time he comes to pick up our son. Or will he send Beau because he doesn't have the guts to look me in the eye? Will Uncle Beau be the go-between? Maybe we'll never actually be face-to-face again.

I'll probably just see pictures of Zander online here and there. Will he try to keep our son locked up as well?

A hand rests on my leg. I look over at my mom. She shakes her head as if she knows my thoughts are spinning out of control, and I'm moving ten paces forward instead of staying in the here and now.

Once the SUV pulls up to my parents' house on the ranch, we all file out. DeSoto's clearly been instructed to stay with me until further instruction.

My mom raises her hand at him. "Okay, DeSoto. You're staying here, and I'm taking my daughter with me."

DeSoto looks at my mom, knowing there's no arguing with her, and he nods. But I have no doubt he'll be hopping in his own UTV and following a couple yards back.

"Mom, I don't want to go anywhere. I just want to go to my bed and lie down," I say.

"Well, I'm sorry, Romy. Everybody has to do things they don't want to do. You're getting in the UTV, and we're going to Daisy Hill."

Lottie laughs behind me. "What analogy are you gonna use for her, Mom?"

My mom shakes her head. "Get in, Romy. It's time."

"What does that mean? It's time?" I look back at Lottie.

"It's the weed talk. You're gonna get the weed talk." Lottie grins.

"But I didn't do anything wrong. Are you suggesting I did?" I cross my arms and rest them on my bump.

Lottie shrugs. "Can you tell us one thing we were talking about on the ride back?" She cringes as though she's sorry, but she's taking Mom's side on this one.

"Let's get this over with," I mutter.

So I climb into the UTV, knowing my mom won't let up. I'll have her stupid talk, then I'm going home to wallow.

Chapter Forty-Five

ROMY

We drive to Daisy Hill—the cemetery where all my ancestors who've passed are buried. The daisies don't grow on the hill this time of year, which always makes me a little sad. As if I needed any help with that today.

We walk up the path. It's already been cleared of few inches of snow. Mom must have sent my dad ahead, knowing this was our destination.

She holds my hand as we walk up and opens the small white gate of the fence that surrounds the cemetery. Even in the dead of winter, someone has placed fresh daisies on my aunt's grave. I wonder if my Uncle Bruce comes here every day and what it must be like for him to live his life without her.

My mom walks over to her parents' grave and sits on the bench. There's a blanket over the seat. The second sign that she's already had conversations with someone about setting this up.

"Okay, Mom, so what am I? Lottie's a weed, and Bennett is a Jack Russell. What am I?"

She rolls her eyes. "You guys are relentless. I'm just trying to make your lives better."

"All right, I'm just kidding." I pat her leg.

She exhales. "I don't know if I have a word to describe you. I've been thinking about it really hard because I want to give you a word—but I just can't find one that encompasses everything you are. I can't relate you to anybody or anything else."

"Wow. This is a promising conversation."

"I've thrown some around. A balloon, a compass..."

"Is this some joke about my sense of direction?" I ask.

"What? No. Why would you think that?"

"I don't know? Because a balloon just floats in the air, taking it wherever the breeze goes, and a compass would be a sarcastic joke."

She laughs. "No. Jeez. I just meant—" She stops, knowing we're going off on a tangent. "All I can say is, Romy—you're a hopeless romantic. You've always been that way. You'd make me read all the fairytales twice every night. For Halloween, you were a princess every year until you were ten years old. All those fake weddings you'd put on when you were little. I swear you could find anything to use as a veil." She laughs. "The first novel you ever read was a romance you stole from Aunt Bette."

I shift in my seat, trying to get more comfortable in this pregnant body. "Nothing wrong with any of that."

"You're right. Nothing is. But you truly believe that everything is fate or kismet. And I don't know... for a while, I worried about you because of that. I thought that you were only going to be disappointed when you got older."

"Well, I am disappointed. Guess you're psychic."

She places her hand on my thigh and squeezes. "No, I mean that... I thought you wouldn't be able to settle. And maybe there's nothing wrong with that. You know, you were always looking for a specific connection that something meant something. Or a sign. And I thought, maybe she's just gonna meet someone as she's dropping off the mail at a post office. Like, it doesn't have to be this big, grand thing. And I wondered... if it was just an ordinary way of meeting someone, would you give it a chance and believe in them? But then... it kind of happened to you."

"Yeah, Mom. I got picked out of a crowd because a country singer wanted to fuck me."

She taps her hand on my thigh. "My god, Romy, stop talking like that."

"It's the truth, Mom. Zander didn't pick me out of the crowd because he had a feeling I was the one."

"How do you know that he didn't point at you and ask security to get you because he felt something different?"

I laugh, a fake hysterical one. "Because he pushed me away. After the third time I went to see him. On the fourth time, he had DeSoto tell me I wasn't on the list." All that pain is present again, but so much worse now. Because we've gotten close, and we're having a baby, and I was naïve to think he'd changed.

She sighs. "You know, the thing is... sometimes men just don't know what they want."

"I don't want to hear that, Mom. I don't want to hear that he's out there somewhere yearning and pining away for me when I'm in as much pain as this. He's not. It became difficult, I didn't want to play by his rules, so he pushed me away. That's the way he works." I cross my arms and stare at the words on my grandparents' graves. Wife and husband. Maybe mine will just read mother, sister, daughter. I need to be okay with that.

"I don't think that's true. And I know that you're probably going to tell me I'm wrong, but... you know, Zander didn't grow up with this." She puts her hands out and circles her head around, indicating our surroundings. "He didn't grow up with love. Definitely not unconditional love. I mean, he grew up with people taking him in who didn't always have the kindest hearts. Sure, there are great foster families out there —people who want to help the kids and give them a chance at life—but they're not all that way. And it sounds like Zander wasn't lucky enough to be placed in those families."

"I get it, Mom, I know it wasn't easy for him. He had a rough childhood."

She frowns. "It forms the person you are, Romy."

"I know." My voice comes out rough.

"You clearly don't." Her angry tone makes me turn to face her.

"What don't I get?"

"You protect what you love. It's a reflex. Like breathing. He and Beau probably know what love is before anyone else does because they know how it doesn't look. They spent their childhoods with strangers constantly turning them away. So, when Zander finally found something real, something he loved"—she nods at me, then my stomach—"he gripped it so tightly, with everything he's got, and God help the world if it takes it away."

"He just let me leave," I say, but she continues as if I didn't say anything.

"Now, he has an instant family. A woman he loves and a baby he wants to give every opportunity that he didn't get—"

I groan, and tears fall down my cheeks. "Stop saying he loves me. He can't love me. Not when he deliberately hurt me."

"Oh, stop it. You know what that man feels for you. And if you don't, then you need to go back and look at some of those pictures of you two. There're plenty of them on the internet. Go search them up. That man loves you."

"Then why would he push me away, Mom?" I wipe the tears on my face.

"If I had to guess? Because there's a part of him that doesn't think he's good enough. That you being in his world puts you at jeopardy, and he'd sacrifice himself before he ever let anything hurt you. And if you looked at the internet right now, I'm pretty sure you would understand—"

"What? What is it?"

She shakes her head. "It doesn't matter. But people don't always want the best for you. And I think, to a certain degree, you are a little naïve. I blame myself for giving you such a great childhood." She gives me a cheeky smile.

"Mom." I roll my eyes and give her a small smile.

"But people... even people who claim to care about Zander... they don't always want the best for him. And that's a hard pill to swallow. But that's the life he knows. He's lived it for how many years? And you haven't. So, he's trying to save you from that pain because he loves you."

"So, what do you expect me to do? He's the one who broke it off with me. Isn't this supposed to be some talk to get my head out of my ass?"

"I don't think you did anything wrong, Romy. I think it wasn't working between you two, and something had to change. But I think maybe he might need a little more reassurance than most that you're going to stick around. That you're not going anywhere."

"Mom, what do you want me to do? I have been—I've been doing everything I can."

"I know you have, sweetie. All I'm saying... just understand a little bit from where he's coming from on this, when he comes to talk to you."

"Oh my god. You think he's going to come and talk to me?" A disbelieving chuckle leaves my lips.

"Yes. He's going to come and talk to you."

A cold breeze blows my hair in my face, and I tuck it behind my ear. "Why would he?"

"Because he loves you. Believe me—every man, at some point, gets their head out of their ass. And when he does, he's going to come to this ranch, and he's going to declare his love for you. And he'll tell you that he's a changed man. All I'm saying is—he's not. But if he sees his faults and what he did, how it affected you... just listen to him, come together, and work this out. You guys are too good together for it to end."

"He doesn't seem to think so."

"I know. Sometimes they're really hardheaded." She puts her arm around me and slides closer on the bench. "You're a good egg."

"An egg. I get an egg?"

She laughs. "I'm just saying, your heart is so full and so open. Zander is lucky to have found you and fallen in love with you." Then her hand falls on my stomach. "You're going to give them a great life." Tears slide down my mom's cheeks. "You guys are going to be so great together. And it just makes me—"

"Mom, why are you crying?"

"I just love it when somebody goes through something really bad, and they get something really great out of it. And Zander is going to get you. I think he's really, really lucky."

She kisses my cheek. We sit there, and we hug, and the desire to see Zander is greater than ever.

"Oh!" She pulls away. "A peach. You're a peach!"

"What?"

"Yes. Sweet and easy to like."

I stare at her blankly, then I tilt my head. "Better than an egg, I suppose."

She settles next to me again, putting her hand on my stomach, and I lean my head on her shoulder. This is what she's talking about. This is what Zander never had, and I've taken it for granted because I don't know what I would do without my family.

As we sit there quietly, I try to fill myself with the same hope and confidence my mother has that Zander will come for me. For *us*. His son and me.

Chapter Forty-Six

ZANDER

Beau parks the truck at the corner and kills the engine. His hand taps the steering wheel before he finally turns to look at me. "You recognize it?"

Of course I fucking recognize it. The neighborhood hasn't changed at all. The sidewalks are still cracked. The same chain-link fences still sag from years of neglect. Same patchy grass struggles against the Texas sun. And I swear, one look, and I'm twelve again, swearing I'll do whatever it takes to get out of here.

I swallow, my throat dry. I can't even say I grew up here. I *survived* here.

Beau studies me, waiting for my reaction. "You want to get out?"

I huff out a laugh. "Why the hell are we here, man?"

And I knew. As soon as we hopped off the plane, I knew this was where he'd take me.

"Because you need to be here."

I want to refuse. I want to tell him to take me anywhere else. But a part of me knows that if he dragged me here, there's a damn good reason for it. Maybe I'm so screwed up he had to bring me here.

When we get out of the truck, he points at the duplex. The one where we met. It was my third foster home. The paint is peeling off the house in sheets, the window AC half hanging out the window.

"Home sweet home," he says.

"Did you bring me here to depress me further or something?" My boot kicks at the broken pavement.

"I brought you here as a reminder. Look at this place. Really look at it."

And the funny thing is, this is probably the happiest house I was ever in. Because this is where Beau and I crossed paths. Two foster kids. It was only a year before we were split up. Our foster mom said we were too much trouble, that we weren't listening to her rules. And when we were wrestling and broke a cat figurine, that was the end of that.

"You're not that kid anymore," Beau says softly.

My head snaps toward him. "What?"

"You heard me. You keep living like you're clawing your way out of this dump. Like if you don't grind yourself down, you'll end up back here. But look around, man. You made it out. We both did."

I let out a sharp laugh, shaking my head. "Made it out? Yeah, sure. I'm living in hotel rooms and chasing deadlines."

"Bullshit," Beau fires back. "You've got more money than you know what to do with. You've got talent most people would sell their souls for. And you've got a woman who actually gives a damn about you."

I roll my eyes. I don't know why I roll my eyes. It's the truth. Romy gives a damn about me. The note she left on the nightstand after she took her suitcase and left Chicago still burns a hole in my back pocket.

I'll never keep you from him. No matter what happens with us, you are his father, and he is your son.

I never told Beau, but that last night in the hotel room, I finally broke down, realizing that I'm the one destroying it this time. It's not some foster dad who can't handle his anger or alcohol. It's not a neglectful foster mom who uses the money meant for us to get her nails done. It's not even the caseworker's fault. This time, it's nobody's fault but mine.

"Romy's different," he says. "And you know it."

God, just the mention of her name stabs me in the heart. "That doesn't mean she's meant for this life."

Beau snorts. "You need to stop acting like a coward. Jesus. You love her. She loves you."

I glance at the duplex again. "You just... you don't get it."

"I do." When I try to respond, Beau cuts me off. "More than anyone. We grew up in the same damn system, remember? I get it. Foster kid rule number one: don't let anyone in. Because the second you do, they're gone. Whoosh. Disappeared from your life. But that rule doesn't work anymore. You're not that boy waiting for a caseworker to show up and free you from a shitty situation. You're a man. You can walk out whenever you want. And Romy isn't going anywhere—unless you push her out."

I press my palms against my jeans, trying to ground myself, but the memories creep in, nonetheless. The cold nights huddled under thin blankets. Pretending not to be scared when her boyfriend grabbed us by the shirts and pushed us up against a wall. Trying to act as though we were too cool to care. The ache of wanting someone, anyone, to claim us as theirs.

I blink against the burn in my eyes. "You make it sound

easy." My voice is as rough as the gravel driveway in front of me.

Since when did he become this well-adjusted? Why isn't he as fucked up in the head as I am?

"It's not easy," Beau says. "But you don't have to keep pushing yourself. You worked your ass off to escape this. You don't need to prove you can do it anymore. You deserve the life you built for yourself."

My throat closes.

"Listen, I'm not saying it's perfect—your lifestyle. Hell, it's a circus. Cameras, travel, fans. But you've got choices now. And you don't have to keep bleeding yourself dry like it's the only way to survive. You survived. And you're allowed to want more."

"Want more, huh?" It comes out quiet.

"Yeah. Like a future with Romy. Like not screwing it up because you're too scared to admit you're worthy and that if it came down to it, she would choose you every time."

His words land in the hollow places inside me. Places I've kept locked for years. And for the first time in a long time, I let myself imagine it.

A life with Romy. A home. Her laughter filling the family room. Waking up next to her warm body every morning. Her hands sliding with ease into mine as we walk through the fields. Watching her hold my son—our son—knowing he has the best mom in the world.

The image nearly cracks me open.

Beau claps me on the shoulder. "You need to get your head out of your ass, brother. Because if you let her go, you'll regret it every day of your life. And you don't deserve that."

The weight of his words settles somewhere in my chest, but something else stirs.

"She'll run," I whisper. "As soon as she sees what this life is really like. The pain it'll bring her."

He shakes his head at me. "It's kind of funny that you can't see it. She didn't run. She wasn't running. You pushed her out the door."

I think about it. And I know why I pushed her.

"It's admirable you want to protect this love that you have for her," Beau says, "and I know that you want to shelter it so well that nobody can destroy it, but it's suffocating her. She needs room to breathe. You need to let up and trust that she'll be there through the worst of it. She's stronger than you're giving her credit for."

"I know she's fucking strong. It's just... I—" What? I don't even know anymore.

"You know you're one helluva a guy, right? And she knows that. She understands your life. Sure, it will take some time with all the stuff that comes with you, but I'm pretty sure you're worth it to her. She wants you, and everything else is just noise." I don't say anything, and he continues. "But by all means, fuck this up for yourself."

I turn to Beau. "I need to go to her."

He grins. "Damn right you do." He walks toward the truck. "Let's get you to Nebraska, brother."

Chapter Forty-Seven

ROMY

I stare at the mirror, running a tissue along the edge of my eye to get rid of the smeared mascara. I haven't stopped crying since I arrived back home, and Zander hasn't called. I'm trying to hold onto hope that he'll return like my mom said, but my cheeks are flushed from crying, and the stupid knot in my stomach refuses to loosen.

A knock sounds on the bathroom door outside my office.

"Romy," Scarlett's voice singsongs.

"I'll be out in a minute."

"Okay. Hurry. I have a surprise for you."

I don't want to know what the surprise is. Her last surprise is part of what led me to this heartbreak. She's probably out there with the rest of my cousins and Lottie with some sympathy heartbreak cake or something. I'm not in the mood for them to try to raise my spirits.

Another knock sounds. Lighter this time.

"Hey, Romy. Come on. Come look." It's Scarlett again.

I roll my eyes. "In a second."

I look at myself one more time, then wet my face with water and dry it with a paper towel. I don't want to be cheerful. I want to sit here and wallow over the breakup and wonder why he hasn't even called.

Still, I can't hide in here forever, so I open the door. The moment I do, Scarlett's arm is entwined with mine, leading me down the hall.

"What's going on, Scarlett?"

"You'll see." She seems more pleasant than she usually is in the middle of a workday.

She leads me into the venue area of The Knotted Barn, and my breath catches.

Zander's standing in the middle of the room with his hands shoved in his pockets, his shoulders up to his ears. He looks up, his gaze slowly finding mine.

Scarlett's arm slips from mine. "Surprise," she whispers, then leaves and shuts the big barn doors, leaving Zander and me alone.

My throat tightens, and I try to put on a brave face, as though I haven't been crumbling since my departure from his life. "What are you doing here?"

He steps closer, his boots scraping against the wood floor. "I screwed up." His voice cracks. "I screwed up because I don't want to lose you."

I cross my arms as though I'm going to fight him on getting back together. But my mom's words come back to me, and I soften my stance. "Go on."

He drags a hand over his jaw. He looks like shit. I mean, he's still gorgeous, but he looks... like I feel.

"That night I pointed to you in the crowd, you drew my attention. And not just because you're gorgeous, but it was your smile. I told myself the next day, that would be it. That I would forget you. Then I asked Beau to fly you out, and I extended the time you were supposed to stay. The third time, I didn't want you to leave at all. But you were so kind and sweet, and I didn't want to hurt you. So, I told DeSoto to deny you backstage entry even though it was the opposite of what I really wanted. That's the night I wrote the single."

"Are you saying..." I had suspected that maybe... but he'd never mentioned it to me.

"I wanted to wait until it was done to tell you. But I wrote that single about me becoming the man you deserve. Beau heard me playing it one night and said I had to record it. I didn't think you'd ever find out, or maybe you'd hear it at some point and wonder, but you'd never really know."

Tears flow down my cheeks. "Zan."

He toes his boot on the floor for a second, staring at it before he looks back at me. "Then I came here, and you knocked me over, Romy. Not just because you were pregnant, but because of who you are. After I finally decided to give this a chance, it was better than I could have imagined. I never thought my life could be like this. Your family, the ranch, all of it... it's not anything I've ever had or dared to dream of having. So, I was scared. Not of you. Not even of these feelings I have for you. I was scared of what would happen when you saw what my life is really like. I thought if I kept you hidden and I kept you safe, I could protect you. That you wouldn't see the bad parts of being with me, and you wouldn't be hurt by everyone on the outside. And then maybe..." He swallows. I watch his Adam's apple bob. "Then maybe you wouldn't leave me."

His confession slices through me. "But you don't get to decide that for me, Zander."

"I know. Believe me, I know." His shoulders sag.

"You can't keep me locked away, and you can't protect me from everything in this world. You think I don't know what it means to be in this life with you? I do. I understand the ugly parts. The messy parts. But I want to be in it with you. Together. As long as it's the two of us against the world, that's all that matters to me."

For a moment, he says nothing. Silence hums between us. Then he's closing the gap.

"You really mean that?" he asks with tears in his eyes.

"Yes. I wouldn't be standing here if I didn't."

He reaches for me, his fingers grazing mine tentatively, as if he doesn't know if I'll accept his apology. I give him an opening, locking my pointer finger with his. He takes my olive branch, tightening our hold and pulling me forward, his forehead resting on mine.

I breathe him in.

I missed him so much.

"I'm sorry," he whispers. "God, Romy, I'm so damn sorry. I was so afraid of the outside world ruining us that I did it for them."

"No more hiding. We're in this together. It's the two of us. Do you hear me?"

He nods against my forehead. "Yeah. I hear you."

"You cannot run away from me anymore. You cannot push me away anymore, understand?"

"Never again. And I'm changing up my schedule. I'm going to take some time off and slow down. And when I leave this ranch, I want you with me. And not to sit in a hotel room. I want to show you and our son the world, but we'll limit the time we tour. We'll do everything by consensus, and if it doesn't work for you, it doesn't work for me."

The *we* sounds like heaven.

His hand leaves mine, and he cradles my head. "Will you take me back?"

I nod, and he presses his lips to mine. All our fear and longing and love crashes between us.

The door creaks open behind us, and a flicker of light seeps in from outside.

"Oh, glad you two finally figured your shit out," Beau says. "Now let's do some damage control."

I bury my face against Zander's shoulder. "This is the shit side of the business, huh?"

We turn our bodies to face Beau.

"Hey," Beau says.

Zander stiffens for a moment, but he squeezes my hand. For the first time in weeks, I believe we're going to survive this —together.

Chapter Forty-Eight

ZANDER

T he lights are bright. I've done a shit-ton of interviews, but I've never been this nervous. Mostly because we're going to be candid today. I won't be a country superstar promoting a new album. I'm just going to be me. A guy in love with his girl.

I settle next to Romy on the couch and put my arm around her shoulders. "You okay?"

"I'm okay." She squeezes my thigh.

And I believe her because if she wasn't, I'd shut this whole thing down and carry her out of here.

The Getaway Lodge's conference room has been made into a pop-up studio, with the lake in view through the window like a reminder that we're real, and we're not in some manufactured studio.

Beau talks with the producer and the interviewer, Kira.

Kira comes over with a kind smile. "Okay, so are you guys ready?"

We nod, and Romy glances at me for a second. Her smile assures me that we got this.

Kira sits, and the light on the camera flicks to red and someone says, "Rolling."

"All right," Kira says. She starts by introducing me and lists all my accolades, then turns from looking at the camera to look at Romy and me. "So, this is quite the change of pace for country's biggest superstar. You've never been reported to have been in a serious relationship before, Zander. Tell us— how did you guys meet?"

I glance at Romy, and she raises her hand.

"Well, I was a groupie."

"You weren't a groupie." I laugh.

"Yes, I was. Very much a groupie." Her grin is contagious.

"I saw her from the stage, on the Jumbotron when the camera scanned the crowd." I take Romy's hand.

For her part, Kira puts her hand over her heart and sinks back in her chair.

"I guess it is kind of romantic when you say it." Romy leans her head on my shoulder for a second before popping back up.

"During one of the songs when I was changing out my guitar, I told my security detail to give her a backstage pass and bring her back."

"And you went?" Kira asks Romy.

"Of course I went! He was like my dream come true. *Is* my dream come true. Although I didn't know what I was in for, going back there. As soon as I was past the security line, I had an NDA shoved in my face." Her eyes find Beau behind the camera, and he shrugs.

"So then, okay. You signed the NDA. And then what? After the concert?" Kira leans in a bit, seeming interested in the next part.

"I was just brought to his dressing room." Romy squeezes my hand.

Kira turns to me.

I clear my throat. "And from there... well, I don't think we all have to know everything that went on after that."

"Yeah, let's keep this PG," Kira says with a chuckle. "So, it sounds like it started as a whirlwind romance. How did it become more?"

Kira digs a little further. I'm sure Beau told her to be patient and not push too much, but I don't care. People are already saying shit, making up stories on the internet, so what's the difference if I tell them the truth?

"Romy came to see me two more times after that," I say.

She puts her hand on her swollen belly. "It was a fairytale. Literally. I was swept up in it. I mean—it's what you think happens when a superstar is interested in you, right?"

I laugh. Romy faces me and touches my cheek. I kiss the inside of her wrist.

"And then..." I place my hand on her stomach. "Somewhere in those three visits, we made this little one."

"He's forgetting the part where he blew me off." Romy shakes her head and rolls her eyes playfully.

Kira's eyes widen, but I can tell she's completely charmed by Romy. As she should be.

"Zander," Kira scolds like a mother.

"I have no excuse other than I was a stupid man. But fate intervened because I ended up here on Plain Daisy Ranch, filming a music video for the song I wrote for her."

I glance at Beau behind the cameras. I never asked him how he found this place. I figured he stayed away from Texas since that's where we grew up, but how did he find this small town in Nebraska to film the video?

"And you haven't been shy on socials, letting everyone know the new song is about Romy." Kira smiles and looks between us.

"Yeah, it is."

"That really is a fairytale, Romy."

Romy shakes her head. "I've learned there's no such thing as fairytales. But I think we come pretty damn close."

"Did the two of you immediately fall in love when Zander arrived on the ranch?"

I can't help the scoff that comes out of me. "Not at first. She was hell-bent on making sure I paid for blowing her off."

"With good reason," Kira says good-naturedly.

"I couldn't resist in the end." Romy looks at me, and I kiss her forehead.

Kira asks, "So do you want to fill us in on what you're having?"

Romy looks at me because we discussed this before coming here.

"We're going to leave a few things secret." I wink at Romy.

"Fair enough," Kira says, looking at the cards in her hand. "Zander, you've been a really private guy until now, so I have to ask—why are we doing this today?"

I look at Romy to answer.

"We're sick of reading the lies about us?" Romy laughs. "Honestly, we're giving the public our truth, and hopefully they reciprocate by allowing us to live our life with some element of privacy."

I squeeze her hand. Romy's so much better at this than I am.

"And how does it feel to be public?" Kira presses.

"Like I can breathe with both lungs." Romy smiles at me.

"I used to think it was easier to stay quiet, but I met this really smart woman who made me see different." I look at Romy—who's given me the strength to live my life for real—and am overcome with gratitude.

"And what do you love most about each other?" Kira asks.

Romy laughs under her breath. "What is there *not* to love about this guy?"

She doesn't go into specifics, and I kind of like that.

Because I know the things she loves about me aren't what the public sees, and that makes me feel loved for *me*.

"And what about you?" Kira asks me.

"I've never met someone who can take the air out of my lungs… and someone who makes me feel like I'm home. Romy walked into my world with both eyes open and made room for me in hers."

Romy whimpers, and I grab a tissue, handing it to her.

"Oh jeez, you two are sweet." Kira fans her face as though she might cry at any moment.

Romy waves the tissue in the air. "It's just the hormones." She laughs before kissing me on the cheek. "I'm kidding."

"And your schedule… is this new single the start of a new album and maybe a tour?"

I place my hand on Romy's stomach again, and our son kicks as if he knows it's me. "We're taking this one day at a time right now."

"I know the fans will be disappointed to hear that, but I have a feeling you probably don't care." Kira smiles at us, then looks at the cards in her hands. "Last one—what do you hope people will see when they see you two?"

Romy looks straight at me. "A family. Two people trying to make something real. And good."

"I lied. I have one last question." She meets my gaze. "What do you see when you look at Romy, Zander?"

I smile, holding nothing back. "Home."

"Sounds like the best place to be. Thank you both for joining me, and we can't wait to find out the little one's name. I want to wish you the best of luck with the delivery and the start of this new chapter in your lives."

We say our thanks, and the red light flicks off.

I nuzzle Romy's ear. "You were perfect."

"I don't know about that," she says. "But I'm glad it's over."

"We're going to be late to the family dinner."

"They'll wait."

I help Romy stand, and she stretches.

After everyone has packed everything up, Romy looks at Beau. "You ready for dinner?"

"I thought you'd never ask," he says, leaving The Getaway Lodge with us and heading to her parents' house.

I kiss Romy's temple for always knowing what I need before I do.

Chapter Forty-Nine

ROMY

"**O**h my god."

The contraction hits me like a freight train, and I bend as much as I can, reaching for my stomach.

"Where is he?" I grit through my teeth.

"Romy," Lottie says, rushing to my side, "I told you. I'm your partner. We're in this together. I'm here for you."

"You're fired!" I shout, and she rears back.

"Jeez, I was just going to be here until he came back."

I grab her hand. "I'm sorry, I just... where the hell is he?"

"Dad went down to get him," Mom says, her phone in her hand, probably trying to call Zander, Beau, or Dad.

Zander went down to the cafeteria fifteen minutes ago to get a drink and a snack with Beau. The nurses said he could, that it was fine, there's lots of time, then suddenly the doctor comes in and says I'm ready. And now, suddenly, I'm in rapid labor. Everything's happening so fast, but I am not having this baby without him here.

Dr. Rojas touches my leg. "You're at ten centimeters, honey. It's time. We're gonna push."

"No. I'm not pushing without him."

"She's definitely not a peach right now," Lottie says to Mom, and they both laugh.

I give them a scathing look signaling that now is not the time, then I tug on Lottie's sleeve. "Listen, weed, get him here."

"That's not an insult. I'm happy to be a weed." She lifts her chin.

"I called his phone twice," my mom says. "Maybe there's no signal down there."

This entire time we've been waiting for our baby boy to come into this world, Zander's been paranoid, not letting me do anything he thinks might harm the baby, then he needs something to drink right as I go into labor?

"Call Beau," I grit through my teeth.

"Same thing," my mom says. "Hopefully Dad will find him, and he'll make it before the baby comes."

"He *will* because the baby isn't coming out until he's here," I say.

"Romy," my mom says, "you can't control that."

Another contraction builds like a rising wave and crashes into me. I scream. The urge to push overwhelms me, but I somehow hold it at bay. I'm not sure how much longer I can.

"Romy"—Dr. Rojas gives me a serious look—"the baby needs to come out."

I sob and shudder. "No, we have to wait."

The nurse comes to the side that Zander should be on. "We can't wait, sweetie. I'm sure your dad will find him before he's delivered, but it's time to push."

The door to the room bursts open and bangs against the stopper.

"I'm here!" Zander's feet skid to a stop by my bedframe as he grabs my hand. "God, I'm here. I'm here. Jesus, I'm sorry."

He's breathless and wide-eyed, cheeks flushed. He must've sprinted and taken the stairs or something.

I cry harder, but it's the good kind of cry—relief. *Love.*

"You just *had* to get a Coke," I snipe.

He presses his forehead to mine. "I know. I know. I will never get a Coke again. But it's time? He's coming?"

He sounds so happy my tears freefall down my cheeks.

"It's time," Dr. Rojas answers.

Zander looks down, finally noticing my legs in stirrups and the doctor already positioned between them.

"Holy shit, I almost missed it." He grabs my hand. "Scream at me. Break every bone in my fingers. I'm yours."

"Well, you just made it a lot easier, since you had to go get a Coke and almost missed the delivery."

I push. I scream. I sweat. And Zander's there the whole time, telling me what a great job I'm doing and how much he loves me. He talks about how much our baby boy appreciates the agony I'm going through. Maybe not now, but someday— and Zander promises to tell him this story.

Lottie tells him our son won't want to hear his birth story as she places her hands on my shoulder. My mom is right next to Lottie, her hand in mine.

I push again.

The nurse counts down.

And I push again.

Then there's a cry. A beautiful wail of a cry that fills the room.

"He's here," the doctor says. "But I need one more."

Zander pushes his head into mine. "Just one more good push. Okay, Romy? One more."

I do, and our son comes into the world still screaming. He must have inherited that set of lungs from his father.

Zander pulls his hand from mine. "Shit, you're strong." He waves his hand to get blood flow back.

"You said no swearing," I say through happy tears.

"I know. I know. God—darn it."

Everyone in the room laughs.

Dr. Rojas places the baby on my chest. He's warm and pink and wrinkly and perfect.

Welcome to the world, Rhodes Shaw.

LATER THAT NIGHT, EVERYBODY'S GONE, AND THE room is dim and quiet. It's just us. Our little family that's a piece of a bigger pie.

My body aches, but I'm still running on adrenaline.

Zander's in the chair, cradling Rhodes against his chest. I've never seen anything hotter in my life.

"I'm gonna screw up," Zander murmurs. His voice is soft in the dark. "Not on purpose. But I will. But you'll never wonder if I love you. You'll never have to earn my attention or compete with a schedule. I'm gonna be there. Baseball games. Science fairs. Choir shows. Front row. Always."

Rhodes makes a small sound as if he understands his daddy.

Zander laughs softly. "I'm gonna give you stability. A home. I swear I'm gonna give you everything—everything I didn't have. And your mom, we hit the jackpot with her. She's going to make sure our home is full of love and warmth and understanding."

He glances toward me and sees that I'm watching.

"Hey," he says. "I'm just letting him know how lucky we are."

Zander walks over and places Rhodes in my arms, leans down, and kisses both our foreheads.

"I don't think I can ever thank you for this," he whispers.

I place my hand on his cheek. "I could say the same to you."

We stare at our little guy. The person who is probably the reason we were brought together.

Life has never been sweeter.

Epilogue

ROMY

The minute I open the door to the girls' house, something seems off.

I ran in here to grab a jacket since it's a little cooler tonight, and Zander and I were walking along the path with Rhodes in a stroller. We've been staying at my parents' since Rhodes was born, but I'm ready for us to find a place for ourselves. There's just nothing on the ranch. We might be renting Brooks's old house until ours is built. But Zander seems to love it at my parents', so I might have to drag him kicking and screaming. My mom babies Zander more than Rhodes.

As I pluck my old jacket off the hook by the back door, I hear a man's voice. I freeze mid-step. Who would be here? Is Poppy or Scarlett hooking up with someone, and I don't know about it?

I pause when I hear footsteps coming down the stairs, and the voice carries. He says something I can't make out to the person he's here with.

Oh shit. It's Nash.

I blink and peek around a corner where he can't see me to double check. He's running down the stairs, buttoning up his pants.

Oh my god!

What the hell is Nash doing here—upstairs at that—and now he's buttoning his pants?

I stay hidden, hoping he doesn't want to go out the back door. He turns and leaves out the front door.

Footsteps on the stairs sound again, and I rush back to the back door, which I open and shut. I don't have time to slip out without her hearing the door and knowing someone was here, so maybe I can convince her I just arrived.

"Hello," Poppy calls.

"Hey. Just me. I forgot my coat." I have no idea how I'm pulling off my casual voice.

She comes into full view. Her hair looks like a bird's nest, and her shirt isn't even buttoned correctly.

"Hey, what happened to you?" I ask.

She looks down at herself. "Oh... I took a nap."

"Just napping?"

"Yeah." Her eyes narrow slightly, and she turns toward the front door. I have no idea if Nash drove here or walked since I came in the back door.

"By yourself." I don't phrase it as a question.

"Who would I be napping with?" She opens the fridge and takes out a water. "Why are you here again?"

"Just grabbing my jacket. We're doing s'mores if you want to come."

"Nah, I'm still pretty tired. I've had a headache all day. Might just go back to bed."

I have no idea how she's playing this off so easily, but she is. "Oh, well, feel better."

"Have fun and give Rhodes a kiss for me."

I rush out the back door and practically run to Zander.

His head is buried in the stroller, cooing at Rhodes. "I think it's too cold for him."

I look over Zander's shoulder. Rhodes is bundled up and has two blankets over him. He's fast asleep. "He's fine." I swat Zander's arm. "You're never going to believe this."

Zander doesn't grant me any of his attention.

"Hey."

He finally looks up at me. "Let's get him home before he freezes."

I roll my eyes. "So, I think I just... I think Nash and Poppy are messing around."

"Really?" He's walking a little faster than normal, causing me to double my pace to keep up with his long legs.

"Zan, like sleeping together."

"Well, I didn't think you meant they were wrestling."

"They are, but in a bed during the day!" I draw back as though this is juicy gossip, but he's busy staring through the little plastic window of the stroller.

"Thought they hated each other."

Finally, he's in on this gossip. "It's complicated. Nash is Jensen's best friend. It would be like Lottie sleeping with Beau."

He twists his head in my direction as though that's the most absurd thought. "What? Brooks would be hella pissed at you for making that comparison."

"Whoa." I hold up my hands. "It was so you could understand. I love Brooks, and Beau... I mean, he's not ready to settle down yet..." I wave. "Anyway, I want to talk about Nash and Poppy. Her hair was—" I motion with my hands to indicate that it was all over the place. "And he was doing up his pants. Do you think they're just friends with benefits or something more—"

"They'll tell us if they want us to know."

I stop walking and look at Zander as he continues to walk away. "That's not the way gossip works in this family. Have you not learned that yet?"

We walk the short path, me arguing with him about how he needs to be just as invested in the fact that Nash and Poppy are messing around and speculating on how Jensen will feel if he finds out his best friend is sleeping with his sister.

When we get to Mom and Dad's, everyone's already gathered outside, so I have to shut up about it. I don't need to warn Zander because he doesn't seem to care.

Mom comes off the porch and picks up Rhodes.

"I think he's cold, Darla," Zander says.

"He's fine," I mouth, but my mom coos at Rhodes and takes him inside.

"You're gonna have to let the kid live a little." I arch an eyebrow at Zander.

Wren and Leia run over and ask Zander to twirl them around, which he goes out to the grass and does without objection.

I sit down next to my dad. Lottie is on Brooks's lap. Mack's at Beau's feet, probably recuperating from whatever workout Wren and Leia just gave him. Bennett and Delaney are inspecting the flower boxes, his hand on her back.

My mom comes out to hand me Rhodes, but Lottie snatches him up as Mom says, "I put him in a warmer onesie."

"You said it was my turn," Brooks argues as Lottie stands and walks away with Rhodes.

"Fifteen minutes," Lottie says, nuzzling her head into Rhodes's.

"Is this how it will be when our baby arrives?" Brooks asks us.

"No. When she has one all to herself night and day, she's

going to be happy to pass them off to you, Brooks," my mom says.

"Just so you know, I'm the number one uncle," Beau says before sipping his beer.

I laugh at Beau and Brooks, going back and forth over who's the better uncle.

My mom walks over and hands me a large roll of paper. "A present for our peach."

"Um... thanks." I frown, having no idea what this is about.

"Don't thank me. Thank him." She nods toward Zander.

He stops spinning the girls, and Bennett calls them over. Zander walks up to the porch. He actually looks nervous, which is odd for him.

"What did you do?" I ask.

"Just open it." He nods toward the paper in my hands.

I slide the rubber band off, and the paper unfurls. It's a blueprint. "Zan?"

He chuckles.

The top reads Romy Owens's House in big black printed letters.

Everyone suddenly finds an excuse to leave. My dad claps Zander on the shoulder and corrals the kids to go inside.

My mom kisses my temple and tells me, "Just look," before disappearing with the rest of them, including Rhodes.

The door creaks shut, leaving me alone with Zander.

"It's your house," he says simply. He steps closer, then sits beside me, hand touching my leg. "I've been working with Darla. The land—your piece of land. These are just blueprints. Four bedrooms. Big kitchen. Wraparound porch. Rhodes deserves a real home. And so do you."

Emotion hits me so hard I can barely breathe. "You deserve one too."

I should be mad. Really, I should. He didn't ask. He didn't consult me. He just did this.

But looking at him, I see that it's not arrogance that made him do this.

"I should be furious with you. It's pretty presumptuous of you to do this."

"I know." His voice is quiet, lacking any of his usual swagger. "And if you want to be, I'll take it. But I did it for you. And Rhodes. You needed the security—whether or not I was part of your life."

"You did this before…"

He nods. "The day after you showed me your parcel. I just… wanted you guys to have somewhere to be a family."

"And what about you?"

He drops to one knee and pulls a jewelry box from his pocket, lifting the box and opening it. The descending sun catches the huge diamond on a gold band.

"I'd like to share the primary bedroom—as a married couple?"

I laugh, tears toppling down my face.

"I'm hoping that's a yes."

"Of course it's a yes," I say, the word bursting out of me.

He takes the ring out and slides it on my finger before pulling me up to stand. His mouth finds mine in a too-short kiss before I throw my arms around his shoulders and hug him tightly.

Then everybody comes out—congratulating us, hugging us, welcoming Zander to the family. Although he was already part of it in all the ways that matter.

My dad makes a joke about how *Zander Owens* has a good ring to it.

Somebody hands me Rhodes at some point, and I nuzzle him as Zander pulls us into a small huddle.

"Our family," I whisper, staring at my soon-to-be husband.

"Um... you're forgetting about us," Wren says.

One by one, everyone swarms us in a giant family hug.

Happily ever afters really do come true. Maybe I do believe in fairytales after all.

The End

My Beautiful Neighbor

My Almost Ex

My Vegas Groom

A Greene Family Summer Bash (Novella)

My Sister's Flirty Friend

My Unexpected Surprise

My Famous Frenemy

A Greene Family Vacation (Novella)

My Scorned Best Friend

My Fake Fiancé

My Brother's Forbidden Friend

A Greene Family Christmas (Novella)

Lake Starlight

The Problem with Second Chances

The Issue with Bad Boy Roommates

The Trouble with Runaway Brides

The Drawback of Single Dads

The Complication with the Best Man

The Nest

Mr. Heartbreaker

Mr. Broody

Mr. Swoony

Mr. Charming

The Nest Before Christmas

Hockey Hotties

Countdown to a Kiss

My Lucky #13

The Trouble with #9

Faking it with #41

Tropical Hat Trick (Novella)

Sneaking around with #34

Second Shot with #76

Offside with #55

Chicago Grizzlies

On the Defense

Something like Hate

Something like Lust

Something like Love

Kingsmen Football Stars

False Start

You Had Your Chance, Lee Burrows

You Can't Kiss the Nanny, Brady Banks

Over My Brother's Dead Body, Chase Andrews

Modern Love

Charmed by the Bartender

Hooked by the Boxer

Mad about the Banker

Single Dads Club

Real Deal

Dirty Talker

Sexy Beast

Hollywood Hearts

Mister Mom

Animal Attraction

Domestic Bliss

Bedroom Games

Cold as Ice

On Thin Ice

Break the Ice

Chicago Law

Smitten with the Best Man

Tempted by my Ex-Husband

Seduced by my Ex's Divorce Attorney

Blue Collar Brothers

Flirting with Fire

Crushing on the Cop

Engaged to the EMT

White Collar Brothers

Sexy Filthy Boss

Dirty Flirty Enemy

Wild Steamy Hook-up

The Rooftop Crew

My Bestie's Ex

A Royal Mistake

The Rival Roomies

Our Star-Crossed Kiss